HEARTS ON
LOVING FRANKIE

Dixie Lynn Dwyer

MENAGE EVERLASTING

Siren Publishing, Inc.
www.SirenPublishing.com

A SIREN PUBLISHING BOOK
IMPRINT: Ménage Everlasting

HEARTS ON FIRE 5: LOVING FRANKIE
Copyright © 2015 by Dixie Lynn Dwyer

ISBN: 978-1-63259-390-0

First Printing: June 2015

Cover design by Les Byerley
All art and logo copyright © 2015 by Siren Publishing, Inc.

Printed in the U.S.A.

PUBLISHER
Siren Publishing, Inc.
www.SirenPublishing.com

DEDICATION

Dear readers,

Thank you for purchasing this legal copy of Hearts on Fire 5: Loving Frankie.

It is not easy to lose the only family you have and the special things that remind you of them. Frankie is holding on to that perfect image of a cop. Men like her father and brother who gave their lives to the job and lost their lives on the job. So when her brother's best friend, a cop, promises to care for her and love her, she accepts because she's used to what good cops do and how a brotherhood so strong cannot be broken.

It's too late when she realizes that her brother's friend Kevin is a good cop gone bad. Now his troubles and problems become hers. She needs to disappear after being stabbed and a witness to confessions of murder.

A woman set on freeing herself from the past and some bad mistakes, Frankie heads to Bayline near Treasure Town to begin a new life and remain under the radar. The last thing she expects is to fall in love and learn to trust the Hawkins brothers.

Just as she's learning to trust them and reveal her past and what she ran from, the men she escaped from have found her and they're ready to take her back.

But Frankie's a different woman. She'll give her life to protect her lovers, her best friend, and the kind, giving people of Treasure Town. True love is worth fighting for even in the darkest hours while staring death head on.

May you enjoy Frankie's story and her fight for true love.

Happy reading!

Hugs!

~Dixie~

HEARTS ON FIRE 5: LOVING FRANKIE

DIXIE LYNN DWYER

Prologue

Francesca "Frankie" Sonoma stared at Kevin as he spoke into his cell phone. He was tall and handsome, a street cop, a detective with the attitude and charisma of a gangster. She felt that tightness in her chest at her own description of her boyfriend, her lover, the man she thought she was destined to be with. A street cop gone bad guy, Kevin was corrupt every which way from Sunday. She should have seen it coming.

How had she been so stupid? Why was there such a deep need to keep a connection to a first responder, a cop? So what if her father was a cop, as were her brother, Mickey, and her uncle, who had all died in the line of duty. She was alone. Her aunt had lost her mind after her husband passed away, and she had been no help to Francesca, a woman finishing up college and trying to get a job. That had been a few years ago. Now here she was, twenty-three, successful in the advertising firm, and thinking that she needed to leave town. She had to disappear, but how could she with Kevin knowing her every move and keeping his hold on her tight?

At first she'd found his possessiveness arousing. But as the months passed, and she finally slept with him, he'd become obsessed. She realized that a very fine line existed between possessiveness and obsession. But now it was too late. Now she was stuck, with no one around to help her.

Francesca knew that a psychiatrist would have a field day with her. She was weak and all alone. Now Kevin was in deep with some other dirty cops and a group of drug dealers. She sat at clubs and bars where Kevin would meet up with these men in private rooms and discuss certain transactions. At first they used code words, so as to not only keep things secretive but also to protect themselves from incriminating evidence. It wasn't as though they really believed that the Feds were listening in. It was more a macho attitude that they were so good, so successful in their crimes of illegal money laundering, drug and gun dealing, and God knew what else, that they were unstoppable. That arrogance apparently had led to Kevin's frantic state of mind today. He picked her up for lunch, and she had been prepared to try and break things off with him. She recited her speech. The one about needing some time apart to breathe and to work on her career. She was moving up the corporate ladder in the advertising firm of Franklin and Hursch. She could be a CEO, but she feared Kevin's reaction.

It was time. She'd had enough. Enough of the lies, the manipulation, and the constant promises that Kevin was getting out, was going to take her away from Chicago to live a normal life. She was done wasting her youth on him. The older, gorgeous, strong cop she'd fallen in love with had turned out to be the complete opposite of her father and Mickey. She started thinking more like a cop than his lover and girlfriend. In fact, she'd recently taken notes, writing down names he mentioned, locations of events, shipments, and even the code words and what she thought they meant. She figured she never knew if she might need those. It was information that she could probably be killed for, but it was also a little extra security. This new way of thinking made her realize it was definitely time to get out and get away from Kevin.

Frankie watched him pace. The holster and gun, the detective's shield, and his well-maintained body were no longer enough to make her stay with him. Her heart pounded. Her mouth felt dry. She anticipated his reaction to her breaking things off. He would be angry. Kevin angry wasn't a good thing, especially how he lashed out at her. In the last several months, he would yank her hair or squeeze her wrist to get her attention. When they had sex, it went from slow and passionate to rough, him hurting her as he took from her body. She had bruises on her ribs and her hips from his manhandling. The kisses he applied afterward, and the profession of passion and lust he felt for her body and how he lost himself because of her, was no longer acceptable and erotic. It was abusive. She knew it in her gut that this wasn't right. That she didn't want to feel like an object but as an equal, a precious gift to love and cherish.

She had fallen for his charms and his sexual experience as an older man in his thirties, but it wasn't enough. He would only bring her down. She was a good girl, a college graduate, a woman who came from a law enforcement family that had all died in the line of duty. It was too late, and she was in deep with him when she realized the truth. Kevin wasn't the man she'd made him out to be.

She was alone with no family, and she thought Kevin had represented everything she wanted and everything that reminded her of her own family. She had been wrong. Hearing his conversation now, as well as the names he was throwing out there, she knew things were worse than she had suspected.

They were names she read about in the newspapers. Gangsters, corrupt businessmen, politicians, and criminals. Well-known ones. Ones she knew the Feds or, at the minimum, local special crime units should be investigating. It made her feel sick, used, and stupid. Now how the hell was she going to end this and start over? Would Kevin give her the space she needed so she could slowly distance herself until he got the message? Or would he freak out, perhaps strike her or threaten her? She looked at him. He was more than capable of that. He was capable of worse.

"Details. I need details," he yelled into the cell phone.

Kevin glanced at her as she jumped from his intense tone and gave her a wink. He reached out and stroked his finger along her jaw then gently brushed his thumb along her lower lip. That sexy expression used to set her body on fire and make her putty in his hands. Not now. Not anymore. She also couldn't minimize the fact that he cheated on her. It was time to draw the line and end it all.

He pulled back and yelled into the cell phone. Something about a deal and the wrong guy delivering drugs to some place Carlotto owned. Louie Carlotto, the notorious entrepreneur. Carlotto seemed to maintain the attention of the FBI yet remain free instead of behind bars for all the criminal activity associated with him and his various companies. She knew a lot of crap on him. She'd heard a lot of the discussions between him and Kevin, but more importantly, and what she feared the most, was the way Louie Carlotto looked at her. He called her by her first name, Francesca, with authority, with power, and what sounded possessive to her own ears. She never told Kevin about Carlotto's advances or how he had the nerve to send one of his henchmen to her office with a rose and an envelope containing a phone number. The guy had told her that Mr. Carlotto said to call him. She didn't.

A week later she received an envelope at work. No return address, no verification of whom it had come from. Most important were the contents of the package and the words indicating a schedule of Tuesdays and Thursdays at the Hyatt hotel and lounge downtown. It also contained eight-by-ten photographs of Kevin with his tongue down some redhead's throat and then other pictures. Intimate ones with the whore's mouth wrapped around Kevin's cock and others with him screwing her every possible way. Her heart had broken that day, and her entire world shattered. But, still, she couldn't let go. She didn't want to believe that the pictures were real or recent. She looked at the address and noted the date as Tuesday.

She grabbed her purse, her keys, and the address, and headed out of her office. She got downtown in record time and took the elevator to the eighth floor. After pulling out the key card that came with the envelope, she slowly swiped it and watched the red light turn green. Time seemed to stand still as she quietly pushed the door open.

She heard the sounds. The moans, the banging of furniture. Her legs nearly gave out on her, and her heart sat in her throat ready to choke her.

She'd rounded the corner and gasped. Never had anything hurt so badly. Never had she wanted to die, to end the heartache, the insult, and the disgust she felt. She would never trust another man again. She would never trust a cop, and she certainly would find it difficult to ever let her guard down and trust anyone.

Today she'd come here to tell Kevin goodbye and to make him realize that nothing he could say or do would make up for what he'd done to her. Nothing.

She couldn't help but be scared. After all, besides sleeping with whores, he was in bed with gangsters.

"Goddamn it! They fucked this shit up. I don't believe this. This is the biggest deal of my fucking life and some dick rookie fucks it all up. Fuck!" Kevin roared as he closed up his phone and paced the room.

She didn't want to hear about the crimes he was committing. She didn't want to know anything more. She needed to sever the ties between them. She needed to forget that he was her brother's friend and the only person she'd had to lean on when Mickey died.

She stood up, straightened out her skirt, and reached for her bag.

"I need to go," she whispered, unable to look at him. If she stared into those dark eyes and that handsome face and saw his controlling expression, she would falter.

She didn't want him to restrain her. To put her in one of his bear hugs and make her listen to him. Then she heard him say Oscar Finery. She knew him well. He was the son of a good friend of her father's. Like her, Oscar came from a family of law enforcement officers. In fact, she'd seen Oscar the day before she received the pictures. She'd told Oscar that Kevin wasn't the man she thought he was and that things were getting complicated. Oscar had touched her cheek then squeezed her shoulder and offered his support. She smiled at him and had gotten an odd sensation.

As they'd parted and Oscar told her to call him, she noticed one of Kevin's so-called friends. That was when she knew he had someone following her.

She closed her eyes as he stopped ranting and moved closer. She saw the picture of the redhead. Fake boobs, big ass, and a very wild look in her eyes as Kevin fucked her in the ass. She saw it again. She heard the moans and saw how turned on he was.

Frankie wouldn't do that with him. It had taken six months before she gave Kevin her virginity. It took six more for her to suck his cock the way he begged her to do. She had been a virgin, an innocent, inexperienced twenty-one-year-old. She knew nothing about pleasing a man in bed, and Kevin knew it all.

"Baby, where are you going? You know you can't leave right now. It's not a good time. I need you here where I can watch over you."

She used to love when he said that. That he was watching over her and protecting her, and that she was his everything.

He had men spying on her, watching her every move to make sure she wouldn't cheat on him like he cheated on her.

"How many have there been?" she asked. He reached for her shoulders and squeezed. She pulled away and took a few steps back.

"How many what?"

"How many women have you fucked behind my back, Kevin?"

He squinted his eyes at her and released a long sigh.

"I told you that I love you. I only want to be with you. I fucked up, baby. One fucking time and I'm going to make it up to you. This deal, this was supposed to be our ticket out of Chicago, hell, out of the country."

"I don't want that, Kevin. It's over. I don't want anything to do with you, your criminal lifestyle, or to pretend you love me and are committed to me. It's over."

"No, it's not over."

"It is," she yelled at him.

"Where are you going to go? You're nothing without me. You have no family and no friends." He taunted her. He had caused that. He'd made it so every waking hour she wasn't at work she would be with him. The few friends she had moved on to dating, working on their careers, and enjoying their early twenties. She didn't. She thought she was in love with Kevin.

"I have friends. I'm not alone."

"Who? Who the fuck do you have? There's no one but me."

"That's not true."

"Oh, you mean Oscar, that dumb fucking rookie? Yeah, well, guess what, he's fucking dead. So shut up and take a seat," he yelled at her, and she gasped. She couldn't believe it. Was he saying that Oscar was really dead and that he'd killed him?"

"You hurt him? You killed him?" she asked, voice cracking.

"I said enough. He should have stayed away from what's mine. That includes you."

"I need to go. I'm not staying here. I came here to say goodbye and to tell you that it's over." She started to take a step, but before her high heel reached the carpet, he was pulling her back by her upper arm, making her slam against his chest. Her purse fell to the floor, and she gasped.

"What the fuck are you talking about? I don't need your sophomoric bullshit right now, Frankie. I'm dealing with a serious situation with work."

He was calling her sophomoric? This was his MO, making her feel naive, uneducated, weak, unknowing so that he could manipulate her actions and her thoughts. Her mind scrambled for control. Part of her wanted to just ease back down to the couch, be a good girl, and listen to Kevin. A killer, a bad cop, the man who supposedly killed Oscar. God, this was too much. *My God, poor Oscar.* Was it true? Was he really dead?

She felt the tears roll down her cheeks. She didn't know what to do. Her mind raced as she wondered how she would get out from under Kevin and even Carlotto. She needed to get to the police, but maybe there wasn't anyone she could trust. Maybe they were all like Kevin. Kevin would protect her and keep her out of harm's way. But then came the reality of the situation and this relationship. It was a dead end. If she stayed, she was headed for disaster or, worse, becoming the wife of a cheating, manipulating crook of a cop, everything her father and her brother were the opposite of.

"No, Kevin. I'm leaving. You deal with your situation at work. I want nothing to do with you, especially if you killed Oscar. I can't go on like this."

"Go on like what?" he yelled, shoving her arm as he released his grip.

She shuddered a moment. He had been known to strike when he was upset or angry over something. She took a retreating step backward, and his eyes widened and then squinted with anger.

"You're not going anywhere. Sit your little ass down and keep your fucking mouth shut."

Her eyes instantly filled with tears. He really was a bastard, a heartless, manipulative bastard.

"Go to hell and take your whore with you," she spat at him and then began to flee toward the door. Kevin pulled her back by her hair. He smacked her face. She screamed out and grabbed her cheek, shocked at the pain he inflicted.

"Whore? What the hell—"

He stopped talking and stared at her. At first, his expression seemed remorseful, but it quickly changed to anger.

"You bitch. You spying on me? You don't trust me?" he roared.

"Obviously you can't be trusted, Kevin. The Hyatt? The Tuesday and Thursday schedule every week? Yeah, I was there, and I saw you screwing her from behind. I heard and saw it with my own eyes, so don't stand here and lie to me." She screamed at him as tears rolled down her cheeks. She was shaking, so scared and so angry.

He gripped her shoulders and shook her so hard her neck wrenched.

"You're not leaving me. You're mine. I own you, and we're going to be together forever. You're nothing without me. You hear me? You're fucking nothing."

The tears streamed down her cheeks as she cried out at him.

"I hate you. I want nothing to do with you."

He struck her. She'd nearly fallen to the floor when, suddenly, the door to the apartment was kicked open. Two men came charging in and one closed the door behind him.

"What the fuck are you doing here?" Kevin roared and shoved her behind him.

Frankie didn't know what was happening and tried to run to the left and get out of the room, but the guys pulled out knives. Kevin went for one, and the guy struck forward.

"No one double crosses Carlotto," he roared.

She jerked and cried out as the knife sliced into her hip, hitting the bone. She screamed, and Kevin roared as he attacked the two men at once. She held her hip as the blood oozed from the wound. The door opened again, and there stood Louie Carlotto with three other men. His main guys.

"Enough!" he roared as Frankie cried and leaned against the wall, shaking.

Carlotto stared at her, anger in his eyes but also wearing an expression of concern. She wasn't stupid. She knew his concern was for selfish reasons. He wanted her. He'd wanted her since the moment they'd met four months ago.

"Carmine, take her to Vito. Fix her up and make sure she knows the deal to not talk."

She shook her head as Vito reached for her.

"Come with me, doll. You don't want to make the wrong choice here. Your freedom depends on this," Vito told her.

"No. Where are you taking her? She's mine," Kevin roared from the rug. Two of the men were on top of him, holding him down.

Tears rolled down her cheeks.

Carlotto held her gaze.

"Go with Vito. Everything will be okay," Carlotto told her.

She looked toward Kevin. She wondered if she would ever see him again and what was in store for her with Carlotto removing her from this scene.

"Come on, doll. We'll get you all patched up," Vito told her as they exited the room.

The door closed, and she heard the roar of pain. She couldn't help but think they were going to kill Kevin. Her heart ached, but that innocence, that quality of inexperience, disappeared the moment the thought went through her head with the hope that Carlotto killed Kevin. All her current troubles would be over, but new ones would start. Beginning with owing Carlotto her life and her future.

Chapter 1

"You are so funny. With your body and gorgeous face and eyes, you could be in magazines, and you won't sunbathe in a bikini on the beach? God, you have so much to offer, and I've seen the men you've turned down at Prestige. I'm starting to think something is wrong with your brain."

Frankie chuckled as she leaned back in the beach chair under the umbrella, as if she were barely listening to Cassidy's rant.

"I'm not looking to get involved in a relationship with anyone."

"How about a booty buddy then? No strings attached and you can get some relief."

"Relief?"

"Yeah, girl, you are so uptight sometimes I'm just waiting for you to snap. But every time you look close to it, you pull back, gain control, and are the usual sweet, soft-spoken Frankie we've all come to know and love."

Frankie smiled.

"Who is all?"

"I can tell you for a fact that half the male staff, including the owners at Prestige, would like to taste your cookies."

"Get out of here. You are so full of it. Besides, all those men are older and single and want to keep it that way."

"Booty call. You can have your pick. I think if I wasn't breaking up with Keith and wanting a break from men for a while, I would move in on Shark or even Charlie."

Frankie sat forward and pulled her sunglasses off.

"Shark or Charlie? Are you crazy? Those guys, Lure included, are the most intense men I've ever encountered. They have like secret pasts or something. I'd stay clear of them, Cassidy, and just make sure Keith doesn't manipulate your mind."

"He had that capability for a while. If it weren't for you and your insight into such controlling, abusive relationships, I may have fallen deeper instead of staying free."

"I know. It sucks, and you might even second-guess your decision to leave him, but it was the right one. If he can hit you, put you down, and make you feel worthless, then he's not the man for you."

Cassidy stared at Frankie. "So when are you going to tell me all about this ex of yours and how you know so much about men like Keith?" Cassidy asked Frankie.

"Never. It's in the past, and I made a promise to just move forward. So, what are you going to do tonight?" Frankie asked.

"No plans. I'll wait for you to be off so we can check out Riley's or the Beach House in Treasure Town. There's supposed to be a great live band there on Thursday night."

"Ugh, you just reminded me. Gloria is supposed to be working tonight. God, my feet are going to be killing me, and I'm going to be exhausted," Frankie complained.

"I don't know why Lure and Charlie haven't fired her. She has shown up late like three times, and she barely even works the floor at the club."

"Tell me about it. Then I do double the work and have to share the tips."

"Maybe when we work with her we should be lazy and do what she does. Nothing," Cassidy suggested.

"That would only hurt us in the long run and Charlie and Lure. They're onto her. I'm certain. In fact, if I had to bet on it, I would say the next time she shows up late they'll fire her."

"I don't know. She has big tits and great legs and thinks nothing of flirting with the customers and talking them into buying top-shelf liquor. That means money," Cassidy told her.

"But Lure and Charlie seem like good bosses and men. I've seen them reprimand Gloria for her behavior."

Cassidy chuckled.

"Hell, you weren't working the night she was doing a table dance in the back room with some dirtbag. If Charlie hadn't walked in, she probably would have fucked the guy right there with other men watching. Prestige isn't that kind of place."

"Thank God I wasn't there. I probably would have quit," Frankie stated seriously.

"No you wouldn't have. You need money just like I do, and no one is hiring right now during the season. It's crowded with tourists and vacationers, and, of course, horny men, both young and old."

"I know. I can't even get motivated to go look for another job for during the week. There just isn't anything out there, and I hate hearing the words, 'sorry, we're not hiring,' all day long."

"The tips are so good at Prestige, so why do you need another job?"

"I don't know. I've never been a server before, and it's not exactly what I want in my future as a career."

"What did you do back where you came from? You still haven't told me."

Frankie felt bad. She liked Cassidy, and they had become great friends, but the less she knew, the better and safer Cassidy would be.

"Let's just say something more professional and businesslike."

"What? Squeezing your thirty-six double Ds into an extra-small V-neck T-shirt that says Prestige is not appearing professional? Never mind the short black skirt that shows off your ass and your tan legs. Huh, really now. I'm insulted." Cassidy crossed her arms and gave Frankie a sassy look.

Frankie chuckled.

"It's different than what I'm used to. That's all."

"So no to accepting any offers of dinner or dates from patrons of Prestige, too?"

"No accepting any offers of dates period. I'm taking a break from all that drama," Frankie told her.

Cassidy giggled.

"Me, too. That's why we should hit one of those places I mentioned on Thursday. Maybe the Beach House. I hear a lot of people hang out there."

"We'll see. Maybe," Frankie said and then leaned back in the chair.

"You really should remove that cover-up and lay out a little. A nice tan will bring out those blue eyes of yours even more."

"Yes, Madam Cassidy," Frankie teased. Cassidy shook her water bottle at Frankie, hitting her with cold water.

"Hey." She sat forward, laughing. "Enough with the Madam Cassidy stuff. I'm not your madam. I'm just hoping that you'll find someone that you like and who can help you forget about the guy from your past."

"No need to worry. He's already forgotten," Frankie said then pulled off her cover-up and moved her chair off to the side and out from under the protection of the umbrella.

As she got comfortable in the chair, she closed her eyes and thought about Kevin and her past. He wasn't out of her head. She could never forget about him because she knew this wasn't over. Running away, getting out of town was the only way she could save her life.

Frankie thought about the last week of hell in Chicago. She thought about Oscar Finery's funeral and how sad his parents and family were. His murder had been shocking and hit the entire department pretty damn hard. It was torture to go to that wake, to see all the officers paying their respects. It brought back memories of her own father's and brother's funerals and the reality of the job of law enforcement officers.

She had to sit there and listen to old friends of the family talk about the case, the investigation into Oscar's murder, and how hush-hush it was. She waited, listening carefully, and hoped to hear some inkling of a clue that a special team to investigate had formed and that they had suspects already. But nothing. There was nothing, and it made her wonder who were the good cops and who were the bad ones.

Then, of course, Carlotto came to visit her. He'd threatened her. He threatened to take other officers' lives, including Oscar's cousin who worked as an investigator for a special crimes unit in Chicago, if she were to go forward and rat him and Kevin out. Carlotto made his intentions known that night. He caught her off guard when he brought her hand to his lips and kissed the knuckles as he held her gaze. She knew his intentions. She read the hunger in his eyes and felt the power of his abilities. Frankie would never forget his words to her that night.

"You deserve better. The best. You remember the chance I have given you, Francesca. When I call you to come to me, to be mine, you better come."

She shivered from the memory of his words.

She got home that night and thought about her options.

She thought of going to Oscar's cousin and his team and confiding what she knew, but when—not if—Carlotto found out, both she and Pete would die, just like Oscar had. Oscar had been into something big. There had to be a team working with him, knowing he was undercover. Why weren't they coming forward? Why weren't they willing to help bring justice to Oscar's family, and more importantly, why weren't they coming to her?

Were they all bad cops? Were they all so callous and unfeeling that they viewed Oscar's death as a part of the price an exposed undercover officer paid? She didn't know, and in order to stay alive, she had done what she needed to do. She left without a word, without giving notice to her perfect job, and without Carlotto or Kevin knowing. She needed to be smart, to stay out of trouble, and to stay alive. The best way to do that was to remain under the radar. That shouldn't be too difficult in a small touristy area like Bayline.

* * * *

Mike Hawkins hung up his gear after he rechecked his firefighting equipment. He was tired and longed for a good night's sleep. But the crew was going to the Beach House to hear some new band play, and his brother Rye was meeting him there. Another brother, Turbo, was working late at the sheriff's department so he could take off the weekend for the party they were all attending, and his brother Nate would stay home as usual. It was amazing enough that they'd gotten him to say he'd attend the party on the weekend.

"Hey, you heading over there around eight?" Marcus Towers asked him. He was a fellow firefighter in Engine 19, along with his brother, John.

"Yeah, I'm supposed to meet Rye there. He was heading over early to help Daniel set up the stage."

"That's pretty cool that his old Army buddy is playing in a band showcasing at the Beach House. I can't wait to hear them. They've been all over the Internet and have great reviews," Marcus said as they grabbed their regular stuff from their lockers.

Eddie Martelli met them on the way out.

"Hey, enjoy the weekend, Mike. Give Jessy, Larry, and Dudley my best and try not to be so hung over that you work like shit on Monday," he teased.

Mike chuckled.

"You know I don't party like that. Too old."

"Too old my ass, Hawkins. You're thirty-three. That's one year younger than I am."

"Like he said, Captain, he's too old," Marcus teased.

Mike gave Marcus a shove as he chuckled and walked ahead faster, afraid they both might tackle him for his comment.

"I'd watch that if I were you, Marcus. Thirty is breathing down your neck. Enjoy the next year or two," Eddie told him.

"I will, old man, and you can just sit there at home and be envious of us youngsters."

"Have you seen my woman? I think I know who's envious," Eddie said and then walked away.

"Envious? Me?" Marcus said as he and Mike headed out.

"Well, Tasha is pretty hot," Mike said.

"Damn straight she is. That's what I need to find. A sassy redhead. That's now my goal tonight."

Mike chuckled.

"Whatever. I'll see you there."

"Later, bud," Marcus told Mike as Mike headed to his truck.

* * * *

"This is fun," Frankie told Cassidy as they sat at a table and listened to the band, Exodus, playing. There were six men in the band, and each of them seemed very talented.

"What did you say?" Cassidy asked her.

"I said this is fun." She raised her voice and drew the attention of a few guys who had been checking them out.

"Want to check out the bar outside on the dock?" she asked.

"Sure," Frankie said, and they stood up, walking through the crowds of people.

It was very crowded, and as she passed by a few men who were talking, one of then stepped back between her and Cassidy. He was laughing about something, and he was very attractive. She saw his tattoos on his arms, and he had dark, serious eyes.

He looked her over as he said, "Excuse me."

"No problem," she whispered as she walked by him. When she looked back over her shoulder, he was watching her. His eyes roamed over her body then back to her face. Quickly, she turned around.

"Damn, that guy was gorgeous. His friends were pretty fine, too. Sure you don't feel like mingling?"

"Not tonight."

"Party pooper," Cassidy teased, and Frankie chuckled.

"You'll thank me when you're able to get up in the morning and go to the gym with no problem."

"Honey, if I take home a hottie like that one you just passed up, I wouldn't need to go to the gym. There'd be plenty of working out in the bedroom."

"You're crazy," Frankie said as they stood at the bar and ordered margaritas.

Then they took their drinks and walked toward the railing to look out at the water. There were tall tables with high barstools out here, and the docks were filled with boats and even some yachts.

"Look at that one." Cassidy took a sip from her drink.

"Too big."

"Ladies."

Frankie and Cassidy looked over their shoulders at two guys who approached. Cassidy recognized them immediately while Frankie adjusted her body, turning fully toward them.

"What are you doing here?" Cassidy asked one guy, and Frankie immediately felt on the defensive.

"Hanging out getting a few drinks and listening to the band just like the two of you," he said then eyed Frankie over.

"Who's your friend, Cassidy?" he asked, and the other guy crossed his arms and looked like a troublemaker.

"None of your business."

"I'm Tanner, a friend of Cassidy's boyfriend, Keith." He reached out his hand, and Frankie stared at him, never moving to shake his hand.

"You mean ex-boyfriend, don't ya?" Frankie asked.

He gave a smug look and then let his eyes roam over her body before he looked back at Cassidy.

"About that… Cassidy, don't you think you're giving Keith a hard time? I mean the man cares about you a lot, and he's miserable without you."

"He should have thought about that before he cheated on me," Cassidy replied.

"That's not true, and he's been trying to get in touch with you. Can't you give him a minute of your time?"

"We're leaving, actually," Frankie said and stepped away from the table, taking Cassidy by her hand.

Tanner tried to stop her. "He'll be here momentarily."

"Good, then you can tell him she said bug off," Frankie stated, and as she turned with Cassidy to walk away, she bumped into the guy she'd seen earlier.

She gasped as he held her by her arms and stared down into her eyes then at Tanner and his buddy. She was shocked at the warm feeling she got from his hold and the instant attraction. He was very tall and muscular and smelled really good. She cleared her throat and turned to look at the guys following her and Cassidy.

"Are these men bothering the two of you?"

She exhaled.

"Not anymore. We're leaving," Frankie replied then Cassidy pulled her through the crowd.

Frankie couldn't help but to glance back at the good-looking guy with the tattoos. He looked sincere and as if he really was concerned. But then again, considering her inability to judge characters well, she wasn't giving that expression or action another thought.

"Let's get out of here," Cassidy said, and they called it a night.

Chapter 2

Frankie crawled out of bed feeling the dull, annoying pain in her hip. She had to trudge through it. She needed to work, even though she hated waitressing at a bar and nightclub. But tips were great, and there wasn't much for a woman trying to lay low. She longed for her business attire, her high heels, and professional work setting. She couldn't believe she missed sales reports, advertising brainstorming meetings, and everything from red-eye flights to boring board meetings.

She'd needed something that made quick money and kept her out of any potential trouble. Also something where she didn't need to get paid on the books, where her name would be in a computer system and constantly pop up everywhere.

Miles Campbell had hired her in the middle of the summer when no one was hiring. His partners, Charlie and Lure, two very attractive men, were now her bosses. Although Miles was a bit creepy and seemed intense, he didn't ask her a lot of questions or push for personal information. He was out of town a lot. The employees at work had bets going that he was in the witness protection program or a spy. He was something. But he wasn't Louie Carlotto or Kevin Lang. In fact, she was pretty sure she wasn't the only employee working at Prestige who was trying to keep a low profile. Except maybe for Cassidy.

She smiled to herself. Making a new friend so quickly had been surprising. But they both had so much in common it was inevitable. Cassidy was a great woman. Frankie hoped that Cassidy's ex would leave her alone and that Cassidy would find someone perfect.

If Cassidy could, she would hit on their bosses, Charlie and Lure, but they were pretty private men who ran a very busy and well-known club. So busy that Cassidy had been right. Frankie really didn't need to look for a day job.

None of the employees dated one another, at least as far as she knew. Most were male anyway. She would never date her boss or even a fellow employee, although Lure was pretty damn good-looking. He was one of the many heartthrobs of the place and always drew a crowd at the bar as one of Prestige's top bartenders, never mind that he was part owner of the place, along with Charlie Spar.

Frankie made her way to the bathroom to wash up and prepare for the long night ahead of her. Friday was ladies' night, and Prestige was always jam-packed. But the tips were too good to pass up. At least for now and while she saved enough up to get back on her feet again. Kevin had done a number on her. She'd nearly married the jerk. Him getting jammed up had saved her. A dirty cop, a man who led multiple lives and was unfaithful. How could she have been so stupid?

She shook the thoughts from her head but couldn't shake that tight sensation in her chest. She knew the reality of this situation. Despite being behind bars, Kevin still had friends who could be watching her. Just like Keith's friends tonight at the Beach House. They'd approached them and called Keith to tell him Cassidy was there.

Guys had some kind of special loyalty and bond to one another. They didn't even care that Keith struck Cassidy and pushed her around. In fact, they might be just like him.

Kevin was the same, and no matter how badly he treated Frankie or how he spoke down to her, Kevin didn't see anything wrong. He actually thought she would take him back and that he still had that hold, that control over her life. That had been six months ago. He was a killer. Hell, he'd gotten away with murder, or at least the one she knew of. Poor Oscar. She had cried for days. She'd even looked up information on his obituary, looking for any pictures she could find about his service, a full law enforcement service with officers from around the United States. She had stood there, feeling like shit for keeping her mouth closed about his murder.

God, she hated police funerals, funerals for firefighters, and military ones. She'd gone through multiple on her own, and she never wanted to go to another one again.

She ran the brush through her hair and fixed it into a fancy style to the side of her head. Maybe she would wear it like this tonight. She had to wash it first.

She felt guilty. Guilty for knowing that Kevin had gotten away with Oscar's murder and she couldn't do a damn thing about it. It was her life on the line. She not only feared Kevin's wrath and possessiveness but also feared Carlotto's. Kevin was the one who'd killed Oscar. Carlotto was part of that, and she needed to keep her mouth shut about Kevin's confession because it would destroy their multi-million-dollar drug operation back in Chicago. Back in a life she'd put behind her.

She'd escaped that life and put the past behind her. At least she prayed for that to be true. If Carlotto or Kevin ever found her, they would force her back into their criminal world or put her in a grave.

She established some guidelines and rules for her future and for men in general. Staying clear of them entirely was ridiculous, especially with men like Lure and Charlie constantly around. But she didn't feel the deep attraction she fantasized about with any of the men she'd met so far. She wanted more. She didn't want lust, infatuation, or just sex. She wanted to be loved, and in wanting something so perfect, she pretty much knew she was destined for loneliness. How could she ever trust a man? How could she put an innocent man in jeopardy of getting hurt or, worse, killed? That was a realistic outcome if Kevin or Carlotto ever found her. They would kill any man she was with. There was no lying to herself about that. Maybe a quick fling would be the best option for her? That thought had her shaking her head. She wasn't like that. Kevin had been her first and only lover.

She didn't think she wanted to get that close to another person again. To be bound that intimately and always fear getting hurt and used. No, it wasn't for her. Not now anyway.

Francesca had a new life now, with no more fears that one of Kevin's thug friends could find her and keep tabs. Or at least she hoped none of them knew where she was. She wasn't planning on staying in Bayline anyway or even saving enough money to live in Treasure Town a few towns up and on the water. Rent wasn't cheap in resort areas, even on the outer limits. She loved the area, but Carlotto's reach went far. If she stayed in one place too long, he might find her. She didn't want to be owned. She just wanted to be left alone to live her life the way she wanted to and not be controlled and directed by a man.

She turned on the shower and prepared to maneuver under the hot water. That should ease her hip, an injury that was getting better and better every day. An injury that showed the scars from the knife wound the night Carlotto's men had tried to take out Kevin. At least Kevin had cared enough to shove her out of the way and take a hit from Carlotto. But that didn't mean she forgave Kevin for all he had done to her.

Carlotto got her out of there. Carlotto had saved her from being questioned by police and even interrogated for information on Kevin and Carlotto. He helped her get the medical attention she needed, and then she took off as Kevin went down for a minor crime.

She read that a special team of investigators was looking into Oscar's death. But then she left town and didn't look back. Carlotto set up Kevin to take the fall for drug possession while he tried to get Frankie in bed.

The illegal drugs landed Kevin in jail for a year. But she knew how these things worked. Kevin had friends all over the place, and he wouldn't serve his full time. Her hope that Carlotto would kill Kevin and then the police would bust Carlotto never happened. She had to run. She took off the moment she had the chance and never looked back. She needed out of Chicago and fast.

She withdrew her savings and took off. She didn't even pay the rent she owed on her apartment, and she felt bad about that, but she couldn't waste any time. She didn't trust a soul, and she planned on keeping it that way.

Frankie shivered as she stepped under the spray of water, hip throbbing, which was more psychological than anything else. Late at night, while she lay in bed listening to every small sound, fearing Kevin's men or even Carlotto's might have found her, the pain increased. But then the sounds of fighting, men and women in drunken stupors in the older, beat-up apartment complex replaced those fearful thoughts.

She would grip the handgun. The one she slept with every night.

I can't go back to him. I can't let him manipulate me like he did before. He cheated on me. He's a criminal, and everything he told me was a lie. Lies to manipulate my mind. To make me fall in love with an imaginary man who was evil and a killer. So why does it still hurt so much? Why do I feel so weak, so foolish and worthless? Because that's what he told me I would be without him. Nothing. No one. And all alone.

Francesca closed her eyes as the tears emerged. Her chest tightened, her breathing grew rapid, and she pressed her forehead against the tiled wall. *Twenty-three and broken. That's all I am.*

Thirty minutes, two cups of coffee, and a meal replacement shake later, and Francesca was off to Prestige. She entered the club through the back door after walking the four blocks to work. The town was alive with music, a nearby amusement park that stayed open until midnight and a strip of bars and restaurants along the way. As the sun began to set, the beachgoers went home to rest, shower, and change in anticipation of the nightlife and all Bayline had to offer in the evening hours.

"Hey, gorgeous, how's it going?" Lure asked as she entered the back door where he prepared the guest list for the private back rooms for the night.

"Good. How about you? Is it going to be a busy night?"

Lure assisted with bouncing as security. He was in his thirties but had this mysterious look in his eyes like he was analyzing everything or suspecting everyone of being guilty before innocent. From what she'd heard, he used to work for the government and was some sort of agent or something. No one really knew. He had nervous energy though. That was why he worked all the time and barely rested. Plus, he had loads of money from what she heard. It added to the mystery of the man, who was tall, had wavy, slicked-back black hair, and a chiseled jaw and cheekbones, making him appear stronger and capable. His deep, dark eyes always looked so serious. A lot of the workers thought he was mean, but he had never been mean to her and always gave her a welcoming smile.

He glanced down at the clipboard he held in his hand.

"Looks like we have a few parties tonight on top of the regulars. I'll need you to handle the big one if you're up to it?" he asked and eyed her over.

His gaze landed on her hip, and she turned slightly, as if that would stop him from singling out her weak spot. After she'd worked at the place only a few days, Lure had noticed her favor that hip and rub it late in the evening. He asked her about it, and she told him it was an old injury that acted up when she was on her feet a lot. From there on out, he tried to get her to rest in between performing her tasks, but of course, she refused. She tried hard not to show weakness even in the eyes of compassionate strangers.

"Sure thing. How many are expected for this party?" She hung up her hoodie and bag then reached for her black apron. It was short and held only her two pens, a notepad she hardly ever used, and her lip gloss. She smoothed out her short black skirt then began to adjust the T-shirt she wore with the Prestige insignia on it. Her breasts were too large for the tank top and the T-shirt, but she had to wear one of them, so she chose the T-shirt. It was annoying, but the truth of the matter was that showing off her deep cleavage really brought in the big tips. If there were a lot of males at this party, she should make a killing tonight. Still, she missed her office job and the professional dress code and using her brain and business instincts to get the work done.

She glanced over her shoulder to find Lure watching her with his arms crossed.

"What kind of party is this tonight?" she asked.

"Bachelor."

Her heart raced a little. The fear that some wild, drunk guys could get a bit rowdy made her nervous.

He seemed to read her mind.

"Don't worry. I personally know the men who are hosting this party. They'll be sure to keep the guys under control. There are only about twenty-five of them. You'll handle the appetizers and drink orders while Gloria does cleanup, if she ever gets here. Her attitude sucks lately. I'm sure they'll move on to the bar area within a couple of hours."

"Okay. If you say so." She pulled out her lip gloss and ran the small tube along her lips.

"Anyone gives you a hard time, you tell me or Charlie. You hear?"

"Yes, sir." She smiled. He held his serious expression and turned and walked away.

She gulped. Lure was very stern all the time, but she trusted him with doing his job and watching over his staff. He would ensure her safety. Now all she needed to do was prepare herself mentally for this bachelor party. She glanced into the mirror by the lockers.

I really don't like showing off my body like this. Maybe I can find another job where the uniform is less revealing?

She took a deep breath, stared at her blue eyes and platinum-blonde hair, and got ready to start her night at Prestige. She placed her purse into the locker and used her hoodie to cover it. She brought her gun with her everywhere, but she didn't need to advertise that. She wasn't sure how much longer she could stay in Bayline, but wherever she moved to next so Kevin and Carlotto wouldn't find her, she hoped for a better job, one that didn't make her feel like the easy, gullible tramp that Kevin made her feel like. All she could do was hope for a better life now that she'd gotten away from him.

* * * *

Deputy Turbo Hawkins stood next to his brothers, Mike, Nate, and Rye as they got out of Nate's truck. They were all together tonight, an unusual event they were usually too busy to enjoy lately. Turbo had been looking forward to this bachelor party all week, anticipating a good time with his brothers and some of the friends they'd all grown up with. Jessy Parker and his brothers, Larry and Dudley, were getting married to Priscilla.

"We haven't hung out like this in months," Mike said as he held the door to Prestige open for his brothers.

"More like over a year, Mike," Rye said as they all entered.

"We've all had crazy schedules with work. But with Mike off of nights for the next month from the firehouse, we should be able to hang out together more often," Turbo added.

Before anyone could respond, the cheers started as their friends greeted them.

Jesse and Dudley were already drinking as they gave them hugs then hello slaps on the backs.

"What are ya drinking these days?" Larry asked as he leaned against the bar.

"I'll take a Bud for now," Turbo told him then glanced at Mike, Nate, and Rye.

Nate was talking to the owners of the place, Charlie, and Lure. Lure and Nate went way back to their jobs in the service and with the government. Turbo took a sip of the beer Larry handed him as he watched Nate talk to the two men. All three of them were straight faced and hard looking. Nate worked construction with Rye but more so to stay in shape and keep busy. Money wasn't an issue for any of them.

"How are the prospects looking tonight, Shark?" Gary asked one of the main bartenders.

He smirked as he wiped out the inside of a clean beer mug.

"Charlie and Lure hooked you guys up. Starting with the hottest waitress and bartender of Prestige to the extra special guests your buddies all lined up in the private room."

"Oh man, not the platinum-blonde one with the big—"

Lure slapped Gary on the back interrupting him before he continued.

"You've got Frankie. I expect you to behave. Now if you all will follow me, I'll escort you to the area we have set up for you guys," Lure told him, and then the others followed.

Turbo took his beer and walked with his brother Mike, following the other guys. They were talking and laughing, all excited about the night ahead of them, and Turbo wondered who Frankie was and what had Gary rubbing his hands together and appearing excited. He was fixing his shirt and then the waist of his pants as he whispered to Murphy, and Murphy shook his head.

The moment they headed toward the large table in the back of the club, Lure introduced Frankie.

"Gentleman, this is Frankie, your server for the evening. Anything you want, you just ask Frankie and she'll try her hardest to accommodate your request or get me to assist. Enjoy the evening, and the first round is on Prestige."

The guys cheered, but Turbo was caught off guard by Frankie's beauty and body. He wondered why the hell she went by a guy's name as his brother Mike gave his arm a nudge. He glanced at him.

"Holy shit," Mike whispered.

Some of the guys took seats at the table while others stood around talking and ordering drinks from Frankie. He couldn't get himself to sit down. Turbo watched Frankie like a hawk, taking in all her assets and the movement of her body as she walked between the men. She was petite, too, and had sexy, toned thighs that led up to a nice, round ass. But her deep cleavage drew all his attention until he locked onto her baby blues.

"Can I get you another beer, sir?" she asked him, making him feel old.

The strike to his ego had him barking the word Bud to her, and she quickly wrote it down then looked at his brother Mike.

Her eyes widened, and then she looked down at the note pad then back up toward him. Turbo wondered what was going on.

"This is where you work?" Mike asked her, and she just nodded and held the pen then looked down at the pad again.

"I saw those guys trying to follow you and your friend out of the Beach House. My buddies and I stopped them. They didn't catch up with you, did they?" Mike asked her.

She looked shocked and then squinted at him.

"You did that? Why?" she asked, on the defensive.

"I didn't like the looks of them. They seemed up to no good, and they scared you off. That meant I couldn't get to know you better," Mike added, flirting.

Turbo just watched Frankie's expressions change. At first she seemed thankful that Mike had intervened at something and then annoyed. He wanted to know what happened, what sounded like some guys bothering her at a club. But then Frankie released an annoyed sigh and changed the subject.

"And you, sir, what would you like to drink?" she asked Mike, and then Turbo didn't feel so hurt.

Apparently Mike had met the woman somewhere before. Mike was probably closer to her age at thirty-three than Turbo was at thirty-six. He would have to ask Mike where they'd met.

"Darling, you can call me Mike." He winked at her, and she smiled.

"Sure thing, Mike. I'll try to remember your name, but there are a lot of you guys."

He reached out and tugged on a strand of her platinum hair.

"You'll remember me, just like I'll remember you, Frankie." He released her hair and winked again.

She shook her head.

"Smooth," she whispered and moved onto Nate and Rye.

Mike smirked, and Turbo shook his head but watched Nate and Rye give her their drink orders.

Nate kept his arms crossed in front of his massive chest, intimidating the poor young woman, while Rye leaned closer to pretend to see if she had the order straight.

She blew them off, too, in a friendly way and continued on.

"So how do you know her?" Turbo asked Mike.

"I don't really know her. I saw her at the Beach House the other night. Some guys came over, bothering her and her friend. I went over to see if they were okay, but she seemed to have it under control. Whatever went down, she and her friend disappeared. I couldn't keep my eyes off of her while she was there. Caught her looking back a couple of times. I don't know what her deal is."

"Maybe she has a boyfriend," Turbo suggested and felt his own disappointment thinking that.

"I sure hope not. I was hoping to get to know her. Don't you think she's beautiful?"

Turbo glanced back toward the platinum-blonde who seemed to have snagged all the guys' attention, including the married ones.

"She sure is." He just watched her like the other guys did and wondered more about her.

The conversations went on as appetizers were brought out and more guys arrived. It got louder and more crowded as Frankie delivered drinks and cleaned up plates. She was looking a little flustered when Lure showed up midway through. He squinted his eyes at her, and she shrugged and barked at him. He looked around as if he were searching for someone then walked away, pissed off. She ran her hand along her brow and exhaled then rubbed her right hip.

"What's that expression for?" Mike asked him.

"Did you see her rubbing her hip? She's in pain." Mike squinted his eyes and watched. Then Mike gave him a nudge.

"Looks like Nate and Rye noticed, too. She's working this entire party on her own. We better be sure Gary and Murphy tip her well," Mike said.

"Why wouldn't they?"

"Because she keeps declining their advances."

Turbo shook his head and took another slug of beer. He felt that inkling of jealousy hit his gut. It was stupid. She wasn't his, so there was no reason for jealousy. Besides, she'd declined their advances, too.

* * * *

"You work too hard, Frankie. Why don't you come on over here and sit on Jessie's lap? You know he, Larry, and Dudley are getting married next week?" Gary told Frankie.

"All three of you are getting married? I thought just Larry was." She placed her hand on her hip. It was aching, and she still had hours of work to go once the men went into the other room.

"We're marrying Priscilla. She's beautiful like you," Dudley said then downed another shot of Fireball. The men cheered around him, and Gary placed his hand on her shoulder.

"Come sit," he told her.

"No, that's okay. Remember what I told you? I'm not on the menu. I think your treats are waiting for all of you in the other room." Just as she said that, and the guys started whining and flirting with her, she heard the roar of anger and turned to the right. There stood

Gloria, half dressed and suddenly charging toward her. Lure and Charlie were far behind her and looked really pissed off. Frankie wondered what had happened. Gloria had never shown up to help Frankie take care of the party, and she'd been forced to do it all herself. But the expression on Gloria's face had Frankie backing up

"You bitch!" Gloria yelled out and slapped Frankie across the face, hitting her cheek and upper eye.

Charlie and Lure grabbed her.

"Bring her to the back room, Charlie. The police are on their way," she heard Lure say as someone lifted her up and pulled her onto their lap.

"Are you okay? Jesus. Rye, grab ice."

She felt the tears stream down her cheek and the pain radiate against her cheekbone and eye, causing her vision to blur a little. Instantly, her eye began to swell as she tried to focus on what had happened and also tried to get up off of whoever was holding her.

"No, honey, sit still. You're hurt, and I've got you."

She blinked her eyes opened and saw Turbo holding her. With short dirty-blonde hair and a hard expression, the man was like steel. His hard thighs pressed firmly against her ass, making her feel sensations she wasn't used to feeling. Mike was there, and the other guy Nate, who appeared hard and serious and had an expression of pure anger. She was shaking and had no idea why Gloria had struck her like that.

"I don't understand," she whispered.

"What the fuck is going on, Lure? Who was that woman, and why did she hit Frankie?" Nate demanded to know.

Lure placed his fingers under Frankie's chin and tilted it up toward him. He cursed. "Fuck. Damn, baby, I'm sorry she got to you. She was a raging lunatic. If we'd known she would go after you, we would have kept watch on her better in the back room," Lure told her.

"Here's the ice," Mike said, handing the plastic bag of ice to Turbo, who gently laid it on her eye and face.

She tried to take it from him and hold it there, but she was shaking.

"I got it. You just relax. You're safe with me," he told her. She gulped. Safe with him? Who was this guy? Who did he think he was, taking control of the situation and taking care of her? She tried to move. His hand gripped her thigh a little snugger. "No. Sit still and let the ice work."

She was overwhelmed. She felt the attraction and a sincere appreciation for the man's good looks and chivalrous actions. She needed to get a grip. All men were sneaky, manipulative dickheads. She'd learned that the hard way. She looked away from him and focused on Lure and Charlie.

"Why did she do this?" she asked, voice cracking.

"We caught her in the back room. She was snorting coke and banging some asshole instead of working and helping you. Turns out she was selling the shit here, and that dick was her supplier. We're taking care of it. The police are on their way," Lure told her.

"The police are here," Nate said and then walked away toward them as two uniformed cops and what appeared to be a detective in plain clothes arrived. Nate seemed to know them and so did the others as they greeted one another.

"Don't worry, honey. Just keep the ice on there. We'll take care of everything."

Take care of everything? This is ridiculous.

"I need to get up. I have to get back to work," she said, and Lure, Turbo, Mike, and Rye all said, "No, sit still." She gulped, taking the ice from her eye and cheek. Rye cursed, and Turbo ran his hand along his jaw.

"You might need a paramedic to check this out or a doctor."

"No. No I'm not. I don't need to go. It's just swollen from the strike of her hand. The ice will bring down the swelling. No, I'm not going. That's stupid." She stood up and lost her balance.

Mike wrapped an arm around her waist to steady her. "All right, relax. If you don't want to go, then I'm sure the cops can take a picture of your injuries so you can press charges."

"Let's bring her to my office," Lure said, joining them again.

"No, I'm okay. I need to clean up and help with the party."

"We got it covered, honey. Come on now. We need to look over that eye. Nate?" Lure said to him, and Nate nodded as they escorted her to the back office.

She noticed the other employees helping with the party and the guys in the bachelor party headed toward the other room. She hoped their night wasn't ruined because of this.

Those thoughts left her mind a moment later as she felt Mike's large, heavy hands on her waist, guiding her down the hallway. The others followed, including several police officers and a detective. But she was shocked that Nate and Rye followed, too, and took protective positions around her as if guarding her from everyone else. That gave her an odd sensation in her gut.

She was shocked at the tingling sensations she felt just from Mike's hands on her, guiding her. She was attracted to all four of the good-looking men. When had she become needy for a man's touch? An attractive, masculine man's attention? She needed to clear her head. Men were pigs.

As they entered the office, it appeared all the men knew one another. Mike helped her into a chair, and she crossed her legs and held the ice in place. Nate knelt in front of her. He placed a hand on her thigh and one on the arm of the chair.

"I know a bit of first aid, sweetness. Let's take off the ice and see how it looks, okay?"

She stared at his firm expression and absorbed his dark-brown eyes and the mature, hardened lines of his jaw, and then she inhaled his cologne. She felt an instant attraction to him, just as she felt to Mike, Rye, and Turbo. They were all older, big, muscular, and handsome, but she had been down that road before. Look what falling for the charms of an older, more experienced man had gotten her. Nearly killed.

She gulped.

"I'm sure I'll be fine if I just ice it." She began to lower her head, and he raised one of his eyebrows at her.

"I'll be the judge of that," he replied firmly.

He was sexy, big, and had what appeared to be a tattoo on his neck peeking out from the collar of his button-down white shirt. She felt so tiny and fragile next to him. When he touched her chin, his thick, large fingers aroused some inner need inside of her to feel the safety and protection of such a charismatic and large man. She surely would know what it felt like to be hugged and protected in his arms.

But that couldn't happen. She needed to put a little space between them and set these men straight.

"You should be at the party enjoying yourselves like your friends are, really. I'll be fine, Nate," she whispered, and his eyes seemed to brighten and show some emotion before he was serious again.

He gently lowered the ice bag and her hand. He squinted hard and kept a firm face. He turned her chin slightly.

"It's a good one. I think the ice will keep the swelling down. But it seems Gloria was wearing a ring. It cut your skin by your eye."

He didn't look away as he spoke to Lure, and she didn't look away from Nate either.

"I need a first aid kit, some ointment, and a tiny Band-Aid," he said, and she felt his large, heavy palm caress her thigh.

The man was big and solid, like a linebacker but trimmer. This close, she could see what appeared to be a tattoo on his shoulder through the white dress shirt he wore. It must have extended from his neck then lower. She wondered what it was. She also wondered how much it hurt to get that tattoo. But a man his size with such a hard, dark look in his eyes probably never felt pain.

"I really need to get back to work," she told him as she absorbed the gruff look on his face and the darkness of his eyes. The man looked almost haunted.

"Honey, you're done for the night. I'll be bringing you home once you sign the papers and press charges against Gloria."

She locked gazes with Lure.

"Do I have to press charges? Won't it be enough that she was selling drugs here and that she got fired?"

Nate squeezed her thigh.

"Definitely not enough. She assaulted you, Frankie. That's unacceptable."

She instantly felt on edge, nervous and intimidated. The man was so forceful and disciplinary. It was as though he was giving an order, and she needed to comply. A bunch of thoughts went through her head, including telling him to mind his own business, but then Lure spoke up.

"You can fill everything out and then decide. But as far as tonight is concerned, you're done."

"But I need to work." She wrung her hands together. She was embarrassed and looked away from Nate and to Lure.

"I need to. I'll be fine, Lure. Really."

Nate released his hold and stood up just as Frankie put the ice down and stood. Her eye and cheek throbbed, and she teetered a moment getting up so quickly.

These men all made her nervous, including Charlie and Lure.

Nate held her, steadying her, and she heard him curse under his breath. It sounded like he'd called her stubborn.

"I don't think you'll need to work for the next month. Not with the tips the guys left you, and considering you didn't get any help, it's all yours, Frankie. You can afford to take tonight off," Charlie said as he walked into the room.

"I've got the paperwork ready, miss," the officer told her as he came to stand by Mike and Rye.

She felt Nate's hand glide along her lower back nearly to her ass, and then he released her.

"Sign the papers and we'll get you home."

She was shocked as she looked from him to Charlie and Lure.

"Nate?" Charlie said his name as if questioning him about him saying he would take Frankie home.

She answered the officer and signed where he told her to but listened to the conversation behind her.

"She's our responsibility, not yours."

"Says who?" Nate replied to Charlie.

"'You fucking just met her."

"And your point is what? I'm taking her home. Is there a problem? Is she yours? Are you claiming her?"

She didn't know what was going on. What were they talking about, claiming her? She didn't belong to anyone. She was far from belonging to a soul. In the back of her mind, she recalled some things she'd heard around town. Comments pertaining to the way certain men protected their women. Then she thought about the ménage relationships, and her belly tightened so quickly she thought she might lose it. Were these men trying to stake a possession or claim on her?

"What's going on?" Frankie asked, on the defensive as she handed the pen to the officer and turned toward Nate, Charlie, Lure, and Turbo. Then she felt Rye and Mike each place a hand on her shoulder.

"We're going to take you home and make sure you're safe," Mike told her.

She swallowed hard and shook her head, stepping from them.

"No, no you're not. I'm staying here. Charlie or Lure can take me home later when it slows down. I don't know you, but thank you for the offer. I need to use the ladies' room and get back to work." She felt her voice shaking. It was bad enough she would have her name on the file in a police computer system. She sure didn't need four older men thinking they could claim her for their woman for the night because they'd come to her aid after she was attacked.

She was surprised no one said a word as she exited the room. But she did hear the deep voices and then the door to the office closed. Captain, one of the main bartenders, was there and escorted her to the ladies' room.

"I never liked that bitch Gloria. You sure didn't deserve to get assaulted," he told her as they stopped in front of the ladies' room. A few people were walking by, and she avoided their stares.

"I don't know why she took it out on me. I was just doing my job."

He placed his hand on her shoulder. "That's exactly why. She was caught not doing hers and selling drugs. You know Charlie and Lure don't allow that shit. And listen, having men like Nate Hawkins and his brothers wanting to protect you isn't such a bad thing. Nate and Charlie and Lure go way back. Secret military government shit, and Turbo's a deputy. It's always good to have a cop in your corner." He winked.

She felt that unease feeling in her gut turn to fear. Turbo was a cop. Nate was involved in the military and government stuff. What horrifically bad luck she had. These men were too similar to Kevin to ignore. She had to keep her distance.

"Well, I can take care of myself. I'm not in the market for any protection."

"I'll wait out here," he said, and she nodded, but as she went into the bathroom, she couldn't help but to think about what Captain had just told her.

This could be a lot worse than she thought. Kevin was a cop, a detective who knew other dirty cops looking to make quick cash. She had never seen Nate or his brothers in Prestige before. They could be working for Kevin or, worse, for Louie Carlotto.

* * * *

"So you're going to let her go back to work?" Mike asked Charlie as he and Lure stood there staring at them.

Lure couldn't help but smirk slightly.

He leaned back against his desk, his arms crossed. "I understand you two being Good Samaritans, but Nate and Rye, I just don't get it. I can't even believe you two showed up to this bachelor party."

"Very funny, Lure. But seriously, who is she?" Rye asked.

Lure looked at Charlie. "She's only been here a few months. She's real quiet, keeps to herself, and is a hard worker."

"Always shows up on time, never missed a shift, and is real easy on the eyes. She aims to please," Charlie added, and Lure watched his four friends' expressions change.

"What is that supposed to mean?" Mike asked, on the defensive.

"She's a good-looking woman. Young and inexperienced, but sweet and needs looking after."

"You two doing that? Looking after her?" Turbo asked.

"You know we take care of our own," Lure told them.

"That's not what Turbo means, and you know it. We just want to make sure she's okay. That was a hell of a hit, and she's going to have a nasty bruise," Nate told Lure.

"We'll be sure to make certain she ices it."

They were all silent, and Nate gave a nod to Rye.

"Let's get back to the party. Seems Lure and Charlie have this covered after all."

Nate exited the room, and the others followed, Mike closing the door behind him.

Lure looked at Charlie and raised one eyebrow.

"Frankie is a special young woman. You know you thought about hitting on her just like the rest of us," Charlie said as he walked over toward the wet bar and poured himself and Lure a drink.

"But you knew the moment we interviewed her, along with Miles, that she was hiding something. She wasn't too keen on pressing charges either."

"Lure, she wasn't too keen on getting paid on the books. She talks about things being temporary. Never says anything about buying things for her apartment like other women do. You know as well as I do that something is up with her."

Lure took a sip of scotch.

"So what do you think? Let Nate and his brothers see how far they get with her and maybe it all works out?"

"Either that or it turns out she's some criminal in hiding and our four friends get their hearts broken."

Lure smiled. "I'm still not sure Nate and Rye have hearts."

Charlie chuckled.

"Mike and Turbo have to. They work too closely with the public to become desensitized like that. Besides, I think Frankie will blow them off just like she blows off every other guy who hits on her."

"We'll see. In the meantime, one of us needs to take her home and make sure she ices that eye. I don't like that shithole she lives in. We pay her well enough for her to live in a better place. I don't know why she's hiding in the projects of Bayline."

"You just said why, Lure. She's hiding, and no one that sexy and attractive would be caught dead in the apartment she rents."

Lure squinted his eyes and thought about that a moment.

"Maybe we need to ask Frankie a few more questions."

* * * *

They were making her nervous. Frankie tried to focus on working instead of the pain by her eye and upper cheek. But every time she paused to take a breath, she felt the eyes upon her. The Hawkins brothers, as Shark had told her. It seemed Shark was filled with lots of information on the four brothers and their interest in her.

It put her on edge, especially when she found out that Turbo, the tall, muscular blond was a deputy. Mike, who had lots of tattoos, scruff on his face, and a long-lost look in his eyes was a firefighter and just as intimidating. When she'd seen him the other night at the Beach House, she'd instantly thought he could be another mistake for her to make. He was that attractive. Frankie understood the type of relationships that took place around Treasure Town and Bayline, hell, all over the place, but she'd never really associated with people into ménage relationships. Cassidy explained about them and the difference between the real ones and those just out to have a good time with no commitment. A bit of a wild twist on the one-night stand idea.

Frankie swallowed hard. She would never do a one-night stand, despite how attractive Mike and his brothers were. Could they seriously be sticking around and watching her thinking she was interested in them? God, that instantly made her feel panicked. She watched as various women tried to hit on the four attractive men, but the men blew them off. Some of the women were gorgeous, too. A little slutty looking, but still very attractive.

"You got yourself some bodyguards tonight, Frankie. I'm jealous," Cassidy whispered as she gave Frankie a nudge in her shoulder.

Cassidy placed the drinks Shark made onto the tray she had to carry.

"Bodyguards? I don't think so."

"Well, they can guard my body any time. They're delicious. You can't tell me that you're not interested. Hell, it's like fate or something. That guy Mike showing up here and recognizing you from the Beach House. He has eyes for you, and I think his brothers come as a package deal. That's sexy."

"Not interested," Frankie said, and Cassidy raised her eyebrows up and rolled her eyes at Shark.

"The woman needs psychological help. I'm on the rebound. I'd take them on in a second if one of those men over there wanted me."

"Sure you would," Shark told Cassidy, rolling his eyes.

None of them like Keith, Frankie included, but she felt a bit upset at Cassidy saying she would go after one of the men. It was so strange, and she didn't want to analyze it. The idea of talking to more than one man was nerve wracking enough. Having sex with more than one? Anxiety attack big time.

Cassidy turned away to deliver the drinks as Shark began to place the drinks Frankie had to deliver to a table near the Hawkins brothers. They hadn't even joined the rest of the bachelor party in the private back room. She wondered why as a few of their friends came from the back room and joined the regulars.

"After you deliver those drinks, you're to take a break and ice that cheek and eye. It looks like it's swelling more," Shark told her, looking pissed off. She reached up and winced at the pain.

"Goddamn it. I wish Charlie or Lure had let me at that bitch. I would have given her a kick in the ass or, at the minimum, sicced Cassidy on her ass. She'd mess her up good."

Frankie chuckled. "I still don't understand why she took out her frustrations on me. I was just working and doing my job." Frankie placed two olives into the martini on the platter.

"Because you've been a threat to her since day one."

"Me?" she asked, pointing at herself.

"You really don't know how beautiful you are, do ya, gorgeous?" he asked as he licked his lower lip and held her gaze.

"Oh brother," she said, thinking he was hitting on her, too.

He chuckled. "Don't worry. I'm not moving in on Hawkins's territory. I'm just stating the facts. You're a stunning young woman. Kind of remind me of Carrie Underwood, except you have that real long platinum-blonde hair. And a better body." He winked.

"I'm not even from the South," she replied as she lifted the tray.

"Where exactly are you from?" he asked, and she felt her chest tighten, and immediately she lost her smile. Shark definitely picked up on that.

"Far from here," she told him as she headed away from the bar and to the guys whose drinks she needed to deliver.

On her approach, she took in the sight of the brothers. Rye appeared to be the youngest. He was very handsome, with spiked, crew-cut hair, hazel eyes, and very smooth skin. He seemed like the type who shaved his chest so his muscles would show better in the summertime.

Mike was the opposite. He had lots of tattoos and looked in need of a shave, which she surprisingly found very sexy.

"Hey, babe, we thought you forgot about us," one guy said as he eyed over her chest and bit his lower lip.

"Nope, just really busy tonight. Sorry for the wait." She passed around the drinks.

The other guy tipped her and paid the bill.

"Your eye looks like it might need some ice," he told her.

"Yes, I'm planning on taking a break and doing that right now."

"You want some company?" he asked, and she felt the hands on her waist at the same time she heard the deep voice next to her ear.

"She's taken care of."

Frankie heard Turbo's voice and gulped. "Take your tip, Frankie, and then come with me so you can ice that eye."

She reached onto the table, saw the annoyed expressions on the guy's face, and then said thank you.

Turbo held her by her waist and walked away from the table with her in tow.

"You're on break. Charlie said to come to the back room."

He escorted her, and she noticed the eyes upon her and Turbo as they walked together. Now people would think they were an item. Was that a bad thing? She couldn't help but feel her body hum with an awareness she wasn't accustomed to. But her fear, her distrust was more powerful. The moment they got into the hallway so she wouldn't make a public scene, she pulled from his hold. As she turned around, he nearly collided with her, and she wound up against the wall palms, flat behind her. She gasped, and he held her gaze.

"I don't need an escort for a break. I also don't need some guy I don't even know acting like I belong to him. Go back with your friends," she told him, her voice cracking and giving away how intimidated she was of Turbo. He was so muscular and defined that she could see the cords of muscle in his neck leading under his dark-blue dress shirt. It didn't help that he smelled really good, too.

His expression held steady. Confidence, control, and something else oozed from his gaze, making her hesitate walking away in a huff, as she expected she should after her statement.

He held her by her arms, gently. The feel of large, masculine hands against her skin did a number on her.

"You have an escort, whether you like it or not. I was there when that woman attacked you for no reason. I'm concerned about your cheek and eye."

"Why?" she snapped at him.

He licked his lower lip, and she couldn't help but watch him and wonder what it would feel like to have a man like Turbo kiss her, hold her, and make her feel safe. Instantly, that word, safe, made her chest tighten and had her stepping back. He stepped closer. Now she was pinned between him and the wall.

"Are you kidding me? I know you feel it. That deep sensation, that inner instinct that says there's something happening between us. Between all of us."

Her eyes widened. Was he talking about his brothers, too? A ménage? A relationship of some sort with four men and her? Was he out of his mind? She'd sustained the abuse and lies from one older guy whom she thought she could trust. Why would she set herself up for such torment and pain again?

She shook her head.

"I don't know what you're talking about. I don't feel a thing."

He ran his thumb and pointer along her chin, gripping it gently as he looked down into her eyes. The man was tall. She felt feminine, petite, and protected just standing this close to him. How would she feel with their bodies entwined and his cock deep inside of her?

She was shocked by her own thoughts and felt her heated cheeks give away his ability to get to her. He didn't smile, smirk, or give any facial indication that he read her like a book. Instead, he gently stroked that thumb of his along her jaw to her neck and then leaned forward as though he was going to kiss her. She turned slightly. Enough to make his lips press against her jaw then to her ear.

"Don't be sacred of my brothers and me. We'll take things slow, Frankie. As slow as you need." He kissed her earlobe. She couldn't help but to close her eyes and relish the feelings he drew out of her. She'd never felt anything like this before. She was stunned.

"Let's get that ice and make some plans so my brothers and I can see you again."

His words snapped her out of the fog she was in as he took her hand and led her down the hall. She pulled her hand from his gentle hold, and he paused by the office door, staring at her as though she'd hurt his feelings. It was so crazy, this instant attraction and this need for her to not like another man or take another chance. Kevin had really screwed her up big time.

He stared down into her eyes and opened the door. Charlie and Lure were in there, waiting for them.

"Damn, Frankie, it's swelling up good. I think you're done for the night. Let's ice this and call it a night," Lure told her as he took her hand and escorted her to one of the chairs in the office.

She sat down, crossed her legs, and accepted the bag of ice from Charlie. As she looked at the three men, she noticed Turbo exchange looks with Lure. Something was going on, but at the moment, she didn't care. Her cheek was aching, and the ice was very cold. It cooled down her libido, bringing her body temperature to a normal level. But one look at Turbo standing there in the office, looking so big and sexy, made her feel as though the ice was melting, and she was not going to be able to resist his advances for long.

Chapter 3

"Getting arrested is not keeping a low fucking profile," Sal Baletti told Gloria as he gripped her upper arm and escorted her out of the local police station. She couldn't believe Sal was here to spring her.

"It wasn't my fault. That bitch had it coming."

He squeezed her arm a little harder, and she gasped from the pain. Sal was a mean son of a bitch and a big shot around New Jersey. He didn't say a word more until they were in the parking lot and his driver opened the door to the black SUV with the tinted windows.

She felt a little scared now. She'd fucked up in more ways than just striking Little Miss Sweetheart.

Before she could get a look inside the SUV, a hard hand gripped the back of her head and hair, pulling her across the seat. Her face hit the hard leather and the door. She cried out.

"You stupid bitch," Gino, Sal's cousin, yelled.

"Get us the fuck out of here. Bring us to the warehouse. This bitch is done," Sal ordered as the SUV took off.

"No. No please, Gino, Sal, please give me another chance. I know I screwed up. I know I lost my shit and let my anger get the better of me."

Smack.

"Oh!" she cried out after Gino gave her a backhand to her mouth.

She grabbed onto Gino's knees as she knelt on the floor, crunched up in the small space.

"Please. Please don't kill me."

Gino glanced at Sal, and Sal leaned back in his seat. He wouldn't look at her.

"You cost us thousands of dollars. You fucked up a good operation at that club. We were bringing in a shitload every week."

"I'll make it up to you. I'll get into another place and get it hooked up in no time."

"That's time we don't have. It's not all our money, Gloria. The dough we made at Prestige selling drugs covered our loan and interest from Carlotto. In fact, while you were fucking that sleezeball in the back room, we were negotiating terms and selling the Prestige business entirely to Carlotto. He's been interested in taking over some of the Jersey connections. This is really bad. I had to call him and tell him it wasn't going to happen because one fucked-up, stupid bitch addicted to coke and cock screwed us all. And do you know what he told me?"

She shook her head and felt the tears roll down her cheeks.

"Kill the bitch and get me my fucking money. He upped the interest on our loan. We're fucked, Gloria, absolutely fucked, and you're a liability."

The SUV stopped, and Gloria looked at Gino. He moved his jacket to the side, revealing his gun. "Don't try to run. Just accept your fate. When Louie Carlotto issues an order, there's no negotiating."

* * * *

Deputy Turbo Hawkins was on the scene along with Detective Buddy Landers and Sheriff Jake McCurran. It didn't take a seasoned detective to see that someone had tried to get rid of a body in the bay near the inlet that led to the ocean. Treasure Island did have its share of homicides over the years. People got crazy or even violent when they were drinking all day or night, but rarely did people try to dump bodies in the ocean from the shoreline.

As he approached the scene, he heard Buddy say that the body hadn't been in the water long. But when Turbo glanced at the body as the forensics team did their thing, he noticed the black T-shirt immediately.

"Oh shit." He stated took a closer look. The letters spelling out Prestige were nearly masqueraded in blood.

"You know her?" Jake asked him.

"Not personally. She works at Prestige. She was fired three nights ago after she was caught selling drugs and then attacking one of the other women who work there."

"You know this how?" Jake asked.

"That must have been a hell of a bachelor party for the Parker boys. I heard something about it getting rowdy and some hot little platinum-blonde that turned everyone down," Buddy said as he stood back up.

Turbo knew exactly whom Buddy had heard about. Frankie. She'd turned him and his brothers down, too, and refused to exchange numbers or let them drive her home. They'd all thought about her for the last several days and were planning on hitting Prestige this Friday just to see her.

"Not sure who you mean. But I can tell you that this woman was pissed off. We were all there when she raged through the room and struck Frankie."

"Frankie? A guy?" Jake asked.

Turbo shook his head. "No, a woman. Her name is Frankie."

"That's it. That's the name of the woman the guys have been talking about. A woman with a guy's name. Said she was a knockout."

"We'll need to go talk to her and the owners of the place," Jake told them.

Turbo felt his gut clench. Was Jake thinking that Frankie, Charlie, or Lure could have done this?

"I doubt Frankie had anything to do with this. She was shocked by the attack and insulted by it. Plus, she's like five foot three and a tiny little thing. Real sweet."

"Heard that, too," Buddy said and chuckled as he winked at Jake. Jake kept a serious expression.

"If you have some sort of relationship with this woman, tell me now. It may be better if Buddy and I go to talk with her."

"We just met her that night. As Buddy said, she wasn't showing any interest in anyone."

"Turned the Hawkins men down flat, too, huh? Damn, I can't wait to meet her. Smart girl." Buddy started walking away so the coroner could do his thing. Jake chuckled.

"Why do I get the feeling that this is going to get complicated?"

Turbo tried to laugh off the conversation and teasing, but he couldn't. What if the woman they were all attracted to wound up being involved with this or a killer? *Damn, my life sucks.*

Thirty minutes later, he, Buddy, and Jake had located Frankie's apartment in the downtown area of Bayline. It was a shitty, crime-infested neighborhood.

"Are you sure about this address?" Turbo asked Jake as Jake pulled the sheriff patrol truck alongside the curb by the front of the building.

It was an apartment complex, ten stories high and huge. He saw garbage all around as they got out and headed toward the building where she supposedly lived. Some homeless people, or maybe just drunks, sat on benches or against the side of the building. There were even some along the dark, narrow sidewalks between the units.

"This is a very unsafe area. Who is this woman?" Jake asked as he searched for her name on the list of residents. The board was behind broken glass, and names were all screwed up.

"I think the door isn't locked. She should be on the fifth floor. Apartment 5B," Buddy said as he glanced at his notes. Jake pulled the door open, and they headed inside.

The place needed everything from new paint to new doors. It wouldn't take much to bust through one of these doors and break in. He felt sick.

As they got to 5B, he saw a guy sitting on the ground a few doors down.

"Don't bother. That bitch has a gun," he told them, and Jake looked at Buddy and then at Turbo.

Jake knocked on the door. "Frankie, this is Sheriff McCurran. We'd like a word with you please."

"Who?" she asked through the door, and Jake identified himself again.

Frankie asked for ID, and Jake held the badge up to the eyehole so she could see it. Then they heard a series of locks and what sounded like dead bolts being opened.

She creaked the door open slightly, and Jake smiled and showed her his badge and ID.

She slowly opened the door. The moment she looked at Turbo, she gasped. She looked over his uniform and pulled her bottom lip between her teeth.

"What's going on? What are you doing here?" she asked.

But Jake had noticed her holding a revolver in her hand.

"Maybe you'd like to put the gun away?" Jake asked, his hand on the butt of his gun.

"Oh, sorry. Force of habit." She let them in. She walked over toward her purse and placed the gun inside but not before she clicked on the safety.

"You have a license for that firearm?" Jake asked.

"Of course."

"Do you always answer the door with a gun?" Buddy asked.

She eyed him over. "You saw the neighborhood. What do you think?" she countered.

Turbo took in the sight of her and of her apartment. It was the complete opposite of the neighborhood. It was neat, beautifully decorated, and feminine like her. Even now she wore a pretty sundress, her breasts well hidden but accentuated by the tight bodice.

"We sure did. We have some questions for you in regards to what happened a few nights ago at Prestige," Jake told her.

"Is that bruising still remnants of the assault?" Buddy asked.

She reached up and ran her finger along it.

"Afraid so." She glanced at Turbo.

"Looks a lot better. You iced it like Nate suggested."

"I iced it like Lure and Charlie suggested," she countered, and he squinted at her.

It seemed as if she was still putting up a wall and fighting the attraction.

Jake cleared his throat.

"Turbo told us about the assault and how Gloria came out of nowhere," Buddy began to explain.

Turbo listened, and Frankie explained what happened and what Charlie and Lure had told her about the drugs, the sex, and the confrontation.

"Your gun is a 38? Do you own others?" Buddy asked her. She looked taken aback by the question.

"I think one is sufficient. Yes, it's my only gun."

"What's with the suitcase?" Jake asked and nodded toward the sidewall by the door. Turbo hadn't even noticed it. He was preoccupied with Frankie.

She turned away as she replied, indicating to him that she was hiding something. Turbo put aside his attraction and began to ask his own questions.

"The suitcase?" he pushed.

She looked at him with a firm expression. "My emergency bag. In case I need to leave quickly. You know, fire, bomb threat, a riot. Why are you asking me all these questions? Is this normal protocol for pressing assault charges?"

Jake looked at Buddy and then exhaled.

"Gloria's body washed up along the shoreline near Treasure Town. Our town," Jake told her.

She gasped and covered her mouth with her hand.

"What? Her body? You mean she's dead? How? What happened?"

"It appears she was shot and then someone tried to dump the body," Buddy told her.

She looked at him. Her eyes darted to each of them, and then she lost the coloring in her face.

"You came here because you think I killed her?" she asked, sounding insulted and angry.

"We came here because of the incident the other night at Prestige, and it's part of doing this investigation. This is what we do, Frankie," Jake told her.

"Well, that's wonderful. I get assaulted, and suddenly I'm the first one you look at as a suspect? How about the many guys she sleeps with? Or maybe the drug dealers and her connections to the goods? How about these people? The criminals and repeat offenders have more rights than I do? Are you kidding me? I mind my own business and work my butt off, and I'm a suspect in a murder investigation? You want to take my gun and check to see if it has been fired? You want to search my apartment for weapons, evidence, blood-stained clothing, forensic stuff?"

"Frankie calm down," Turbo said to her as he placed his hand on her shoulder. She looked at him with such fear and terror he felt his gut clench with some sort of reaction.

"No one is accusing you of anything. We're following our leads and determining where to go next. Just cooperate, and it will be fine," Buddy told her.

"Do you need to take my gun?" she asked him.

He shook his head. "The victim was killed with a Glock, not a 38," Buddy told her.

She sighed and looked relieved. Turbo felt as though she was really scared living in this place, and the fact that she carried a firearm upset him.

He pulled away. "Why do you live here?"

She widened her eyes and then looked panicked.

"What do you mean?" she asked.

"The place is unsafe. You have it nicely decorated, but you carry a gun and have a suitcase packed and ready to go."

She didn't say a word, and Jake and Buddy didn't add any comments. Her lack of response concerned him, and then she looked at him.

"I don't know why you're interrogating me. I haven't done anything wrong. I told you if you need to take my gun to ensure I haven't used it you can. Why I live here is none of your business, deputy."

She called him deputy with such disgust and disrespect.

"We may need to talk to you again. Do you have a cell number we can reach you at or a home phone?" Buddy asked her.

She shook her head.

"I work at Prestige Friday and Saturday nights. But I've been job-hunting for something else for during the day. Lure lets me use his cell phone number as a contact number. If you need to contact me, I suppose you could try there. You said you were going to talk with Charlie and Lure? They know me well and watch over me." She looked at Turbo as she continued. "I was with them all day and night Saturday and Sunday, if that helps to know."

Turbo clenched his teeth. Was she sleeping with Charlie and Lure? Fuck!

Buddy cleared his throat then pulled out a business card.

"Here's my number. You call us if you think of anything else or if you need to contact us for any reason."

"Okay." She took the card and then headed toward the door. She opened it, and Turbo let Buddy and Jake head out first.

"Be sure to lock up," Turbo told her.

"I always do."

She closed the door, and they all headed down the hallway and out of the building.

"What do you think?" Jake asked Buddy.

"I think Turbo's girl is hiding something, but I don't think she killed Gloria."

"You don't?" Turbo asked.

"Hell no. She is sweet and only seemed to get on the defensive with you, Turbo. I think you need to work on your angle," Buddy teased him.

"Sounds more like she's involved with the owners of Prestige. They know Nate, don't they?" Jake asked.

"They do. But I don't think she's involved with them. I think she's trying to piss me off to keep me at bay. But seeing where she lives, and knowing that Gloria was killed more than likely the night she attacked Frankie, has my gut twisted with concern. Something isn't right."

"Well, what do you know? Deputy Hawkins has a bit of investigative skills a brewing. Should we keep him in the loop?" Buddy asked Jake, and Jake chuckled as he started the truck.

"Only if he promises to not start a fight with Charlie and Lure over Frankie." Buddy chuckled.

"He's a Hawkins. Good fucking luck with that."

Turbo shook his head as Jake and Buddy chuckled.

Turbo felt pissed and disappointed. He'd really hoped he and his brothers had a chance with Frankie. But if she was banging her bosses, sloppy seconds weren't the Hawkins' style.

* * * *

Buddy Landers walked out of the interrogation room with more questions than answers.

Lux, as he liked to be called, was a drug dealer, a little fish in a large pond with useless information. Lux was with Gloria the night she got busted by Charlie and Lure for selling drugs. She'd been having sex with Lux in the back room of the club. Buddy, Jake, and Turbo got a lot of information from Lure and Charlie, who were more than happy to assist with the investigation. Buddy was starting to think that Lux would be his only tool in figuring out who'd killed Gloria. As far as he was concerned, Frankie wasn't a suspect but a victim in the case.

Frankie had not only gained the attention and concern of Lure and Charlie, but also of Turbo and his brothers. Buddy had great instincts, too, and he believed that Frankie was definitely hiding something. It might not be illegal since she'd been more than willing to help in the investigation and even give up her gun to prove her innocence. But when Buddy called her and asked for some more personal information, she'd asked him to not invade her privacy and her past. That things had happened she didn't want to rehash, and nothing was illegal, was just as upsetting.

He was curious, but he respected her wishes. She wasn't a suspect, after all. But he wouldn't be too sure about Turbo and his brothers. They liked Frankie, and it seemed the more she tried blowing them off, the more interested they became.

"Hey, did you get anything more out of him?" Detective Bryce Moore asked Buddy as he joined him outside of the interrogation room.

Buddy pulled out his notes.

"Not much but that he's on the bottom of the totem pole. Looks like Gloria was the contact for their distributor and operator. Lux isn't budging on any names. He'd didn't bat an eye when I suggested he would be charged as a suspect in her murder. He just said he wasn't talking anymore and wanted his lawyer."

"Well, maybe he'll reconsider. Here's a list of all the contacts and recent text messages and calls from his cell phone. I looked into the numbers. Lux is very friendly with Sal Baletti." Bryce smirked.

"Sal Baletti? That scumbag. Holy shit, he's probably their supplier for the club. That's one bad-ass group of men. His brother Gino and the rest of the family have ties to New York and Chicago. This is definitely something we can work with."

"Sure is, and get this, there's some sort of investigation going on into Baletti through the Special Crimes Unit." Bryce handed Buddy a note.

"This is the number of the main investigator. As soon as we started digging into Baletti, we got a call."

"Shit. I knew this wasn't going to be a cut-and-dried case. Looks like some heavy shit is about to go down."

"Sure does."

Buddy glanced at the interrogation room.

"Looks like I'm going to be at this awhile. Let me know when his attorney comes."

Bryce smirked.

"Considering the evidence on his cell phone alone, I'd say he'll be talking to you instead."

Buddy nodded and prepared to enter the room again. He wanted answers, and he wanted Gloria to be the only body to pop up in Treasure Town, but something told him things were going to get worse before they got better. The Baletti family was nothing but trouble, and they always seemed to be able to keep their hands clean. But based on the facts that they were connected to Gloria's murder and they were known criminals, Buddy wasn't taking any chances and letting them make their way into Treasure Town. When he was done here, he would call Jake and talk to his superiors. They needed to handle this accordingly, and knowing how large their organization was, he knew it wasn't going to be easy.

Chapter 4

Frankie was glad that Cassidy had called her to go shopping and grab some lunch today. It took her mind off of the fact that Gloria had been murdered and that Frankie had been initially questioned as a suspect. She had to go to work at Prestige tomorrow night and wasn't looking forward to the third degree Charlie and Lure were going to give her. She'd already received a text message that they wanted to talk and to come early.

They had just sat down when Cassidy's phone began vibrating again. Cassidy exhaled in annoyance.

"What's wrong? Is that Keith again?" Frankie asked her.

"Sure is. He is not taking me breaking up with him too well at all."

Frankie took a sip of her iced tea.

"He hit you. There's no way you should take him back or accept his apologies again. You went through this before with him," Frankie reminded Cassidy, although she didn't have to. Keith was a big guy with a bad temper. He was also abusive, and Cassidy was trying to resist his tactics of charm, apologies, and professions of love. It wasn't easy.

"I know. It just doesn't seem real. I mean that he hit me and lost his cool over some other guy asking me out. I mean, we're not even boyfriend and girlfriend anymore."

"But you decided to meet him for lunch and talk. He took it as a sign that you were forgiving him and you were working things out."

"I know that. You were right. I was stupid, and I guess you know I missed having a boyfriend and going out places. Now it's like I have to worry about every guy I meet or flirt with. Maybe I was just being lazy."

"Lazy? Are you kidding me? Listen, you were comfortable. You truly loved him, and he destroyed that innocence of love. He corrupted it and tainted it by hitting you and by hurting you and calling you all those names and lying. Remember, your other friends saw him with other women, too."

"I know, I know. It will work out. I'm just going to ignore him."

"You can block his number. You can do it right from the phone."

"Hey, look who's walking across the street and headed this way," Cassidy said, and Frankie followed her line of sight.

She felt her belly tighten and her heart begin to race. Nate and Rye Hawkins appeared to be walking from a large black pickup truck. Hawkins' Construction was written on the side of it.

"No wonder they have such incredible bodies. Damn, I bet they work shirtless, too, with those tans they have. Muscles clenching and shifting as they hammer nails and sweat drips from their pecs. Damn," Cassidy whispered as she took a sip from her iced tea glass and stared.

Frankie got annoyed. She instantly felt jealous, and it shocked her. Just then Cassidy's cell phone rang as Nate and Rye walked toward the front entrance and saw her. Nate crunched his eyes together and Rye headed toward her. She looked away, and Cassidy stood up.

"I need to go. Something came up." She grabbed her bags.

"What? What's wrong?"

"Nothing. I just have to take care of something. Shit. I'm sorry, Frankie. I'll see you at work tomorrow night." She leaned down and gave Frankie a kiss on the cheek and a hug.

Frankie watched her leave. She nearly bumped into Nate and Rye, who said hello before they came closer. Frankie watched Cassidy put her phone to her ear and carry on. She seemed upset, and Frankie was concerned.

"Is she okay?" Rye asked as he and Nate moved to stand by the table.

"What? Oh, I don't know. I guess so. She didn't really say."

Frankie swallowed hard as she took in the sight of Nate and Rye. They looked incredible, even slightly dirty and wearing work clothes.

"Can we join you?" Rye asked, pulling out a chair. Before she could decline them, both men sat. Nate stared at her.

She pulled her bottom lip between her teeth as the waitress came over and took their food and drink order. Frankie had already ordered a salad and was waiting on it.

"I'm sorry, but can you cancel the other salad? My friend had to leave in a hurry," Frankie told the waitress.

"Sure thing. Should I bring yours out with their burgers?"

"No, as soon as it's ready please."

She wondered how the hell she would eat with them sitting here with her. She could feel the intensity of their presences, their masculinity, and their appeal surround her. Even the waitress checked them out and smiled.

"How are you doing?" Rye asked and looked at her eye.

She held his gaze. "My eye is much better, as you can see."

"That's good." He held her gaze.

"Were you having a girls' day out or something?" Rye asked as he tapped the shopping bag next to Frankie's chair.

Rye was very handsome, and he seemed to fully focus on her, putting her on the edge. He leaned closer and kept a hand at the back of her chair. She felt his arms brush against her back. It turned her on and made her body heat up. She had to keep reminding herself to keep her distance. No men could be trusted.

"Something like that. We needed new skirts for Prestige, and I needed other things." Like thong panties and a new bra. She couldn't believe while she was shopping in the lingerie store she'd actually thought about the four Hawkins brothers. Here she was telling Cassidy to stay clear of Keith, and meanwhile, she should be taking the same advice about these men. They weren't good for her. It was smarter to lay low. It would hurt when she had to leave. More importantly, they could get hurt if Kevin or Carlotto ever found her.

"Cassidy left in a hurry. Does this mean you're free for the rest of the afternoon?" Nate asked her.

The waitress brought over their drinks, and Frankie clasped her hands on her lap. They were flirting again, hinting toward getting to know her.

She was trying to muster the words to tell them to stop trying, but they never reached her lips. Rye leaned forward.

"Listen, we heard about Gloria and about the investigation. If you need someone to talk to."

She shook her head and squinted at him.

"No. No, why would I? I don't know why anyone would hurt her. I mean I know about the drugs and stuff, but still, I was shocked when your brother and the detective and sheriff showed up."

"That's understandable. Turbo was really concerned. He's worried about your safety coming and going to the club and to your apartment," Rye said.

She felt embarrassed. It had been obvious that Turbo didn't like her apartment and the fact that she lived there. She had to remind herself that she was trying to hide out. So far, so good.

"Well, he shouldn't be. I'm sure when he told you about my lovely neighborhood he also mentioned that I own a gun and know how to use it. I've been taking care of myself for quite some time," she snapped at him.

He held his palms up and leaned back in his chair, somewhat in defeat.

She felt uncomfortable. She was being mean and purposely trying to push him away, and it had backfired on her. She felt guilty, and damn it, she was attracted to Rye as well as Nate.

"You don't have any family?" Nate asked, changing the subject slightly.

She shook her head. Frankie really wanted to reply with "maybe I do, maybe I don't." After all, Kevin had found that out about her and used it as a tool to manipulate her and weaken her resolve to be independent. He wanted her completely relying on him. Perhaps Rye and Nate were the same.

"And you guys?" she asked as the waitress came over with her salad.

"We have some cousins around. But mostly we have one another," Rye told her.

She was affected by that statement, for more reasons than she wanted to acknowledge. Her parents died when Frankie was young. She and her brother, Mickey, had raised themselves from sixteen on. She made smart choices for the most part and even finished college. Mickey followed in her father's footsteps and wound up getting killed in the line of duty. That had been a living hell, but then she'd met Kevin. No sisters, no brothers, aunts, or uncles to ask advice or to lean on. She was alone. And Kevin knew that. He had known Mickey, and that's what made her lower her defenses and let him in. Twenty-one and stupid.

She looked toward the road and where the truck was as she began to eat her salad.

"You two into construction?" she asked.

Nate just watched her as Rye did most of the talking.

* * * *

Nate was trying to figure Frankie out. She was definitely holding back information on herself. When he'd learned that Gloria was murdered and that Frankie lived in the crappiest neighborhood in Bayline and carried a gun, he was concerned. That concern turned to interest and intrigue, and he and his brothers had spent the last several days trying to figure her out. She seemed sweet and somewhat professional. It was almost as though she didn't fit being a waitress at Prestige but more like a career woman in an office or something.

"What do you like to do on your days off when you're not shopping?" Rye asked her.

The waitress arrived with their burgers, and the more Rye talked, the more relaxed Frankie seemed to be getting.

She was quite an attractive woman. Her blonde hair curled at the bottom as it cascaded over her chest. The top she wore was not what he would call low-cut, but enough cleavage showed to reveal a small crystal star necklace with other multiple tiny delicate gold stars spaced along the entire chain. It looked delicate and feminine.

She cleared her throat, and he discovered she was staring at him.

He couldn't resist. He reached out and touched the necklace, letting the gold chain and two of the tiny stars sit along the inside of his palm.

"This is beautiful."

She gulped. He heard her and looked into her gorgeous blue eyes. They were stunning.

"Like you, Frankie."

She inhaled softly, and her breasts rose and fell. This close to her, he got a good scent of her appealing perfume, and like magic, her femininity encased him.

"Ever been to Galileo's? That downtown restaurant and boutique on the water?" he asked, releasing her necklace, even though he didn't want to. The back of his hand grazed her skin, and she widened her eyes at him.

She shook her head.

"It's unique. Has a lot of eclectic art and old pictures and information on everything from astrology to fables and stories surrounding Treasure Town. But what makes it special is the view on the water. On a clear night, you can see the stars so vividly, even without the telescopes they have scattered along the top of the building. You have to see it. You'd love the stars."

"I heard about Galileo's before. It's hard to get a reservation. Especially this time of year."

"Would you like to go there with us?" he asked.

"We'd love to take you. This Sunday is supposed to be a clear, gorgeous night."

"I don't know Nate, Rye," she whispered and lowered her eyes to her salad.

He reached out and used his pointer to gently tilt her chin up.

"Just as friends. You're fairly new to the area, and we know this great place. We'd love to introduce you to Galileo's."

"I don't think it's a good idea. I don't date. I'm not looking to get involved."

He felt his gut clench. Why did he feel as though she was scared of getting hurt and that someone had definitely hurt her?

"Friends first, Frankie. No pressure," Rye added now.

"I'll think about it, okay?"

"You can give us your answer tomorrow night at work," Nate told her.

"You're going to be at Prestige?" she asked.

Rye smiled, and Nate watched her hold Rye's gaze.

"Definitely. You can tell us yes then."

Chapter 5

Detective Bryce Moore was going over the information he'd received from the special investigative unit. It appeared that Gloria had been on their radar for quite some time, along with her bosses, Sal and Gino Baletti. But what grabbed his attention and had him looking around, making sure that no one else could see the file, not even Buddy, was that he'd picked up on one name. Pasqual Carlotto, the son of Louie Carlotto, a big time gangster from Chicago. This wasn't good. Why was Louie's name in this file and part of this investigation? Bryce pulled out his cell phone and texted a message, a code that would let his contact know something was up. Although Bryce thought his days of helping Carlotto were over by moving away from Chicago and into a tourist town like Treasure Town, he knew where his loyalties lay. Carlotto owned him, and no matter what he did, that debt would never be paid. That's what doing business with Carlotto was like. He owned Bryce for eternity. He had to give him the heads-up.

"Hey, did you get that file from the squad? I just left a message for the investigator, and he said he forwarded it to you this morning," Buddy asked.

Bryce swallowed hard.

"Yeah, I've got it right here. Doesn't really say much. Same shit we know. Gloria had ties to Gino and Sal Baletti. Not sure we can prove much considering this special investigative team won't give up any surveillance videos that can help. Looks like we're going to have to rely on any forensic evidence that was gathered from the crime scene or, if we're lucky, any eyewitness reports of anyone seeing

Gloria with one of the Baletti brothers last week." He closed up the file and stood up.

"I think we may want to work that angle."

"I agree. If you're sure there's nothing in there that can help, then let's case the neighborhood where she was seen last. Perhaps someone saw something," Buddy said, and Bryce nodded in agreement as he put the file into the drawer and pushed the chair under the desk.

"I'll drive," he told Buddy.

"Sure thing. Maybe we'll get lucky."

Not if I can help it.

* * * *

Not only were Nate and Rye at Prestige, but so was Mike. They told her when they first arrived that Turbo was working late. She was surprised at how disappointed she felt. The more they talked to her and talked about regular things, the more she forgot about her fears of getting close to them and she lightened up.

Prestige was very crowded, and as the night went on, she wasn't able to talk to them as much. She had a moment and walked toward their table, having to squeeze by a group of people. Mike was sitting on the end seat of the table for four with high barstools.

He wrapped his arm around her waist, pulling her closer so she could hear what he wanted to say to her.

She tensed a moment, holding on to the table with one hand and on to his shoulder with the other. Mike smelled so good. His cologne was light but appealing and his arm solid steel. His fingers splayed over her hip, and she wondered what they would feel like against her ass. It shocked her to have these thoughts.

"What time should we pick you up on Sunday for Galileo's?" he asked her, his lips touching her ear as he spoke to her.

She pulled back and gave him a smirk. "I didn't say yes. Yet." She pulled back slightly, only for him to pull her close again.

Mike, with his dusting of hair along his face and tattoos peeking out from the long-sleeve shirt he wore, looked so damn sexy.

"Come on, baby. We want to get to know you and talk to you where it's not so loud and we have your complete attention." He winked and pulled his bottom lip between his teeth as he gazed over her lips then back up to her eyes.

Little did he know that he and his brothers already had her complete attention. But she was still concerned.

"Listen, I don't know how long I'll be staying in Bayline."

He squinted and pulled her closer, his hand possessively pressed over her hip and ass. She was so turned on by him that she swallowed hard.

"Don't say that. Come on now. It will be fun, and you never know. We may just grow on you."

She glanced at Nate and Rye then heard her name and felt the hand on her shoulder.

"Table seven is looking for another round. I'll put it in, but you need to deliver it, honey," Cassidy told her and winked.

Frankie pulled away from Mike. "Thanks. I'll be right there." She then looked at them. Mike grabbed her hand.

"Say yes."

She took a deep breath and then released it.

"Fine, yes. But I'll meet you there."

They looked at her as though they didn't like the idea at all.

"I have some things to take care of, and I'll be out already. Is seven good?"

"Great. We'll see you there at seven," Nate told her and looked her over with that intense, hard expression of his that did a number on her body.

Her breasts felt full, her pussy leaked, and she couldn't help but to wonder what type of lover he would be. When she turned around and left, her cheeks felt red and warm from her sexual thoughts as her brain caught up. Had she just made a huge mistake? Was she setting herself up for more pain? She didn't know, but she had been lonely and scared for months now. It was time to try and feel normal again. She couldn't worry about Kevin or Carlotto finding her. She couldn't.

Frankie grabbed the drink order from the bar and continued her shift.

A while later, at the end of their shift, Cassidy was sitting with her, counting their tips for the night.

"So what was with the Hawkins brothers? Are you finally going to give them a taste of your cookies?"

"A taste of my cookies? Really, Cassidy?" Frankie asked, and Cassidy raised her eyebrows up and down. Frankie started laughing.

"You're the only person I know who refers to it as cookies. When I heard you say it the other day I wasn't a hundred percent sure what you meant."

"Really? You must be very inexperienced with sex. But don't worry. That will change with four sexy lovers. They're huge guys. They probably have extra large cocks."

"Cassidy," she scolded her and looked around to be sure no one could hear her.

Cassidy chuckled.

"Hey, I'm just teasing you. I know you're a good girl and don't fuck around. Hell, if I didn't know that some asshole hurt you, I'd still think you were a virgin."

"Jeez, thanks, Cassidy."

Cassidy chuckled.

She hadn't told Cassidy about Kevin or her life back in Chicago, just about the fact she'd thought she was in love and her boyfriend cheated on her and was into bad stuff. She got away before it was too late. Frankie wanted Cassidy to know that because she didn't like Cassidy's now-ex-boyfriend, Keith. He seemed abusive and capable of hurting Cassidy, both physically and mentally.

"So did you make plans with them or what?" Cassidy asked.

"Kind of. I don't know. I'm having second thoughts."

"Well, that is a lot of cock to handle at once, but with practice you'll be fine."

"Cassidy, really?" she reprimanded her, and Cassidy leaned back in her chair and looked Frankie over.

"You're sweet and a nice person. Take some of the advice you've given me these past few months and don't settle. Those guys like you. They legitimately seem to care and want to watch over you. If you've never done a ménage, then those four are like hitting the jackpot."

"I haven't given the sex much thought actually."

"What? You're such a liar."

"No, Cassidy, I'm not. I've really been denying any attraction I've felt. I don't know if I'm ready to get into even a friendship with a man or, in this case, men, never mind a sexual one. I guess I'm being cautious, and I don't want to get hurt again."

Cassidy covered Frankie's hand.

"That old boyfriend of yours really messed you up, huh?"

Frankie chuckled but felt the tears fill her eyes as she held Cassidy's gaze.

"You have no idea."

Cassidy gave a sympathetic smile. "Well, that was then, and this is now. Move on with your life and give those men a chance. Since you've been hurt so badly before, you'll know the signs if it isn't right. Just don't go fucking them right away." She smiled then leaned closer.

"Or do fuck them right away. A ménage is hot, and having four huge, bad-ass men taking care of your every need and desire might be the perfect cure to get that old asshole out of your head."

Frankie chuckled. "And what about you? Are you keeping Keith out of your head or is he still trying to get you back?"

Cassidy got quiet and put her money into her bag.

"He's persistent, but I'm not biting. Don't you worry. It will be fine, and he'll eventually get that it's over."

"If you need me, call me. If he keeps it up, I'd tell Charlie and Lure. They'd take care of him."

"I know they would. I think it will be fine. I haven't heard from him in a few days. So what are you going to wear tomorrow to Galileo's?"

"Not a clue. Probably a dress."

"Something sexy yet classy, just like you. Remember to make them work for your cookies." She winked as she stood up.

Frankie chuckled.

Chapter 6

"What if she doesn't show up?" Nate asked as he and his brothers stood outside of Galileo's waiting for Frankie to arrive.

She was five minutes late. They were all dressed nicely in button-down shirts and dress pants, looking their best. Nate couldn't believe his brothers were so into this woman and they knew nothing about her. He was skeptical. She had secrets, and that wasn't a good thing. But he was attracted to her, too.

Nate watched other couples, including some ménage groups, coming and going from the restaurant.

"Look there's the bus," Mike said as a local transportation bus stopped at the corner among the many restaurants and shopping boutiques. Treasure Town was filled with them.

Sure enough, Nate spotted Frankie right away, and so did his brothers.

Mike whistled low.

"Holy shit, I think I'm having chest pains," Rye admitted, and Turbo chuckled.

"She's a damn goddess."

But Nate just watched her and watched the men checking her out as she smoothed her hand down the strapless blue sundress she wore, gripping her purse and a sweater in the other. Some guy said something to her, and she gave him the evil eye and then continued to walk toward them. Mike stepped forward to meet her first.

"You look stunning, Frankie." He pulled her close and kissed her cheek. She smiled shyly and looked at all of them.

They just stared at her in awe then each gave her a kiss hello. Nate held back. She locked gazes with him.

"Hi, Nate."

"Hello, Frankie. You look beautiful."

"Thank you. You guys look great, too."

They just stood there a moment. She looked away from them and toward the restaurant.

"So this is Galileo's? It's pretty big."

Rye placed his arm around her waist and escorted her toward the door. "It is big, and we reserved a nice spot on the upper deck. That way the view will be amazing like we described."

"I can't wait."

She ran her fingers along her star necklace. It seemed she wore that all the time. Nate wondered who'd given it to her. Then he thought perhaps a guy, and he felt angry and jealous.

The hostess escorted them all to the top floor. Nate absorbed the scent of Frankie's perfume and her sexy figure as she climbed the stairs along with Mike and Rye.

The table was just as they'd asked. One close to the balcony, private in its own corner away from any prying eyes. It paid to know people, and apparently Turbo knew a lot of them around Treasure Town.

Rye held her seat out for her, and they all gathered around.

"This is so nice up here, and very private. How did you get reservations? I thought this place was booked up months in advance." She placed her purse on her lap and her sweater on her chair.

"Turbo seems to have those extra law enforcement connections," Rye teased then winked at Turbo.

Nate watched her eyes widen, and then she glanced at Turbo before looking down to her lap. She was nervous, and he wondered if she was intimidated by Turbo's profession.

"Did you work really late last night?" Nate asked her.

"I didn't get home until four."

"In the morning?" Rye asked.

Turbo sat forward.

"That's dangerous, coming home that late at night to your neighborhood," he told her.

She looked at him and swallowed hard. "There's always danger, Turbo. It's being prepared and aware that keeps people from becoming victims. You should know that. Being a deputy and all."

The waitress came over to take their drink orders and to tell them about the specials. Frankie ordered a glass of white wine, and the men all ordered beers.

"So, tell us about yourself. What do you like to do when you're not working at Prestige or shopping with your friend Cassidy?" Turbo asked her.

"Not much. I catch up on my sleep, work out a bit, and keep busy."

"You work out at a gym?" Rye asked her.

"No, I run and had a bike until recently."

"What happened?" Nate asked.

"It was stolen."

"At your place?" Turbo asked.

She leaned back and gave him a hard expression.

"Actually, no, it was outside of the juice bar on the boardwalk. You know, where all the clean-cut teenagers hang out."

Rye chuckled.

Turbo held her gaze. "I didn't mean it like that."

"Sure you did, Turbo. I get it. You don't like where I live, but it's none of your business," she snapped at him.

Nate cleared his throat.

Turbo scooted closer, placed his arm around Frankie's chair, and whispered firmly to her.

"I'm making it my business. You're a very attractive woman. Gun or no gun, you live in a bad neighborhood with criminals everywhere.

I don't like it. I'm worried about you, and I'm sorry if that upsets you."

"It sounded insulting," she whispered.

Turbo ran his hand under her hair and moved closer.

"I didn't mean to insult you. I meant to express that I care."

Turbo pressed his lips gently to hers, and Nate watched, feeling his whole body tighten. He wondered if she would pull away, and he realized that, if she did, he, too, would be disappointed. But his guard was up. Nate still didn't like the secrecy and not knowing who Frankie really was.

Nate released her lips and then smiled.

"Just as I thought. Delicious."

She swallowed and turned slightly to reach for her glass of wine. Nate pulled back but kept his hand on the back of her chair as he stroked her bare shoulder.

* * * *

Frankie wanted to guzzle the wine in the hope that it would calm her nerves. Nate was intense and seemed to be watching her every move and analyzing her answers to their questions. Turbo, as usual, put her on edge. It was the whole deputy thing. She didn't want to go down that path and trust another cop, yet she was interested, attracted to Nate just like she was to his brothers.

She felt Rye place his hand on her knee under the table as they looked over the menus. She bit her lower lip as the wine slowly traveled through her body. Nate ordered her another one, as if he knew she needed it.

"So is it just you and Rye who work construction or Mike, too?" she asked Nate.

Mike held her gaze as he leaned back in his chair looking so damn sexy she wanted to kiss him, too. She cleared her head as Rye talked about the small construction company they owned and the minor home improvements they did.

"Mike's a firefighter in Treasure Town," Rye told her.

She held Mike's gaze and imagined how sexy and capable he must look in uniform.

"As a matter of fact, I was thinking that maybe we could all go to the Station after dinner tonight. Maybe show you around the place so you can see all the memorabilia there. It might be nice for you to meet some of our friends," Mike suggested.

"Cassidy has been trying to get me to go there with her for the past few weeks," she admitted as the waitress set down another round of drinks and then took their orders.

"You haven't wanted to go?" Mike asked her.

"She just has a thing for first responders and doesn't mind flaunting herself to meet someone new."

"How about you? Don't have a thing for first responders?" Mike asked her in a sexy tone as he eyed her over. He lifted his bottle of Bud.

She licked her lower lip as she held his gaze. "Don't want to be just another notch in some cop's belt or on a firefighter's suspenders. I've learned to stay clear of men like that."

"Sounds like you had a bad experience," Turbo told her, and she looked away and out toward the water.

"We're not all the same. We first responders," Mike said, grabbing her full attention.

She looked back at him, hoping they weren't like Kevin then having that sensation in her gut, that fear that warned her to keep her distance.

"Have you all lived around here all your lives?" She found it safer to change the subject, and Mike took a slug of his beer.

Rye lifted his hand off her knee and sat forward. "Mike and I have been around here the longest. Turbo came back here after going to college for criminal justice. He joined the sheriff's department twelve years ago, right, Turbo?" Rye asked.

Turbo nodded.

"That's a long time. Did you join fresh out of college?" she asked.

"No, once I graduated and came back to Treasure Town. Jake talked me into applying, even though I'd already put my papers in for the state police. I was twenty-three."

"How old are you now?" she asked.

"Thirty-six." She pulled her bottom lip between her teeth and lowered her eyes.

"And you? How old are you, beautiful?" Turbo asked her, leaning closer.

She glanced up at him, knowing she should ignore the attraction and how appealing they all seemed. So much older and experienced. Was that really what she wanted?

"Twenty-three," she whispered.

This time Rye clutched her chin and leaned closer. "You do need looking after, beautiful."

He pressed his lips to hers, and she closed her eyes and forgot why she should keep her distance from these older, more experienced men, and then the food arrived. Rye released her lips and winked at her. He was so handsome. How could all four of these men be so appealing and want her?

The aroma of food and the way the night seemed to roll in at such a perfect time as the waitress lit the candles on the table added to the ambiance. The waitress lit more candles along the balcony by the telescopes, and with a glance up toward the evening sky, Frankie could tell it was going to get even better.

They ate and spoke about the area, about Galileo's, and, of course, about the Station. Rye would cover her knee and squeeze it while Turbo ran his fingers along her shoulders and bare skin making her feel flushed and overheated. She thanked them for dinner and wasn't surprised that Nate handled the check. He seemed to be the one in charge, the leader, although Turbo asked the most questions and seemed like the interrogator of the bunch.

Mike got up and then walked around to her chair.

"Take your wine with you. We can move closer to the railing so we can see the stars better."

She stood, feeling the light buzz from the wine, or, perhaps, it was the spell these four men were putting on her. She wasn't certain. She struggled between wanting to give in to the attraction she felt and being fearful of her past, not knowing if the danger was behind her or if she was still at risk. How badly she wanted to believe that she was safe now and could move on with her life. But what if she was wrong? What if Kevin got out of jail and was looking for her or even Carlotto, too? After all, she did know a lot about Carlotto that, at the very least, could destroy his fortune. It made her wonder why he hadn't just killed her when he had the chance.

In the distance she heard the echo of sirens and saw some flashing lights, but they were far from where the restaurant stood, and soon the sky pulled her complete attention. It did make her imagine Mike responding to a fire in full uniform and gear. He would look like some calendar model. He probably had a long line of females wanting to be added to that collection of notches she'd mentioned in his suspenders.

She felt the hand against her lower back as her eyes locked onto the view.

"Oh God, it is beautiful up here." She leaned closer. She felt the arm wrap around her waist from behind and then Mike's fingers moving her hair off her shoulder.

He leaned down closer and kissed along her skin.

"I like this view right here."

His lips kissed her skin, and his mouth moved over her collarbone then down her chest nearly to her cleavage. She felt disappointed as he moved his lips backed up and turned her to face him. His lips touched hers, and they kissed deeply until she felt another hand at her waist as Mike released her lips. Turbo was there as Mike stepped aside, and Turbo pulled her closer.

He ran his fingers under her hair and along her neck, cupping the back of her head.

It was intoxicating, like some sort of dream as Mike kissed her then Turbo took his place all in one smooth transition. Was she drunk? She'd had only two glasses of wine and sipped them slowly. What were these sensations? What was the deep feeling in her heart, her gut that had her returning their kisses?

"We're going to change your opinion of first responders, and for the better."

Turbo covered her lips and kissed her deeply, and she held on, kissing him back, completely turned on by all of them.

She felt overwhelmed as Turbo released her lips. She turned in his arms, relieved to take a breather as she gripped the railing and tried to calm her libido. Then she stared at the evening sky. They had been right. It was a clear, beautiful night, and the rooftop of Galileo's was impressive.

She could smell the salt air and absorb the tranquility of being so close to the ocean in a town that seemed magical. Everyone spoke of Treasure Town as such a place, and she really thought it was corny. Now, being here like this, her views had changed.

Turbo stepped back, and she felt the loss of his hold until Rye took his place. He cuddled next to her and sniffed her hair.

"You smell edible, baby. I love it."

He tickled her, and she chuckled, completely flattered at his compliment and also aroused by his need to get so close to her. His palm pressed over her belly, his fingertips grazed the underside of her breasts, and she yearned for a deeper, more intimate connection. His lips kissed along her jaw, and she turned her head sideways toward Rye, meeting his lips and kissing him first. She was falling deeper and trying to fight the fears in her head and the memories of the lies and pain Kevin had caused her.

They remained around her, all of them murmuring about the town, about work, and about heading toward the Station. She glanced over at Nate, who had yet to kiss her or even get close to her. She was surprised that she wanted him to kiss her, too, considering he seemed the most standoffish and gave off vibes of distrust.

Maybe she shouldn't get involved with them. She could have to leave, and it would hurt only more when it was time to go.

"How about we head out now and grab a drink at the Station? I'd love to show you around," Mike told her, taking her hand.

"Show her off is more like it," Rye teased, and she blushed.

"I suppose for a little while."

"The night is young. I want to learn more about you, Frankie," Mike told her then kissed her lips softly.

As they began to head out and down the stairs, they met some of their friends along the way. They introduced her right away, and their friends smiled. Some of the guys gave them high-fives and winked. She knew they were checking her out as she headed forward along with Turbo. Before they reached their truck, Nate took her hand, and Turbo released her with a wink and a smile. Nate's expression was serious as he guided her around the truck to the passenger side and out of the view of the crowds of waiting people trying to get into Galileo's. Rye opened the door, and Nate stopped her, placing his hands on her waist. She stared up into his dark blue eyes and felt exposed, guilty.

"Where's my kiss?" he asked.

She licked her lower lip and stared at him then realized that he wanted her to make the first move. Was he unsure about this? Was he really worried, too? She felt slightly empowered, and that edge gave her the nerve to lean up on tiptoes and kiss him.

His lips were firm and inviting, and his hands felt amazing as he wrapped her in his arms, deepened the kiss, and nearly made her come in her panties.

84

* * * *

Nate was only going to take a small taste. He had concerns. She was young and inexperienced, or so she appeared, and she was definitely holding back. He wanted answers. He wanted to taste her, feel her in his arms. Hell, he wanted to sink his cock into her deeply and get lost in desire and lust. Who gave a shit what was in her past?

But as he explored her mouth and kissed her deeply, he lost all thoughts and focused on sensations. The feel of her sexy curves against his palms, the scent of her perfume and the shampoo she used, and the way her large breasts pressed tight against his chest aroused him. She moaned into his mouth, and he did the same. It wasn't until he heard someone clear his throat that he realized his hand was halfway up under her dress, her thigh lifted up against his side, and he had her pressed against the truck. He ran his hands along her waist and cupped her cheeks. She was breathing heavily, her lips swollen and well loved.

"You pack a hell of a punch, baby. I don't think one kiss is going to be enough."

She stared up at him with such innocence and femininity he felt an overwhelming sensation of protectiveness over her. He brushed his thumb along her lower lip.

"Hop in the truck, Frankie."

He didn't mean to sound as though he was ordering her around, but he didn't want her out of his sight. Hell, he didn't know how they would let her leave them tonight, but he'd worry about that later. Right now he would enjoy the close proximity of the backseat of the truck and one sexy platinum-blonde who had just turned his world upside down.

* * * *

Mike held her hand as he introduced her to some of his friends. She was nervous about going with them to the Station and how their date might be perceived. That was until she saw the multiple other ménage couples around and, of course, the energy the place emitted.

"This is so cool," she told Mike as she hugged his arm, liking the feel of muscles and thickness against her body.

All four men were big and tall. A lot taller than she was. She felt feminine and sexy around them. She felt safe.

She tried pushing those needy sensations out of her head as she took in the sights. Firefighting memorabilia decorated practically every wall. There were old pictures, some tattered uniforms behind glass, tools firefighters used to fight fires, and the coolest thing ever. In the center of the room was a long pole like the ones used to descend from the upper floor of a fire station.

"It really is a fire station, isn't it?" she asked Mike, and he smiled wide.

"Sure is. Jake's dad, Burt, and his buddy Jerome own the place," Mike told her, and just then Jake, two other men, and a really pretty brunette greeted them.

"Hey, to what do we owe the pleasure of your company here at the Station tonight?" Jake teased, shaking the guys' hands.

"Or, better yet, to whom?" one of the others said as he winked at her. Then he added, "Hal McCurran, Jake's brother." He shook her hand. Then Jake introduced their woman, Michaela, and his other brother, Bear.

"Your call signs, huh?" Frankie asked.

"Get used to it. Most of these guys go by their call signs," Michaela said and reached her hand out. "Nice to meet you."

"You, too."

"Frankie works at Prestige," Jake told his wife.

"Oh, so this is Frankie," Michaela replied, and Frankie felt a little out of the loop.

"I'm sorry, Frankie. I didn't mean to make that sound bad. It's actually kind of funny. Let me explain."

Michaela placed her hand on Frankie's shoulder and began to walk her a few feet away and toward the bar. Frankie glanced over her shoulder and saw the men watching her, and Jake looked serious while talking to Turbo. She felt her belly clench with concern, but Michaela grabbed her complete attention.

"These guys all came in here a few nights after Jessie, Larry, and Dudley's bachelor party and were carrying on about this gorgeous platinum-blonde who worked at Prestige and how she'd turned down all their advances. Some jerks were saying stuff about going there and checking you out when Nate basically threatened them. It was crazy because Nate doesn't date, barely talks to anyone, and, well, just saying, you obviously affect the man."

Frankie lowered her eyes and then pulled her bottom lip between her teeth.

"I wonder why he did that. I hardly even spoke to him or his brothers that night."

"Well, you're with them now. Anyway, it was just awesome to see them here at the Station and walking in with you. Jake and his brothers have known the Hawkins brothers for years, but since Nate came back from serving in the war and working for the government, he's changed. They all had and hardly ever hung out. It's great to see them here. How long have you been dating them?"

"Tonight is our first date actually."

"No. Really? I would have thought, well, it doesn't matter. It's nice to meet the woman who got those guys to come out tonight to the Station. They could have brought you someplace special for your first date though. I'll need to talk with them."

Frankie chuckled. "They took me to Galileo's."

Michaela widened her eyes. "Really? Nice." She nodded. "What would you like to drink?" she asked Frankie as she waved over the bartender.

"I really shouldn't."

"Don't be silly, just one to make a toast."

"A toast?"

"Sure, to new friendships," Michaela told her, and Frankie felt a gush of emotions.

She didn't think this woman was for real. But then, an hour later, as Frankie laughed along with the Hawkins brothers and a bunch of their friends, she knew these people weren't faking anything. They were real. They cared about one another, and she'd never felt so envious in her life.

* * * *

Jake moved across the room to stand next to Turbo. "Galileo's, huh? I guess you went all out to impress her?"

Turbo chuckled. "Hey, you saw her reaction to me at her place. But really I can't take the credit. It was Nate and Rye that got her to accept a date."

"Nate and Rye? No freaking way." Jake replied and then took a slug of beer and looked at Turbo's brothers.

"She's a beautiful woman. I hope it works out for you guys," Jake told him.

"It's a first date. A start," Turbo replied.

Jake gave his arm a nudge. "You sound unsure."

Turbo glanced at Frankie and then back at Jake.

"She's different. It's more than just shyness, youth, and perhaps not being as experienced. There's something there."

"Maybe it's because of the case. You're trying to maintain your professionalism while also pursuing an interest."

"It's more than that. I can't read her. It's like some moments she seems confident, sure of herself, or at least she pretends to be. And other times, she seems intimidated, scared, like she's trying to decide how to react to us."

"You're a pretty good judge of character, Turbo, but sometimes a pretty face and knock-out body can ruin your better judgment. Do you think she's more interested in the fantasy of a ménage than making that type of commitment?"

"I'm not sure what to think, but I know I'll do what's necessary to protect my brothers."

Jake nodded as he looked toward Rye, Mike, and Nate, who surrounded Frankie.

"How about just being honest with Frankie about what you're feeling? Perhaps she'll be honest with all of you in return."

Turbo nodded. "I'll see what happens. It's only a first date."

Jake slapped his hand gently against Turbo's shoulder. "Sometimes it doesn't even take that long to get in deep." He then nodded toward Michaela just as Jake's brother Billy wrapped his arms around her and nuzzled against her neck.

Turbo remembered how they all had met Michaela She had been hiding from serious trouble, too. Maybe he should follow his gut and just ask for Frankie's honesty.

* * * *

"I can take the bus, really," Frankie told them after they left the Station and headed toward the truck.

"Are you out of your mind? We'll take you home. We want to be sure you get there safely," Mike told her, staying close to her as they escorted her to the truck.

She felt pretty good, almost bubbly, as she tilted her head to the side so she could lock gazes with Mike.

"Is this an attempt to get me to let you into my place?"

He turned her around and pressed her against the truck.

Holding her gaze with his beautiful dark-brown eyes, he gave her one of his sexy smiles.

"Baby, inviting us into your place is completely your choice."

Before she could respond, or even recover from that sexy expression and similarly sexy comment, he kissed her deeply.

She felt lost in his arms and in his kiss but reminded herself that this was a first date and taking it too quickly could be disastrous. She pulled back and pressed her hands against his chest.

"God, you make saying no so difficult."

He pulled his lower lip between his teeth and gazed over her cleavage.

"Good, because I so badly would love to explore this amazing body of yours."

She felt her cheeks warm as she pulled back and cleared her throat.

"First date, remember? I think I should take the bus."

"Not happening. Hop in, honey. We'll get you there safely," Rye told her, giving her a light tap to her ass.

Even that aroused her pussy and made her think of making love to these men. Hell, they turned her on so much she truly debated about just letting them fuck her and call it the best most memorable experience of her life. But that wasn't her. She had feelings, and she feared that connection, that bonding of bodies. Kevin had been her only lover, and it seemed she couldn't satisfy him enough that he'd strayed elsewhere. How the hell would she be able to satisfy four men?

She clutched her bag and climbed into the truck with Rye's support.

They talked about town and even mentioned a few newer condominium places that were up for rent. Their hints were thoughtful, and she didn't take them as an insult for they didn't know why she'd chosen Bayline and the worse neighborhood around.

As Nate pulled the truck up to the curb, Rye opened the door and helped her out.

"We'll walk you," he said.

"No need to."

"We want to. It's not exactly well lit, Frankie," Turbo told her.

"Hey, I've got my trusty protection. No worries." She patted her purse. They knew she had a gun. They didn't look too happy about it at all.

"Nonsense. We took you out on a date tonight. We'll walk you to your door," Turbo added, and the doors slammed closed.

Her four huge-ass bodyguards escorted her along the dark sidewalks and up past the even darker pathways to her main door. She turned around to face them.

"Well, I had a wonderful time. I loved Galileo's. Thank you for taking me there."

"We're walking you all the way up," Turbo told her.

"Turbo, I'm fine. I come and go from here every day and night. I can take care of myself."

"I think otherwise. We'll walk you to your door," he added firmly.

She didn't know what to do. She was trying so hard to act independent. To act like having these four amazing, capable, strong, good men around her didn't make her yearn for what couldn't be. They made her feel safe, cared for, and important. She had to be tough. She needed to gain control and think about what she wanted and what was right for all of them.

"I'm not inviting you inside," she told him, pointing at his chest.

Turbo grabbed her finger and pulled her toward him, causing her to step off the top step of the entranceway as he pulled her into his arms.

His hands held her firmly, one palm along her ass and the other around her waist.

"I respect that. It's a first date. But soon enough, you'll ask us to stay, or better yet, you'll come home with us."

He kissed her, and she kissed him back, wondering if this was even real and if maybe, just maybe, the past was well behind her and right here in front of her was her future.

Chapter 7

"So tell me about it. How was the sex?" Cassidy asked Frankie as Frankie joined her on the beach, laying her towel on the sand.

Frankie looked around them as if people may have heard Cassidy.

"Cassidy, could you lower your voice? I didn't have sex with them."

"No? Holy God, girl, what is wrong with you? Or, even more importantly, what did they do to turn you off?"

Frankie exhaled in annoyance, and Cassidy chuckled. She felt sorry for Frankie but also happy for her. It was obvious that Frankie was running from her past or, at the very least, scared of it. To find such great guys like the Hawkins brothers was like hitting the jackpot. It made her think about her own screwed-up relationship with Keith and about the new guy, Peter, she'd met two days ago.

Frankie pulled off her cover-up, revealing her voluptuous figure and the cute little moon and star tattoo she had on her hip. There was also some scarring by her hip bone, and when Cassidy had asked Frankie about it, she told her it was an old injury she'd gotten as a teen.

"They didn't do anything wrong. They didn't turn me off. I just don't have sex on the first date. Not that I didn't want to. God, Cassidy, it was so hard not to," she admitted as she plopped down onto the towel.

Cassidy smiled. She was so happy for her friend.

"I knew it. How could any sane woman not want to have sex with men as hot as those four?"

"Hey," Frankie reprimanded.

Cassidy widened her eyes and then slammed her hands on the towel with excitement.

"Oh my God, you've got it bad. You totally are into them. All four of them. A ménage!" She smiled, and Frankie covered her head and banged her hand down on the towel.

"It's so crazy. I can't even tell you how wonderful and amazing they are."

"So why didn't you sleep with them?"

"Because I don't really know them. I didn't want to come off easy. It was the first date and…"

"And what?"

"I'm scared to."

"Aw, honey." She clutched Frankie's hand. "Does this have something to do with your ex and the past you refuse to talk about?"

Frankie nodded.

"He did a number on me. In some ways he's somewhat like them, yet they're totally different. It's hard to explain. I'm worried, too, because he had cheated on me. I couldn't make one man commit to me completely. How the hell am I going to make four be faithful?"

"Oh, honey, your ex was stupid. A ménage relationship is different. It's sacred, and there's a special bond that exists. They are brothers for one, and they are bound to one another, blood and all. From my understanding, this type of relationship involves a big commitment and no cheating, no hiding information, and being upfront. Men involved in a ménage cater to a woman's every need, desire, and, of course, protection. With more than one man committed, a woman would never feel alone, unprotected, or cared for. It's special," Cassidy told her and then looked out toward the water. She thought about Peter and his brothers and the way they described it to her.

"How do you know so much about these types of relationships?"

She shrugged. "I'd consider it if the right men came along."

"Really?" Frankie asked. Cassidy nodded.

"Well, let's think about this. What specifically reminds them of your ex? Or is it one of them that does?"

"I really don't want to talk about that."

"I think you should. I don't want you to miss out on being happy. After all, it was you who helped me get out of a dangerous relationship with Keith, who, by the way, showed up at my apartment on Sunday with roses and promises of making things up to me."

"Oh God, what did you do?"

"I told him I wasn't interested. I told him to leave me alone. He was pissed off and tried to force his way in, but Manny was home next door. He came out of his apartment with his cell phone and a baseball bat and asked if everything was all right."

"Oh God, you should have called the police. You have that order of protection."

"I just want him to leave me alone. I think calling the cops would have enraged him more. Besides, it is over, and I moved on," she said, and Frankie chuckled.

"Who is he?" she asked.

Cassidy was surprised. Then again, it seemed in the last few months they had become such close friends it was as if they'd known one another forever.

"His name is Peter. He has four brothers, which is why I was kind of hoping that you would engage in the ménage experience."

"Oh shit, you like all five of them?"

Cassidy smiled.

"They're first responders. Cops and firefighters, actually."

"Oh God. Just be careful. Make sure you don't jump into bed with them. Sometimes first responders aren't exactly as perfect as you may think."

Cassidy saw the expression in Frankie's eye before she looked down at the beach towel.

"Is that who hurt you? A first responder?"

Frankie was silent a moment. She looked up toward the beach and then back down.

"He was a cop. I trusted him. I thought I was going to marry him, and he cheated on me."

"Oh man, Frankie. That's terrible. No wonder you're giving the Hawkins men such a hard time. Did you tell them about your ex?"

"No. No way would I talk about him. I'll get past it. It's a long story, and it's from my old life. After Sunday night's date and the way things went, I'm feeling pretty positive that I can move on. I want to move on."

"That's great. I want to move on, too." Just as Cassidy said that, her phone buzzed with a text message.

She glanced down and saw that it was Peter. He was at Sullivan's café with his partner, Todd.

"It's Peter. He and his partner in the police department are having lunch right up on the boardwalk at Sullivan's. They want us to join them."

"Oh, you go. I'll stay here."

"No. Don't be silly. I want you to meet him," Cassidy said.

Frankie gave a small smile. "Okay." She reached for her cover-up as they both stood up. Then she gathered their towels and beach bags.

"It's hot out. I can use one of those big iced teas from Sullivan's," Cassidy said.

"That sounds great."

They both stopped at the top of the beach where the ramp was to wash off their sandy feet and put on their flip-flops. Cassidy reached for her cover-up.

"Hey, gorgeous."

She turned around to see Reggie. "Oh my God, what are you doing here?" She hurried up the ramp and accepted the hug and kiss hello from Reggie, Peter's brother.

"Peter said he was going to see if you were down here, and I was picking up some supplies for dinner tonight. Are you still coming over?" he asked her.

But then she noticed Reggie looking at Frankie. "This must be Frankie." He reached his hand out to her. Frankie smiled and said hello.

"Come on. Join us for lunch, and we'll talk about dinner tonight. You should come, too, Frankie. We have a few friends coming over as well," he offered.

Cassidy grabbed Frankie's hand and smiled. "She would love to."

* * * *

Frankie couldn't help but smile. Cassidy seemed so happy. As they walked across the wooden planks to the entrance to Sullivan's, Cassidy gasped and then gave Reggie a smack on his arm.

"They're all here. You surprised me," she said.

Frankie watched as Cassidy was greeted by men who appeared to be Reggie's other brothers and some friends. Then Cassidy introduced Reggie.

Some of the guys were dressed in dark T-shirts with fire station insignias on the front and others in police uniforms, and a few wore plain clothes. Sullivan's was packed. One of the guys held out a chair for Frankie.

"I'm Max," one of them said to her.

"Hi, Max. Nice to meet you."

"Same here, beautiful," another said, and Cassidy chuckled.

As everyone continued to talk and order food and drinks, Frankie noticed the way Max took position next to her and would whisper things to her to get close. She felt uncomfortable. He was flirting, and she didn't want to be rude. Cassidy looked so happy.

She felt Max's arm against her arm as the waitress delivered their drinks.

"You sure you don't want something to eat?" Max asked her.

"Yes, thank you. I'm fine. Actually, I ate a big breakfast this morning. I think I'll take this iced tea to go." Frankie stood up and so did Max and two other guys.

"Frankie, don't go," Cassidy begged her, and Frankie sat back down.

"Okay, okay. So tell me how you guys met," Frankie said, causing Cassidy to smile.

Reggie pulled Cassidy closer, and Peter took her hand and brought it to his lips.

* * * *

"I can't wait to sink my teeth into Sullivan's pub burger. Damn, I've been thinking about it since last night," Marcus Towers told Mike as they headed toward Sullivan's.

"I've been listening to him going on and on about eating that damn burger. I should sneak the waitress a twenty to bring one well done out to you," Marcus's brother John teased, and Mike chuckled.

Mike peeked down at his cell phone again. Still no response from any of his brothers about Frankie. Nate had called Charlie and Lure to get in touch with Frankie but hadn't had any luck. He was hoping to get together with her this week. Hell, only two days away from the woman and he felt frantic to see her.

"Look who's here," Marcus said as he greeted the other guys who had a large table outside.

Mike looked up as he heard his name and started shaking hands and then his eyes landed on Frankie. She was sitting between Max, a firefighter, and Todd, a cop. She sat forward as though she was uncomfortable as both men kept a hand on the back of her chair. She wore some kind of cover-up that hugged her figure and was partially see-through.

"Mike, oh my God, what are you doing here? Are you having lunch?" Frankie asked as she stood up.

Todd and Max gave Mike the dirtiest looks, and of course, Mike gave his own nasty expression right back. It was funny how it didn't matter how long Mike had known Todd and Max or that they'd gone to the same high school. They were too close to his woman. He would make everyone see that Frankie was his. He'd never felt so jealous or possessive in his life.

"We thought we'd have heard from you today. Nate called Charlie," he told her, and she pulled her bottom lip between her teeth.

"I haven't called into Prestige today. They were doing some changes to the schedule, and I may be working this week for some special parties." She stepped around the table and the guys to come closer to him.

He could tell they wanted to move in on Frankie. He was pissed off.

Mike gently reached for her wrist and pulled her closer. He softly rubbed the skin on her shoulder with one finger as he wrapped his arm around her waist with his other hand.

"Getting some sun, baby?" he asked softly.

She smiled at him.

"I was trying to, but Cassidy wanted to join her friends for lunch. Do you know everyone?" she asked, slightly turning toward the table.

Everyone was just watching them.

"I do. These are my friends, Marcus and John Towers. Guys, meet Frankie."

Frankie reached out to shake the guys' hands as both men smiled and then looked at Mike as though he was a god. Frankie was a stunning woman. He shouldn't be so pissed off right now, but he was. He didn't want other men around her, flirting with her. He needed to do something.

He cupped her chin.

"Join us for lunch? Cassidy's in good hands with these guys."

She didn't even glance at Cassidy. Instead, she locked gazes with Mike and nodded. He was relieved. He felt as though she wanted to be with him as much as he wanted to be with her. Most importantly, she showed him that she wasn't interested in any of the other guys at the table.

He lowered his lips to hers and kissed her softly. When he released her lips, he let his hand slide down over her ass—facing the table of guys and specifically Max and Todd—and gave her a light tap.

"Come on, doll. Later, guys," he said.

Frankie pulled from him a moment. "I'll meet you after, Cassidy, and we'll head down to the beach?"

Cassidy smiled and nodded.

"Max, can you hand me my beach bag?" Frankie asked Max, and he stood up and brought it to her.

"See ya around, Frankie. Probably at Prestige," he said, but Frankie just took her bag and walked toward Mike, hugging his arm to her as Marcus and John held the door to the inside of the restaurant open for them.

* * * *

Lunch had been fun despite the awkward moments when Mike had arrived with his friends to see her squeezed between Max and Todd.

Finally, after lunch, John and Marcus said goodbye and shook her hand, and Mike suggested they take a walk while Cassidy and her new boyfriends finished up their lunches.

She didn't know what to say to Mike or even whether to bring up the scene he'd walked up on. She didn't want him to feel jealous, yet there was a part of her that felt special and cared for that appreciated his sincere reaction and jealousy. She would be lying if she said it didn't turn her on.

Mike took her hand, and they walked a little ways down the boardwalk until he stopped her by a small area and bench. He turned her around, gently pressed her against the railing, and placed one hand on her waist. He held her gaze, and then he let his eyes roam over her cleavage. His move caused her cover-up to lower, exposing her full breasts, covered by the small black bikini.

"You couldn't wear something that covers more of you?" he asked, teeth clenched as he breathed through his nose.

She felt her belly tighten, and for a moment, she was concerned. He must have seen her expression change to fear, and he lowered his head and pressed closer, hugging her to him.

"Nothing was going on, Mike," she whispered, hugging him back.

He pulled back slightly and cupped her cheek but kept his other hand at her waist. It felt so good to be held by Mike and touched this way.

"I didn't look that way when I showed up. They were too close to you and hitting on you."

"Your timing was perfect."

He softly ran his thumb along her lower lip. "I didn't like it."

She gulped. Her breasts felt fuller and her pussy actually tightened. His seriousness and firm statement aroused her.

"Just kiss me, Mike."

He lifted one of his eyebrows before he covered her mouth and kissed her deeply.

When he finally released her lips, his hold still firm, he stared down into her eyes, all serious once again.

"Come home with me."

Her eyes widened, and she tried putting some distance between them.

"I'll call my brothers. They can meet us there, and we can spend the rest of the afternoon and evening together." He kissed her forehead and then along her cheek to her ear.

"I want you, Frankie. I don't want to lose you to anyone else."

This was a huge decision, a big step, and she was so fearful of making another mistake.

"Mike, I'm not ready for that. I need slow," she told him.

He pulled back slightly. He looked disappointed as he glanced over her shoulder and out toward the water. His eyes were narrow and tight, his lips sealed, and she felt compelled to explain a little.

"Mike, there are things that happened to me, I mean that I went through that I need to still work out. Trust isn't easy for me, yet here I am, wanting you and your brothers, too."

He cupped her cheeks and stared down into her eyes.

"Who hurt you?"

She blinked and tried looking away, but Mike wouldn't have it. His fierce dark eyes, the tattoos on his arms, and the scruff on his face all aroused her and intimidated her at the same time. He was a firefighter, a person who was supposed to protect and preserve life, to rescue those in danger. But she had looked to a first responder before, to Kevin, in the hope of getting back those feelings of security, safety, and love she had when her family was alive. The risk of being used and getting hurt was so strong.

"Talk to me, baby. Make my brothers and me understand your fears. We can work them through. You don't think we're afraid of falling for you? You think we're not worried that you might find someone else or perhaps not care for each of us or maybe that you're interested in a ménage just to say you had one? There are lots of fears."

"I would never do that."

He raised one of his eyebrows. "We would never hurt you or use you."

He brushed his lips against hers. "Come back to our place. We'll watch a movie, hang out on the couch, and just get more comfortable with one another."

"Frankie."

She heard her name. Mike released her, and she spotted Cassidy with the guys.

"I'm going to head out. I'll talk to you later or see you tomorrow night at work."

"Okay. Bye." She waved at them and then looked at Mike.

"I guess my plans have changed," she whispered.

He smiled, pulled back, and took her hand. "Good, come on. On the way we'll discuss options for movies."

She chuckled as she tried to keep up with him.

"No girly, mushy stuff," he told her.

"No gore and bloody massacres," she replied.

"Some violence and action?"

"Of course."

"Great, we'll find something to agree on," he told her then kissed her again as they walked.

She loved the feel of his much larger hand holding her smaller one. She loved how tall and muscular he was and also how sexy and wild he appeared with the tattoos and the scruff on his face. She hugged his arm, and he smiled down at her as they reached his truck.

Was she making a huge mistake? She wasn't sure, but nothing would happen that she wasn't ready for. No matter how turned on Mike made her, she would maintain control and not give in so quickly. Taking it slow was the best thing she could do."

He started the truck and placed his hand on her thigh right under her cover-up and against her skin, and she felt about ready to faint.

Perhaps taking it slow and not giving in would be too difficult to do after all.

* * * *

Mike couldn't help but to stare at Frankie as she held on to the railing off the back porch and looked out toward the bay. It was so quiet out here, and he and his brothers loved that about the place. It had needed a lot of work, but they were all handy, especially Nate and Rye.

She turned toward him, leaning against the railing, looking at him watching her. She smiled, and his heart pounded, and his cock hardened for the dozenth time since he'd seen her today at Sullivan's.

"This is such a beautiful spot. It's quiet and so peaceful here. How long have you guys lived here?" she asked.

"Turbo and I have been here the longest, about ten years."

"Nate and Rye didn't always live with you guys?"

"They were off doing their thing. Nate worked for the government after being a soldier in the Army. Rye had some ups and downs for a while until he figured out what he enjoyed doing."

"Construction, you mean?" she asked, walking closer.

She lifted the glass to her lips and took a sip of tea. He still couldn't get over her body. He could see partially through the cover-up, and there was something on her hip, closer toward the front. Was that a tattoo?

"What? Is there something on me?" she asked and looked down at her cover-up, pressing her palms over the material.

He sat forward on the chair and shook his head. "Sorry, I thought I saw something, but I think it's on your skin."

"Oh, my tattoo." She smiled as she clasped her hands in front of her.

He licked his lower lip, and she held his gaze.

"Can I see it?"

She looked around them and then took a step back. He slowly stood up.

"I thought you said something about a movie?" she asked, trying to change the subject.

Mike gently took a fistful of the material and pulled her closer again.

"Come on, baby. I want to see it. I'll show you mine." He released his hold, reached for the hem of his T-shirt, and pulled it up and over his head. He placed it down on the table and caught her staring at his body.

She swallowed hard. "Very nice." Then she tried turning away. He placed his hands on her hips.

"Am I making you nervous?"

"Yes."

"Why?"

"Because I asked you to go slow."

He reached around her waist, pulling her closer as he used his other hand to cup her chin and cheek.

He whispered close to her lips, "I can do slow. As slow as you want."

* * * *

She felt his arm go around her waist, and then his palm caressed down her lower back over her ass. He squeezed and kneaded her flesh as he kissed her deeper. She was lost in all the sensations running through her body. She kissed him back and ran her hands over his tight, hard pectoral muscles then up over his shoulders. His hands moved under her cover-up and against her skin. She felt wild, as though she could lose control when he explored her body further, and his hand cupped her breast.

She loved how his skin felt against hers, the way his hard muscles pressed against her soft skin. But this was going too fast, and things were getting crazy. He pulled from her lips.

"Baby you feel so good."

"We have to stop, Mike. We have to," she whispered against his neck.

He held her tight and squeezed her against him. "But I don't want to," he whispered against her lips.

She heard the floor creak, and she looked over his shoulder to find Turbo standing there in uniform. He licked his lips, and she gripped

Mike's shoulders. Mike continued to kiss her neck and her shoulder as Turbo stepped onto the porch. He licked his lower lip then ran his hand along her ass and the bathing suit that barely covered it. Then his hand trailed up her back under the cover-up until he cupped her head, leaned closer, and kissed her.

Turbo tasted so good. She found herself kissing him back while both men used their hands to explore her flesh. Mike unclipped her bikini top and cupped her breast, making her moan into Turbo's mouth. Turbo squeezed her ass and pressed against her side as he explored her mouth. She was stuck between the two men, and it aroused her to the point where she felt herself letting go and trusting them.

Then came the echo when Turbo's police radio and the sound of the dispatcher's voice interrupted the moment. He pulled back and cursed the damn thing, pressing something on the side of it. She took that moment to pull away and push her cover-up back into place. She crossed her arms in front of her chest, feeling uncomfortable with her top undone and her large breasts and hard nipples pressing against the top.

Mike reached for her, and she stepped back.

"No. That was too fast and too crazy. We need to stop," she said and then turned away from them, reached under her cover-up, and re-clipped her top.

She adjusted her breasts, and when she turned around, Turbo was leaning against the doorway, arms crossed, and eyes glued to her body. Mike had his hands on his hips and looked wild and hungry.

"You were enjoying yourself," Mike told her.

"A little too much."

"Never too much when the connection is like that. I told you my brothers and I want you. You want us, too."

She looked away and felt the anxiety again. The fear of giving in and getting hurt.

"I need more time." She reached for her bag, and Mike stopped her.

"Don't go. Don't run from this."

"Mike, I'm not ready to take the risk. I'm sorry, but I need time."

She heard Turbo move, and now he was closer, placing his hand on her shoulder and looking down at her. They were both so big and tall. It was hard to resist their appeal and to not feel intimidated because they were older and more experienced than her.

"This guy, whomever he was, did a number on you. Maybe if you talk to us about him, make us understand your fears, we can deal with this together."

She pulled her bottom lip between her teeth.

"That would make me even more vulnerable," she told them as she adjusted the bag on her shoulder.

Turbo stepped closer and placed his hands on her hips. He was in full uniform, gun and all, and represented exactly what she feared. Another cop, another good guy with potentially bad intentions, and someone who could hurt her.

She closed her eyes to avoid his appeal and to try and not compare him to Kevin.

"I can't."

"You can," Mike pushed.

She opened her eyes. "No, I can't tell you about him and about my fears."

Turbo squeezed her hips and gave a little shake. "Why not? We wouldn't take advantage of you or make you feel vulnerable. We wouldn't use anything you tell us to hurt you. Can't you see that we care? Can't you feel the deep connection? We want more of you, all of you. Why can't you tell us about him? What is it that makes you fearful to talk to us about the man who hurt you and put this fear in you?"

She stared up into Turbo's dark-blue eyes.

"Because he was a cop and a first responder, just like the two of you."

* * * *

Turbo felt his chest tighten he was shocked He didn't know what he expected her to say, but it wasn't that her ex, a guy that made her fearful of him and his brothers was in law enforcement. It pissed him off and made him jealous.

"Who was he?" he asked.

She shook her head and tried stepping away.

"We need to talk about him and get everything out in the open," Mike told her.

"I'm sorry, but I'm not going to tell you about him. I'm not getting into it. Can't you just give me some time to get used to these feelings? To put what he did to me behind me so I can move on?"

"He hurt you badly. That's obvious, and we want to know what he did," Mike told her.

Turbo stared down into her eyes feeling overwhelmed with emotions. He was angry, jealous, and mostly concerned for Frankie.

"You don't want to talk about him right now, fine. I understand you have fears. We will have to discuss this and get these fears out in the open."

"I understand that, and I'm working it out. I am. Believe me, I never expected to feel like this. I never even considered this type of relationship, and here I am making out with two guys and imagining making out with Rye and Nate, too. It's scary, okay?"

He cupped her cheek and stroked her skin gently.

"We can understand that and respect your feelings. We want you. Do you want us?"

"Turbo."

He gripped her chin and held her gaze.

"Do you want the four of us, my brothers and me?"

She didn't respond immediately, and he feared she would say no and push them away.

"Yes."

His heart beat faster, and his breath caught in his chest.

"Then we can go slow. Just one thing I want to know."

She looked at him and waited.

"This guy, this cop that hurt you, any chance he wants you back or will come looking for you?"

He saw the flash of fear in her eyes, and she pulled away.

"Frankie?" Mike pushed.

She covered her mouth and seemed as though she was trying to stop herself from speaking. Mike placed a hand on her shoulder.

"Frankie, is it over between you and this guy? Is there a chance he might show up looking to get you back?"

She was quiet, and he squinted at her and knew he was being intimidating, but he had to know.

"I don't know," she said and then quickly added, "I hope not. He's the reason I don't stay in one place. If he were to find me, I'd have to disappear again, and that's why I'm afraid to get involved with you guys. I don't want you to get hurt. I don't want to hurt you, but I just don't know if he's coming or not."

"What do you mean the reason why you don't stay in one place?"

Frankie jumped at the sound of Nate's voice.

Turbo held firm. "Explain it," he pushed.

"Stop doing this to me. Just leave it alone." She pulled from his hold and headed around him toward the door, but Nate was there, along with Rye.

Nate took control of the situation. "You're not going anywhere. We heard what you guys were talking about. If you're in some kind of trouble, you tell us now. I won't let you hurt my brothers."

"Turbo." Mike stepped forward.

"I think I should go," she said.

"Maybe it's better if you do," Nate stated then stepped out of the way.

"No, we should talk about this," Mike said.

She looked at them, eyes filled with tears, and ran into the house.

"What is wrong with you? She could be in some kind of trouble. This guy could be looking for her, and he hurt her. How could you push her away like that?" Mike yelled at Nate.

"Because you guys come first. I won't let her break your hearts and use you."

"Use us? Frankie? God, Nate, when did you become so heartless? What the fuck are you afraid of?" Turbo asked him.

"Afraid? I'm not afraid of anything. I just don't want you guys getting caught up in her beauty, her body, and some lame excuse of a broken heart by some dip-shit cop. How do you know any of it is real? We don't even know where she came from. She could be lying. Look at where she lives."

"And what if you're wrong and she is in trouble and this guy hurt her? What if she's in that crappy apartment because she's trying to hide and it would be the last type of place some guy from her past might look? Huh?" Mike asked.

"He's right, Nate. You're assuming the worse. You think she's lying like other women do. We get the whole non-trust issues you have. But Jesus, brother, you could be causing us to lose the best thing that's ever happened to us," Rye told Nate.

"She's brought us closer than we've been in years," Mike whispered.

"Closer? What are you talking about? We've fucked women together. How much fucking closer do you want to get?"

Mike charged at Nate and shoved him against the wall.

"You bastard. Don't you ever compare Frankie to the meaningless sexual partners you've had. Even through those kept your distance. You never gave even an inch of your heart or concern. You fucked them, got off, and walked out. And there weren't even a handful, never mind a few, so drop the tough-guy shit." Mike gave him another shove then stepped back as Rye pulled him.

"He's right, Nate. You've never shown real interest in any woman, and I think you are totally interested in Frankie and were just looking for an excuse to push her away," Turbo told him.

"This is bullshit," he replied and began to walk inside.

"No, pushing away a woman like Frankie and making hurtful accusations is bullshit. Either you're in this with us or you're not. But I won't allow you to hurt her or make her feel like shit. Like you just did," Mike said and stormed past him into the house.

"Fuck!" Nate roared and punched the siding.

"We need to talk to Frankie," Rye said.

"She isn't going to speak to us or give us anything right now. I'll call Lure and see if I can get her last name. Then I'll see what I can find out back at the Station. In the meantime, try not to kill one another and please think of a way to make this right," Turbo told Nate and then walked away.

Chapter 8

Turbo Hawkins stared at a picture of Frankie in business attire. The Franklin and Hursch Advertising Firm in Chicago displayed a series of group pictures on their website and then another link to top-awarded employees. There she was, Francesca Sonoma, twenty-two years old and the youngest to receive such awards. He took a deep breath and released it. She was a successful businesswoman fresh out of college and appeared, from the descriptions and awards, to be headed to the top of the firm.

What had gone wrong? Why did she give that up? What should he do next? Call the company and ask questions? He felt guilty, as if he were invading her privacy, but Nate was so fearful. Turbo just wanted to provide Nate with some concrete information and reasons to believe that Frankie was being honest with them.

Francesca. God, even her name is sexy and beautiful.

Turbo rubbed his hand along his jaw and looked around the office. Everyone was busy. No one was paying attention to him. He wrote down the phone number to the business and then left his desk and headed outside.

Ten minutes later, a bit of smoozing and after speaking with human resources, he found out that Francesca had left with no warning, no written resignation, and just disappeared. In fact, as he explained he was an investigator the person told him they had a series of paychecks for her that they couldn't forward because no one knew where she'd disappeared to. He debated about giving his own address and then knew that would be overstepping the boundaries, never mind he didn't want to push getting more information. The person he was speaking to was giving more info than they should have.

First, he needed to confront Frankie and find out all he could. Everything he was finding out indicated that she'd left Chicago in a hurry and that someone was after her. Was it the ex-boyfriend, the one standing in the way of her letting go and letting them in? Or worse? Was she involved in something bigger, illegal, and trying to run from the law?

That concern led him to calling Nate. Nate had friends across the United States. Nate would find out what kind of trouble Francesca was in, and then they could discuss their next move.

"I'll look into it. Send me what you have so far," Nate said, sounding very serious.

Turbo knew Nate felt upset about what had happened earlier with Frankie. But finding out this information made Turbo even more nervous. He ended the call, and the back door opened.

"Hey, Turbo, Buddy was looking for you. Something about a case you're working on," Deputy Ronnie Towers said as he held open the back door to the department.

"Okay, great. I was just making a quick call."

Turbo took a deep breath and tried to submerge the thoughts going through his head. Perhaps Buddy had some insight or could offer some guidance here. Nate might push too far, and they could all lose a chance at making this relationship work with Frankie. He hoped Nate was careful.

He headed down the hallway to find Buddy standing by his desk. He gave a nod. "You okay?"

Turbo nodded back. "What's up?"

"Well, digging around and having the night shift officers canvas the neighborhood and the block near Prestige paid off. We have two separate witnesses. One across from a small building adjacent to the back door of the police department in Bayline. The other is a block from a warehouse not too far from where Gloria's body was found.

Most importantly, the guy who bailed out Gloria from the police department gave a false name, but Jake had his buddy pulled up the surveillance tapes and then set the picture through the computer system."

"Who was it? You know?"

"Sal Baletti."

"Sal Baletti? Why does that name sound familiar?"

"Because he's a gangster, a thug. He and his entire family operate on old-fashioned mob rules. They're into smuggling anything and everything under the sun and selling it on the streets and black market. Over the years they expanded from New York and New Jersey with connections in Chicago."

"Chicago?" Turbo felt that instant pain in his gut. He had to remind himself that Frankie wasn't involved or even connected to Gloria's death.

"Yeah, but this team of investigators in a special crimes unit have been investigating Baletti and his associates for years. Did Bryce get you the file? Did you look it over?"

"He told me there wasn't anything in it. He said it was minor stuff, and the crime unit wasn't giving up too many details," Buddy told him.

Buddy squinted at Turbo then around the room to make sure no one could hear.

"He's not part of this investigation. I don't know how or why he got his hands on that file first. You look it over yourself and with a clear investigative view. See if anything pops out at you."

"You have other information?"

"I have a copy of the file right here." He showed Turbo the folder.

"And?"

"And I scanned through it quickly. What I did notice was the Baletti name that appeared. Sal Baletti was the one who bailed Gloria out of jail. We have no other eyewitnesses who saw Gloria with anyone else but him."

"So do we go question him?"

"Not yet. I don't want to tip them off that we're onto him or his family. We need to be careful. This isn't just some minor drug operation in Bayline and Treasure Town. This expands to other states, hell across the country. There were a few other names on that list from the investigative team, but they were blacked out. I want to know those names."

"So what are you going to do to find out?"

"If we can't gather enough concrete evidence to pull Sal Baletti in for questioning, then I'm going to have to make some calls. Get some favors. I don't want to have another dead body show up in Treasure Town, so we need to send a message."

"Agreed. Whatever you need me to do, I'll do."

"Good. Take a look at the file. Then let's find out what we can about Gloria's boyfriend, her friends or acquaintances, and, of course, the Baletti family. Then we'll take it from there."

Turbo nodded and took a seat at his desk to prepare to look over the file. His thoughts about Frankie and the trouble she may be in moved to the back of his mind. He'd talk to Nate about it tonight or maybe he'd wait for Frankie after work and confront her himself. His gut clenched, and concern filled his heart. He hoped it all worked out with Frankie. He cared about her already and really felt as though she would be perfect for all of them. He also thought they would be perfect for her, perhaps providing the support and the protection she needed to feel safe and to let her guard down.

* * * *

Sal Baletti was sitting at the card table in the back room of one of his nightclubs. His brother was on the phone with someone, and he didn't look pleased.

Sal spoke to Chino, one of his main security guys.

"You finished getting your ass beat in poker?"

"Not yet. I feel a good hand coming, Sal," Chino said, and Sal exhaled a puff of smoke from his cigar then reached for his glass of bourbon, chuckling.

Ralphy dealt the hand but didn't play. He never was one for gambling. He was a serious guy with psychological problems, specifically violent tendencies, and was an asset to their security and association.

"We have ourselves a potential situation," Gino stated as he ended his call and looked at Sal.

Sal placed his cards down. "What might that be?"

"You were identified as the individual who bailed Gloria out of jail. You were the last one seen with her."

"So what? If they question me, I say I was banging her. I fucked her, dropped her off at her place, and came here for a drink with Ralphy and Chino. They'll vouch for me. We'll get the bartender to vouch for me being here, too. No sweat."

"You may not think so, but you guys fucking dumped the body in the wrong spot. Gloria showed up in Treasure Town. Dead bodies don't show up there. They've got a bad-ass police force, retired government agents, and shit, this is a fuck-up."

"Calm down. It's not a big deal. They won't get shit off her body. It was a clean kill."

"That's not the point. Damn, I fucking wish Gloria hadn't lost it on that other waitress at Prestige. She never would have been charged with assault, never would have been busted selling the drugs and screwing around with Lux."

"Yeah, well, she did. We should put the pressure on Lux, too. Maybe have Ralphy and Chino pay him a visit," Sal suggested.

"No. The cops will be following Lux. Hell, they may have a tail on you, Sal. You need to be careful and lay low a while."

"Not a problem. I think you're worried for no reason. In fact, we have that party for Santino at Prestige this weekend. What better way to act nonchalant than to go there like a normal, local citizen of the community."

"You just want to check out the broad Gloria smacked around," Chino teased.

Sal chuckled. "She did cause some of these problems we're having. I'd love to see what Gloria was so jealous about."

"Just watch your ass. We don't need further attention drawn to us. Plus, you should be working on securing these potential new contracts I've been pushing. Two bar owners are giving our collectors a bit of a hassle."

"Like who?"

"Those guys on the edge of Bayline and Treasure Town. Those two nightclubs the college kids all hang out at and are packed in the summer months. Riley's and the Beach House. Both great establishments that more than make up for the loss of money and product we had from Prestige," Gino told Sal.

"We can handle that, right, Ralphy?" Sal said and then lifted the cards back up to continue to play the hand.

"Sure, boss, we can do that. Tonight," Ralphy said, and Sal smiled as he looked at his brother.

"No worries. We got this. Now can we continue this round before we head out to Riley's and the Beach House? I'm going to need a couple of more drinks before I have to deal with all the noise in those places," Sal said, and Chino laughed.

"But maybe picking up some horny college girls could end the night well?" Chino suggested, and Sal smiled and so did Gino.

"If you're successful, I don't give a shit who you fuck," Gino replied and then walked over to pour himself a drink.

"You say that now, but maybe I'll bring back a few sexy women for you, too, and we can really party tonight."

Chino and Ralphy appeared pleased, and Gino shook his head as he pointed at Sal. "Secure those deals with those places, and remember, business first."

* * * *

Frankie was miserable. She'd thought for sure the longing, the feeling of loss, would disappear because she'd conditioned herself to be hard and untrusting. But she wasn't feeling strong or even good about herself. She regretted not explaining Kevin to the Hawkins brothers. But then she'd gotten angry, especially at Nate, who couldn't seem to care less whether the relationship went anywhere but perhaps to his bed. She wouldn't sleep with four men to experience a ménage and to feel safe, protected, and human again.

She had to be careful though. Kevin was resourceful and so was Carlotto. There was no way Kevin was giving her up without a fight, and it wasn't right or fair to place the Hawkins brothers in the middle. It might be smarter to give her notice here at Prestige and then disappear again.

"Frankie?" She heard his voice and turned around quickly.

"Nate?"

Her breath caught in her throat. She looked him over, and it backfired on her quickly. Shyly, she looked away to gain some composure and not give away the instant effect of his sudden appearance.

"What are you doing here?" she asked.

He stared down at her as she felt a lump form in her throat. Was he going to give her shit again and accuse her of playing games?

"I came to see you," he said and then looked around.

Frankie followed his line of sight and saw Charlie standing next to the bar. He gave her a nod, and Nate waved toward the door to the back offices.

"Charlie said you were wrapping things up for the night. That you just needed to go over your money and the numbers. He told me you do that in the back room sometimes. I'll go with you so we can talk."

He sounded so official and non-emotional. He was like ice, and as she thought that, she shivered with worry. But she needed to be strong. She needed to protect them as much as she needed to protect herself.

Nate opened the door for her, and they walked into the office. She sat down at the small round table in the corner and got out her money and her note pad. Nate watched her.

"Slow night?" he asked.

"One party and a couple of small groups. Pretty quiet," she said as she counted out her cash.

When she finished, she stood up.

"I wanted to talk to you about the other day at the house."

"I think you made it clear how you really feel about me, Nate. You don't trust me. You think I'm a liar. I got that loud and clear."

She went to walk around him, and he grabbed her around her waist and pressed her up against the table.

"No, I don't think you understood."

She released an uneasy breath. Despite his words from the other day and the wall she was trying to keep up, Frankie found herself feeling attracted to Nate. She was aroused by his size, his leadership and control. She was in trouble here and not sure what to do.

"I didn't mean to hurt your feelings or push you away from my brothers. I'm their protector and have always taken on a leadership role with them."

She felt his fingers caress her hips against the tight T-shirt she wore. His eyes roamed over her breasts.

"I hate this shirt, yet I like it."

"How is that?" she replied.

"I like how you fill it out and how sexy you are. But I hate other men looking at this body, wanting you when you belong to us."

She shook her head as she gripped the table behind her.

"But I don't belong to any of you."

He gripped her waist tighter.

"We can change that tonight."

She looked away from him.

"You don't trust me. I get that. I haven't given you enough concrete information on me for you to trust me fully. But the problem is complicated. There's a lot at risk, and I don't think I'm in the position or right frame of mind to give in to the attraction."

"Why not? Why not see where this goes, and when you feel you can trust us with the truth, then you talk to us?"

"But that isn't right either. Nate, you have to understand the fears I have."

"Talk to me. To us and make us understand."

"I can't yet."

"You can," he pushed.

She moved forward, and he kissed her. He cupped her head with one hand and kept his other hand against her waist. He devoured her moans, cupped her breast, and explored her mouth deeply. She ran her hands along the large muscles on his arms and felt the strength and power he had over her already. She would be no match for his strength, and suddenly she feared the repercussions of his anger. What if he turned on her or was displeased with her in some way? Was Nate capable of violence or abuse?

She pulled from his mouth and gasped.

"Nate."

He pressed his forehead to hers, breathing just as rapidly as she was.

"Come home with me tonight. Forget about everything. Forget about what that dick did to you and let go with us."

"Oh God I—"

The door opened, and she immediately stepped away from Nate, and Nate stepped back. Lure was there.

"Cassidy is on line four. She said it's important."

Frankie walked over to the desk and picked up the phone, her head still fuzzy after Nate's kiss as she pushed strands of hair behind her hair.

Frankie heard the worry in Cassidy's voice.

"Keith found out about Peter and his brothers. He's pissed, and he wants me back and wants to talk. I told him no and that I want nothing to do with him. I told him to move on. I think he was drunk, Frankie."

"Maybe you should call Peter or one of his brothers?"

"No. I don't want them to know about Keith. I can't tell them about him and about the abuse. They'll think I'm weak. They'll think the worse."

"No, they won't. They'll understand," Frankie said and looked at Nate, who was standing right there along with Lure. Her own words sank into her head. She was doing the same thing to Nate and the guys. She was keeping secrets and pushing them away.

"What can I do to help then?"

"Can you come stay here with me? Please, just for tonight?"

"Sure. I was just wrapping things up. I'll grab the bus and be there in fifteen minutes."

"Thank you so much, Frankie. I owe you."

Frankie disconnected the call.

"Is Cassidy okay?" Lure asked.

"Yes. I'm meeting her at her place." Frankie reached for her bag.

"She sounded upset. Is that ex of hers giving her a hard time?" Lure asked.

"Just shaking her up a little with his push to get back together with her. But she's involved with someone else."

"She's involved with five other men. She should tell them about Keith," Lure told her.

"It's new, and how do you know about them anyway? They only recently started dating," Frankie said.

"We make it our business to know all about our staff, especially the ones we like." He winked.

She pulled her bottom lip between her teeth and both men squinted at her.

"Well, I need to head over there, and the bus comes in ten minutes."

"I'll drive you."

"You don't have to, Nate. I can take the bus."

He reached for her hand.

"I'm driving you. There's no need to take the bus, and I'll get you there faster."

He had a point, and Cassidy had sounded freaked out.

"Fine. Goodnight, Lure. I'll see you Friday night."

Lure gave her a kiss on her cheek.

"Call me if you or Cassidy need anything. Got it?"

"Yes, sir."

"Ooh, I kind of like that. Watch this one, Nate."

Nate's expression was hard and unemotional as they exited the office.

* * * *

"So what's with this ex-boyfriend of Cassidy's? Has he been harassing her?"

"He's a jerk, and it took a lot for her to drop him. He was bad for her," Frankie told Nate.

Nate's chest tightened, and he felt his concern and anger grow.

"Abusive?"

Frankie didn't answer.

"I won't repeat it. You can trust me."

Her silence made him understand her a little better. She was a good friend and one who kept promises. He didn't like thinking that Cassidy had been smacked around and mistreated. It pissed him off.

"Would this guy try to come to her place and push her to get back together?"

"Not sure, but that's why I said I would come over. I don't want her to be alone, just like she doesn't want to be alone. I know he scares her."

"She should get an order of protection."

"She has one. Besides, he hasn't done anything since they broke up."

"I should walk you in," he said as he pulled up in front of Cassidy's small house. It was one of many little cottage-like homes rented out all year round. There were usually two to three apartments in them, depending on the size of the home.

She opened her door, and he debated about walking up with her.

"You sure you don't want me to come up?"

"No. I'll talk to you tomorrow."

"I can pick you up here. I can come back around noon time?"

"Nate."

"Frankie, we need to talk and work this out."

She was silent a moment, and he truly felt she was legitimately concerned.

"Okay. Tomorrow at noon."

He gave a nod, and she closed the door and headed up to the front door. She opened it and headed inside.

He wasn't sure what made him look back at the house, but just as he made it to the corner and was about to turn, he saw some guy dressed in a hoodie approach the front door. His heart pounded in his chest as the man eased the door opened and walked inside.

* * * *

Just as Frankie put her purse down on the counter and pulled Cassidy into a hug, the front door opened. Keith stood there.

"What the hell are you doing here?" Cassidy yelled.

Frankie looked at her purse. She couldn't reach it, and her gun was in there. Cassidy held on to her.

"I came to talk. To work things out. What the fuck is she doing here?" he asked. His eyes were bloodshot, and he slurred his words.

"I told you that I have nothing to say to you. Please leave," Cassidy told him.

He stomped forward. "You're going to listen to what I have to say. Sit down, bitch." He shoved at Frankie, pushing her to the couch, and then he grabbed Cassidy.

Frankie was shocked when he struck Cassidy across the cheek. Cassidy screamed, and Frankie ran toward him to stop him, but he grabbed her by the shoulders and threw her into the wall and mirror. The mirror shattered, and she felt her shoulder stinging with pain.

Cassidy cried out. "Stop it. Don't do this."

But Keith went to attack her.

Frankie was shocked as the front door burst open, and there was Nate. He grabbed Keith by his hoodie and pulled him off of Cassidy then punched him twice in the face. Keith fell to the floor, out cold as Nate pulled out his cell phone.

"Are you two okay?" he asked, and Frankie nodded as she crawled to Cassidy and pulled her into her arms. Cassidy's cheek and eye were swollen and her lip bloody.

"It's going to be okay."

Cassidy cried out, "I can't believe he did this. I can't believe this."

Frankie felt the stinging in her shoulder and knew she had been injured, too, but all she could do was look at Nate. He hadn't just left as she'd told him to. He'd stayed and must have seen Keith come through the front door. The sound of sirens could be heard in the distance, and she locked gazes with Nate as he kept watch over Keith.

"Thank you, Nate."

She heard the squeal of tires, and then police officers came through the open doorway. There were Peter and his partner, Todd, both in uniform. He ran to Cassidy and Frankie.

Nate explained what had happened as Peter looked over Cassidy.

"Jesus, baby, what the hell was this all about?"

She continued to cry, and he held her until the paramedics arrived. Todd reached for Frankie.

"Shit, Frankie, you're all cut up and have glass or something in your skin.

"Why don't you cuff this scumbag, and I'll take care of my woman," Nate said to Todd, and Todd immediately stood up and pulled out his handcuffs.

Nate helped Frankie stand up. He brushed his thumb along her lower lip and held her gaze without saying a word. She felt the tears fill her eyes. Nate had saved them both. Nate really did care about her.

He went to look at her wound, but she pressed her face against his chest and held him with her one good arm. She was afraid to lift the other one. She knew she'd hit that wall hard.

"I've got you, baby," he said, and she remained against his chest until the paramedics arrived along with Turbo and Jake. She could hear the sirens, the echo of police radios going off as her shoulder stung. It was total chaos.

* * * *

"Holy shit. Thank God you went to see Frankie at Prestige and looked into that rearview mirror," Turbo told his brother as they stood in the waiting room for Frankie to be released.

They had to pull shards of glass out of her skin and do X-rays to make sure that her shoulder and arm didn't have any broken bones.

"I know. My heart was pounding with fear when I saw that dick push open the front door as if he owned the place. When I heard the scream and things banging around, I just went flying in there."

"Yeah, and did a number on that dick. Don't be surprised if he tries to charge you with assault."

"Good fucking luck with that."

"I can't believe they haven't let her out yet. How long?" Mike asked as he paced the waiting room.

"Any minute now. Unless she sustained any broken bones," Rye said.

"Fuck," Turbo said, and just then Frankie emerged with Catalina, a nurse who worked at the hospital and who was a friend of their friends.

"Here she is. A bit medicated for the pain and badly bruised up but no broken bones, right, Frankie?" Catalina said as Mike reached for her.

He cupped her cheek and placed his hand on her waist. "We're going to take care of you."

"My purse, I left it at Cassidy's," Frankie said, sounding worried about it.

"I have it in the truck. Don't worry about a thing," Nate told her, and Turbo watched as Nate approached.

Frankie snuggled into the crook of his arm. He caressed her waist and thanked Catalina.

"You're in good hands, honey. Take care of her." Catalina handed the paperwork and things to Rye, and they all headed out of the hospital.

Turbo was upset, seeing Frankie hurt and emotional. He wanted to hold her in his arms and tell her she never had to be alone again. He anticipated getting her home to their place and taking care of her. But then she stopped by Nate's truck.

"Nate, thank you for being there for Cassidy and me. If you hadn't come there…"

"Shh, you don't have to keep thanking me. I'm glad I was there, that we talked at Prestige. I know we have a lot to work out, but we'll take it slow."

She shook her head and stepped back.

"I should go back to my place. I shouldn't go with you. It will just make it harder."

"What do you mean?" Turbo asked.

Nate took her hand.

"Make what harder?"

Turbo watched her eyes fill up with tears, and she choked on what sounded like a sob and then covered her mouth. She winced at the pain.

"Easy, baby, just calm down. There's no need to go to your place and be alone. We promise to take care of you. We'll go slow," Mike told her.

"'I can't do this. I can't go with you and try not to... not to need you."

"What's wrong with needing us?" Rye asked her.

"I can't, Rye. I can go through what Cassidy did. I can't stand the thought of something like that happening to me."

"Happening to you? You think we would break into your apartment, and assault you?" Nate asked, raising his voice.

Turbo shook his head and grabbed hold of Frankie's hands.

"No, Nate, she means the guy who hurt her back in Chicago. The guy she had to leave her perfect job for and disappear out of fear," Turbo said.

His brothers all asked "what?" at the same time, and Frankie stared up at Nate in shock.

"You know? How do you know? Pease don't tell me you called there. Please don't say he's coming for me."

Turbo shook his head.

"I talked to someone in human resources at the agency where you worked. They said you disappeared. They have a couple of paychecks for you. They have no idea where you are and I didn't divulge any information."

"I did some investigating myself. We'll talk about it later. All that matters right now is your safety and recovering from tonight's events," Nate told her.

"We'll make time to discuss it. I was up to my neck in the investigation I'm involved in. Let's get her to our place and help her to rest." Turbo wrapped his arm around Frankie's side and helped her to get into the truck.

He closed the door, and Nate, Rye, and Mike were there, appearing angry and concerned by the grim expressions on their faces.

"What the fuck? You don't call me or let me in on the fact that you're investigating Frankie?" Mike asked in anger, pointing at Turbo with Rye right behind him.

"I was at my wit's end and thought what could it hurt to find out where she came from. I wasn't expecting to see her name and picture on an advertising firm's website and to learn she was making her way up in that firm, dressed all professional and sophisticated, fresh out of college, and then disappeared. It didn't make sense, so I dug a little more and found out about her leaving her job without notice. She left her apartment without paying off the lease, and she withdrew all her savings, closed her accounts, and closed all her credit cards. Everything indicated she was running from something or someone and feared for her life. That's all I got."

"So you put two and two together, and this ex-boyfriend, a cop, had something to do with it?" Rye said.

"It's what I'm thinking, but I didn't want to search more and red-flag her in case this guy is looking for her. We'll talk about it later. Maybe now she'll open up and tell us all about it," Turbo said and then walked away toward his patrol car.

Rye and Mike got into the truck with Nate and Frankie.

* * * *

Frankie winced as she tried to remove the top they'd given her at the hospital. Her Prestige T-shirt had to be cut off of her as the doctors in the emergency room tended to her injuries.

She moaned softly, trying not to alert the guys that she was trying to look at the damage. Nate had made his way into the emergency room despite the nurses' efforts to keep him outside. But when they asked if he was her boyfriend, she'd shaken her head despite wanting to say yes. They had him leave the room before they cut off her T-shirt.

The nurse Catalina had been very kind and given her a sheet to cover her bra and chest. She was there to assist with the X-rays and to get on and off the machines. Nate and the others waited patiently for her.

It made her think a lot of crazy thoughts. They acted as if they cared, and she felt they were sincere, but there was still a fear that they could turn out to be like Kevin and could hurt her. But when she thought those things, she winced, feeling guilty and wrong. Nate had saved her and Cassidy from God knows what. He had waited and seen Keith enter the house. If he'd just left without hesitation things could have been very different tonight.

But she had to remember what Turbo had done. He'd looked her up. He'd investigated her to try and find out about Kevin. What if Shemar was still working at Franklin and Hursch? What if she'd caught wind of someone asking about her? Shemar could call Kevin or Carlotto. She thought of Shemar instantly because Shemar was the one person Kevin used to watch Frankie at work. It had taken months to figure out who Kevin knew at the company, but then Shemar had delivered some roses from Kevin and told her Kevin wanted Frankie to meet him for lunch. She wouldn't put it past Shemar to call Kevin and inform him that a detective called looking for Frankie. That could make matters worse and send Kevin this way. Her stomach clenched, the paranoia taking its toll on Frankie, exhausting her.

She winced and removed the top then turned sideways. She gasped at the sight. Her entire shoulder and upper arm were bruised badly, and there were slit marks and scratches all over the place.

Keith was a monster. He'd beaten Cassidy up, striking her repeatedly. It was all too familiar to Frankie. It reminded her of Kevin and his abusive ways and his demand for control, respect, and order. He was at that breaking point. He would have crossed the line, too, and struck Frankie, beat her like that. He'd promised that she would always be his no matter what and that he would kill anyone who tried to take what belonged to him. The way things had ended he would come after her with a vengeance. But Keith wasn't Kevin. Kevin had killed before. Kevin had been part of numerous mobster-like murders along with Carlotto, and she knew about them. She'd overheard confessions, plans, and agendas. She was a liability and one handgun wasn't enough, especially in a sneak attack similar to Keith's.

She jumped when she heard the knock on the door.

"Frankie, are you okay?" Rye asked.

"Yes. Um, okay," she mumbled and reached for the shirt she'd dropped. She gasped, and the door creaked open.

"Are you sure?" Rye asked, and when she locked gazes with him, he appeared angry.

"Jesus, baby."

He walked into the bathroom, placed a hand on her good shoulder, and turned her so he could see the damage.

"Catalina said the ointment would work so your skin won't scar." He leaned forward and pressed his lips against her skin. She closed her eyes and gripped the counter.

When she felt Rye's hands grip her hips then gently move up the center of her back, she nearly moaned.

"Your skin is so smooth and tan." His lips, warm, firm, pressed against her skin again, moving higher up her spine, over her bra strap, and to her shoulder. He used one hand to move her hair to the side, and then he kissed the nape of her neck.

"Rye." She whispered his name.

"Yes, baby?"

She slowly turned around to face him. His eyes roamed over her breasts. She completely forgot she was only wearing a bra and her skirt. She was so lost in his touch and the feel of his lips against her skin.

He leaned forward and pressed his lips to her neck then her shoulder and lower.

She held his head with one hand and ran her fingers through the short hair he had spiked in the front. She felt him kiss and suckle her cleavage, and then his tongue rolled under the material and made contact with her nipple.

"Rye."

"Frankie."

She gripped his head tighter and felt his fingers unclasp her bra. His mouth suckled her breast, and she felt the bra fall. He pushed it out of the way. He cupped one breast and feasted on the other.

"Oh God, Rye. Rye." She moaned louder.

His other hand moved down her thigh then under her skirt. She widened her stance, giving him better access to her body and her needy cunt.

"Oh." She moaned as his fingers pressed under the material of her panties and straight to her cunt. In and out he stroked her pussy, reminding her how good it felt to be stroked down there. She thrust her hips against his fingers, and he pulled her nipple between teeth and tongue.

"Oh God, Rye. Rye, please."

He released her nipple.

"Come for me. Come for me now," he ordered her then nipped against her neck, sending her spiraling out of control.

She screamed out and shook as she came. He was relentless in his strokes and in his dirty talk.

"You've got my cock so damn hard right now, Frankie. I need inside this tight, wet pussy. Tell me you want that. Tell me," he demanded to know as he thrust fingers deeper into her pussy.

She gripped his shoulders, and he nipped her breasts.

"Yes. Please, Rye. I want you, too, but…"

"No buts. Just let go and trust us."

She was shocked to hear Turbo's voice. He stood there watching her, watching Rye thrust his fingers into her pussy as she remained in place with no bra on.

"Please." She gasped as Rye removed his fingers then kissed her lips. He gripped her hips and then effortlessly lifted her up into his arms.

"Wait. I'm not sure," she whispered, holding on to his shoulders, her eyes glued to his.

"We'll take you upstairs. Let you get showered and put on something comfortable. Then we'll talk. Take things as slow as you need," Turbo told her while he caressed her hair and glanced over her exposed breasts. She tried to press them closer to Rye, who chuckled.

"I don't think that's going to work, baby. Besides, this sexy body is going to belong to my brothers and me really soon."

Rye's words made her pussy leak some more. She acknowledged that she was indeed in trouble here. There would be no turning back, no running from this deep connection surely developing between her and these brothers.

She pressed against Rye and let him carry her from the room while Turbo took her bra and shirt with them and the others followed.

She was shaking by the time they got her upstairs.

Rye went to set her down, and she held on to him tightly. She was trying to calm her breathing.

"You're okay. None of us are going to hurt you, baby," Rye whispered, his lips pressed against her temple.

She pulled slightly back at the sound of a faucet being turned on and water hitting tile. Her mouth nearly dropped open at the sight of the extra large walk-in shower, as well as Mike completely naked.

She lowered her eyes as Rye set her down on her feet. Turbo was there. She felt his hands on her waist as she took a quick intake of breath. He pressed her skirt and her panties down. Rye licked his lips as his eyes roamed over her breasts while Turbo kissed her shoulder.

"Let Mike help you get washed up. We'll wait in the bedroom," Turbo said.

But before she could move toward the shower on shaky legs, Rye gripped her hip.

"What is this?" he asked, and her entire feeling of being aroused disappeared. Rye had seen her scar.

She could attempt to lie and tell the same story she'd told Cassidy, but these men already knew she was running from her ex. They wouldn't believe her lies, and she really couldn't lie to them anyway.

"An injury."

"What kind of injury?" Turbo asked, and now he knelt down on one knee and ran a thumb along the scar that went close to her groin.

"I really don't want to talk about it."

Rye cupped her cheek and jaw.

"Did he do it to you?" he asked, and she closed her eyes.

"He wasn't the one with the knife, but he was there."

She heard Turbo curse under his breath and then Rye leaned forward and kissed her. He devoured her moans until she was pliant in his arms and no longer thinking of her ex but, instead, of joining Mike in the shower.

* * * *

Mike took her hand as Rye led her under the spray of water. She looked scared, like an injured doe unsure of who was the enemy and who was there to help her. It made him feel sick to think such a sweet young woman was so distrusting and fearful. But he put that aside and just went with his emotions and the power of the attraction between them.

"God, baby, you are so gorgeous." He let his palms caress water down her long hair and then over her hips and up to her breasts. He cupped both extra-large mounds and watched her close her eyes, lean back against the tile, and part her lips. She was a sight, and his cock was as hard as ever.

Lowering to his knee, he licked across one perky pink nipple then to the other. His eyes caught sight of the scar Turbo and Rye had noticed, and he swallowed hard, trying to submerge his anger.

He kissed her belly as he fondled her breasts.

"You have an amazing body, Frankie. Fucking perfect."

He looked up to see her staring at him, holding his gaze but almost frozen in place.

"Touch me," he whispered.

She pulled her bottom lip between her teeth and didn't reach out. He had a feeling she wasn't only afraid and untrusting but also less experienced.

"You ever take a shower with a man before?" he asked then licked around her nipple in a circular motion before suckling a little of her breast into his mouth.

"No." She moaned, and his cock hardened a little more.

"Well, aren't I a lucky bastard?" He reached for her thigh and lifted it up and over his shoulder.

"Hold on, sweetness, you and I are going to do a lot of firsts in this shower." He pressed a finger to her cunt, and she thrust against it.

"That's it, Frankie. Just let go and feel. Know that I will never hurt you, only care for you."

"Oh, Mike. Don't lie to me. Please just say nothing unless you mean it," she said between pants.

He added a second digit and then stroked the cream from her pussy to her anus, applying pressure.

"Mike." She gasped.

"Oh, I mean it, baby. I mean every fucking word I say. I want you. You…this body is going to belong to my brothers and me. We're going to learn every inch of your body, and you're going to learn every inch of ours. Now touch me. You're fucking killing me here."

He thrust his fingers faster and lowered his mouth to her cunt. He nipped her pussy lips then swirled his tongue in the crevice. He continued to thrust his fingers then alternated with his tongue. Finally he felt her hands on his shoulders.

He moaned against her cunt.

"Mike. Oh God, that feels so good."

He licked and sucked harder, and the feel of her feminine hands against his head and cheeks aroused him more. He slid fingers out and used his tongue and teeth to send her higher. Then he pressed a lubricated finger to her anus and pushed through.

"Oh!"

She screamed her release, and he suckled and slurped her delicious cream. Her breasts bounced, and her hands gripped his head. He lowered her thigh and eased his way up her body, kissing her flesh, sucking her breast, then taking her mouth in an exotic, deep, sensual kiss.

He gently pressed her against the tile wall as he held her hips and kissed her slowly. She ran her hands along his waist up his ribs then around his back and hugged him. He released her lips and held her there.

"Is your shoulder okay?" he asked.

She mumbled a yes against his chest. Then he felt her tongue lick across his flesh. He reached up and cupped her cheeks as she nibbled on his skin. His cock hardened.

"That feels so good."

She continued to kiss his skin, exploring his tattoos with her lips and teeth until she tilted her head up to hold his gaze.

"You're beautiful," she whispered, and he chuckled.

"Never been called beautiful before." He stroked her lower lip with his thumb, smiling down at her.

She moved her head forward, tilting it into the spray of the water.

"Well, you are. Even your tattoos are."

He smiled then pressed completely against her, letting his hands stroke over her ass cheeks as he pressed his chest to hers.

"I love your body, too. You have gorgeous breasts, sexy thighs, and a tight, wet pussy." He kissed her on the mouth and then pulled back.

"Ready for us?"

"Probably not. I think I may pass out."

He chuckled low.

"Maybe only from the multiple orgasms we're going to give you."

She chuckled as he reached lower and turned off the faucet.

"Setting the standards high, aren't you, bro?" Turbo asked as he appeared by the shower naked. He threw a towel at Mike and then opened a nice big fluffy red one up for Frankie.

"I've got you," Turbo told Frankie as he wrapped her up in the towel and then lifted her up and carried her out to the bedroom.

Mike dried off quickly. He couldn't wait to make love to Frankie and make her their woman. The thought gave him chills and then a feeling of inadequacy. Would he, hell, would they, be good enough for such an amazing, sexy woman?

He took a deep breath as the words echoed in his head.

We're all about to find out.

* * * *

Turbo helped Frankie dry her body off. He took his time, caressing her large, plump breasts then her taut belly, and, of course, her bare pussy. She tightened up, obviously feeling embarrassed standing there naked. "You're gorgeous, Frankie. You have nothing to be embarrassed or shy about."

He leaned forward and kissed her belly then the tattoo and then the scarring on her hip. She held the towel against her and stepped back, turning so that Nate and Rye couldn't see her backside. She hit her rear against the side dresser next to the bed.

"Come sit down." He patted the bed as he knelt on the rug in front of it.

Her eyes darted to Rye and Nate then to Mike as he approached.

She pulled her lip between her teeth and sat down on the bed.

"Let's get a few things straight."

As Turbo said that, his brothers moved in closer. Mike knelt on the rug on her left side while Turbo remained on her right side. Behind her, Rye climbed onto the bed, and behind Turbo, Nate stood watching over them.

She glanced around at them and then to Nate.

"How is your shoulder and arm? Do you need anything for the pain?"

She shook her head. "It's fine. Just a little achy. The shower helped." Her cheeks turned a shade of red, and she attempted to cross her legs as she avoided Mike's smile. Her foot hit Mike in the knee, and she set it back down and gripped the towel.

Turbo placed his hand on her knee under the towel. He stroked her slowly.

"We were so worried about you when Nate called. A thousand concerns went through our heads."

"Really?" she asked, sounding surprised.

"Of course. The other night at Galileo's meant a lot to us. Some things were said back at our place that came out all wrong. We wanted to talk to you about them. Especially Nate," Turbo told her as he continued to stroke her thigh, moving his hand higher and higher.

She looked up toward Nate. She held his gaze.

"Thank God Nate was there," she said and swallowed.

"Yes, baby, thank God he was. But you need to know he was there and he waited because he cares for you just like the rest of us do."

"We sure do, sweetness. We don't want anything bad to happen to you," Rye said as he squeezed her uninjured shoulder then kissed it.

She closed her eyes and let her grip loosen on the towel.

Mike reached up and kissed her cheek and neck.

"You need looking after, darling. We worry about you." He nuzzled closer, and the towel fell from her chest.

Before she could panic and reach for the towel again, Mike cupped her cheeks and kissed her deeply.

Turbo continued to caress her thighs then stroked a finger over her pussy.

She pulled from Mike's mouth.

"Turbo." She said his name as she panted.

"I want to taste you, Frankie. I want to get your body nice and ready for us. Do you want that, too?"

Mike continued to suckle her neck as Rye kissed along her shoulder and neck on the other side.

"Yes."

Turbo smiled.

"Good girl. We're going to take care of you and make you feel as special and as important as you are to us. You got that?"

She took an uneasy breath and stared at him in shock.

He gave her thighs a little squeeze as he raised both eyebrows at her. "You got that?"

"Yes," she said quickly.

"She's real sweet, Turbo, but you remember you have to share," Mike said as Turbo eased his head between her legs, using his hands to spread her thighs wider.

Rye was there to lower her back gently to the comforter. She cringed slightly, and Turbo stopped.

"You okay?"

"Yes." She held his gaze.

He slowly licked along her groin, making her shiver and shake.

Mike leaned forward and licked her nipple as Nate sat on the bed and cupped her other breast.

"So damn gorgeous," Nate said, and she held his gaze until Turbo licked her pussy.

"Turbo." She moaned.

"Are you on the pill, baby?" Nate asked her between licking and sucking her breast.

"Yes," she hissed as Mike pulled hard on her nipple.

Turbo eased his tongue along her pussy then added two digits. He pressed upward, her pussy sopping wet and ready for cock.

"Damn, you like this, don't you, baby?"

"Yes.'"

"We want you to tell us everything you like and don't like, okay?" he asked as he stroked fingers in and out of her pussy. He leaned down and licked her pussy lips.

She turned, trying to pull her thighs closed, but Mike held one open while Nate held the other open.

"Oh God." She thrust her hips upward.

Turbo chuckled then thrust his fingers faster before pulling them out and swiping along her anus. As he licked her cunt, he maneuvered a finger into her ass.

"Nate. Oh God." She moaned.

Turbo added a finger to her cunt and stroked both holes at the same time.

"How about this? You like a finger in your ass, and one in your cunt?"

"I never... Oh God, it feels so naughty and tight."

Mike chuckled. He pulled on her nipple. "It is naughty and will feel even better when three cocks are inside you, filling this sexy body up."

"Three?" she asked as cream poured from her cunt, and it drove Turbo wild. She'd never had sex with more than one guy at a time before.

"One cock in your pussy," Turbo told her and thrust faster. "One cock in your tight, virgin ass." He thrust his finger faster.

"And one in this sweet, sexy mouth," Rye said, tilting her head sideways so he could plunge his tongue deeply in to kiss her.

She was moaning into Rye's mouth and thrusting upward at Turbo's strokes. He pulled his fingers from her cunt and ass.

"Are you ready, baby?" he asked her as she panted for breath.

"I think I'm losing my mind," she said, and they chuckled.

"Just follow your heart. It won't steer you wrong," Mike told her.

Turbo reached for her hips and pulled her up from the bed. He kissed her deeply, and she kissed him back, running her hands along his arm muscles.

"On your hands and knees. We need to get you ready," Turbo told her.

Mike lay down on the bed, and Turbo placed her on top of him.

"Nice and easy, babydoll. I'm all yours." Mike drew her lower for a kiss.

Rye passed over the tube of lube, and Turbo caressed along her ass cheeks.

"Take Mike's cock inside of you, doll. Make him yours," Nate told her.

She swung her head to look at him then back toward Mike. Her long, damp hair moved over her shoulder, and Turbo saw the line of tiny freckles along her nape.

He stopped what he was doing to lean forward and kiss each one. He reached under and cupped her breast.

"You have these tiny freckles along your neck. Very sexy."

Mike held his cock and aligned it with her pussy as she eased down his shaft.

"Oh. Oh. My. God," she said, sinking onto him completely.

"That's it. Damn, woman, you're tight. Damn," Mike said as he gripped her hips and slowly thrust upward.

"Wait. Wait." She panted. Turbo stopped. Mike paused, and Nate and Rye looked concerned.

"Baby?" Mike whispered as he reached up and cupped her cheek.

She grabbed his hand and held it to her cheek. "It's been so long. I thought I knew. I mean I… Oh God I don't know what I'm trying to say."

Nate reached over and held her chin. His expression was firm as usual.

"You're not ready?" he said, and Turbo's stomach twisted in knots.

"No, I am ready. I want this. I want all of you. I want to feel more of what you make me feel. It's just that… Oh God, I feel so much right now, so right, so much more safe right now with you guys here surrounding me like this than I've ever felt before. It's kind of overwhelming, okay?" she said, raising her tone a bit.

Nate leaned closer.

"You give us all of you. Don't hold back, you hear me? Don't hold back anything. We're not him. We're sticking around forever. You're going to be ours forever. This is a new beginning for all of us. You hear me, Francesca?" he said, and she nodded, reached for him, and kissed him.

Mike thrust upward, and Turbo pressed the lube to her ass.

The atmosphere went from taking it slow to moving fast. A feeling of desperation need and hunger filled Turbo instantly.

He eased his lubricated fingers into her ass. He stroked and maneuvered as she moaned into Nate's mouth, and Nate wouldn't release her. Mike thrust upward, and Rye cupped her breast on the other side. They were all there, all touching her, arousing her.

"I'm coming in, baby. We're all going to make love to you together."

Turbo eased his fingers out and moved the tip of his cock to her anus. She tightened up, and Nate held her, kissed her deeply as Turbo pressed deeper.

"Let him in, sweetness. You're made for us," Rye told her, and she seemed to relax and let Turbo in.

He pressed deeper until he was fully seated in her ass and moaned. "Heaven. You feel like heaven."

Nate released her lips, and Frankie moaned and gasped.

"Oh God, I feel so full. Oh please don't stop. Please." She begged for more.

Mike pulled her lower for a kiss as he thrust upward. Behind her, Turbo thrust into her ass, and then Nate tilted her chin toward him.

The sight of his brother Nate's cock moving closer to Frankie's lips aroused Turbo further. Her tongue darted out to lick the tip, and Nate gripped a handful of her hair.

"No teasing, doll, or you'll get a nice pink ass," he told her, and both Turbo and Mike moaned.

"Don't talk so fucking dirty. I'll come," Mike grunted through clenched teeth.

Nate chuckled then moaned as Frankie pulled his cock between her lips and sucked.

In and out they stroked into her. Mike in her pussy, Nate with his cock in her mouth, and Turbo stroking into her ass. Rye cheered her on and played with her breasts then ran his hands along her ass tapping it, stroking down the crack, and making her moan and shiver.

"Fuck, baby." Nate called out as he came. He panted and caressed her cheeks and hair.

Nate pulled out, and Turbo ground his teeth, thrust three more times, and then came. He hugged her back and kissed her shoulder being careful to not press against her wound as he panted for breath.

Mike thrust up and down, and Nate took Turbo's place. Rye tilted Frankie's chin toward him, his cock in hand, and she pulled him into her mouth. Turbo sat on the bed and watched with a huge smile on his face.

* * * *

Nate was feeling overwhelmed with emotion. No woman, no person had ever affected him like Frankie. He wasn't sure if she was sincere or still hiding stuff, but the more time they spent with her, the more intimate they were, the more truth was revealed. The fucker who'd hurt her had done a lot of damage, both physically and mentally. She had a right to be fearful, but not anymore. Not with them protecting her.

He eased the lube onto his fingers and added more to her ass. She shivered and shook, but Rye kept a hand on the base of her head and her mouth filled with his cock. His brother's face was red, and Nate knew exactly how Rye felt. Her mouth was lethal.

He chuckled then aligned his cock with her anus and began to slowly push through the tight rings. She moaned and thrust onto Mike until Mike held her hips steady.

"Easy, baby. Let Nate in. We all want to make you ours," Mike told her.

She relaxed her muscles, and Nate pushed deeper. He worked his cock into her tight ass until he realized he was holding his breath. As he sank fully into her, he exhaled, and his cock felt on fire.

"Oh fuck." Mike roared, thrust two times, and came.

Rye pulled his cock from her mouth, and Frankie moaned.

"Oh God, I'm coming. I'm coming," she said, and Nate smacked her on the ass.

"Not yet. Not until Rye joins us."

"What?" she asked, sounding so sexy and breathless.

Rye held her cheeks as Nate wrapped an arm around her waist and hoisted her up so Mike could slide out from under her.

"You're mine, too." He kissed her mouth then cupped her breasts as Nate kept her upright with his hard dick still in her ass.

"Move it, Rye, or you lost your chance. I'm going to blow my load in a few more seconds. Our woman drives me wild."

Rye slid onto the bed and held his cock in his hand as Nate eased Frankie over him. She shocked them both when she gripped Rye's cock, aligned it with her pussy, and lowered down quickly, filling herself up and crying out.

Smack.

"Hey," she yelled out.

"You watch yourself. We don't want to hurt you."

"Well, I need…

Rye thrust upward and held her cheeks between his hands.

"You need what, sexy?"

"For both of you to move, damn it," she said, and Mike and Turbo chuckled.

"You heard her, bro. Move," Nate said, and that was it.

In a blur, their bodies slapped together. Their moans and Frankie's screams filled the room as they made love to Frankie. She shook and counterthrust the best she could, but she couldn't keep up with Nate and Rye.

Rye came first and roared. Frankie moaned louder.

Nate thrust into her ass, giving it a smack after every stroke or two. She was panting, moaning.

"Nate! Please, Nate. Please."

"Please what, baby?" he asked as he felt himself getting closer to coming.

"Let me come."

He realized in that moment how trusting she had been, how serious she took his command and order to not come. His heart fell deeper, and his body erupted.

"Come, baby. Come with me now." He grabbed her hips and thrust fast, and she cried out her release as he followed.

He fell to the side, taking her with him as Rye moved from underneath her. Nate pulled her close and kissed her everywhere his lips could touch. He rolled her over, and she winced, but he had to make sure she was real and this intense sexual encounter was more than just sex. It was deeper.

She held his gaze with heavy eyes.

"Incredible," she whispered, and he chuckled as he cupped her breast and leaned his lips close to hers.

"You sure are." He covered her mouth and kissed her as she wrapped her arms around his neck and hugged him close. They stayed like that until sleep overtook Frankie.

Chapter 9

Frankie could hear the deep voices. She could barely open her eyes as she snuggled closer to the warmth. She knew immediately that she was lying on one of the guy's chests. It was Nate. She was certain of it. Her cheekbone dug into his pectoral muscles, and she adjusted. That's when she felt the bed move and the other body close to her back. Lips touched the skin on her shoulder, and a finger trailed down her arm.

She moaned softly.

"Like a sweet little kitten. God, I could wake up to that moan every day for the rest of my life," Rye told her, and she smiled.

She tilted her head up to see Nate's firm expression. Her head throbbed, her shoulder and back ached, and other parts seemed tender, too.

She gasped, and Nate scrunched his eyes together. Rye sat up.

"You're in pain?" Rye asked.

Nate clutched her cheek and chin, tilting it up toward him.

"Truth," he whispered.

"Yes," she said, not holding back, not sugarcoating it. Not with Nate. Nate was intimidating and so damn sexy. She turned her face and kissed his fingers. "I'll be okay." She then lay against his chest again. He adjusted his body and helped her to lie on the pillow.

"A nice, hot bath. I'll get it started." He began to get up. His muscular naked body, tattoos and all, looked so delicious. She gripped his wrist, the move hurting her arm and shoulder.

"Damn it, Francesca," he said in a strong tone.

She pouted.

"I need you close. Just lie with me for a while longer."

He looked at Rye. She tilted her head toward Rye.

"Please. Both of you stay with me?"

Rye pushed a strand of hair from her cheek and smiled softly. "Always, babe." He kissed the corner of her mouth, and she snuggled back against the pillow.

She closed her eyes. "Where are Mike and Turbo?"

"Work, baby. Turbo got called in, and Mike is working days for the rest of the week."

"Oh God, and you guys? You probably have work, too."

"Shh. Lie back down. We're fine. We own the business and make our own hours," Nate told her.

"Which means we have all day to take care of you and make love to you again and again," Rye said then pulled gently on her earlobe.

She chuckled. "Sounds like a fantasy."

"Oh, we're real. I can guarantee every part of us is real," Rye said, and she felt his cock rub against her ass.

Nate stroked her cheek with his finger.

"None of that, Rye. Our woman needs some rest and a good hot bath to soak in."

"After breakfast then," Rye said then placed his hand over her waist and belly and began to outline her tattoo with his finger.

"Why the star and the moon?" he asked.

She lowered her eyes to where his long, thick finger traced the outline of the dainty tattoo. Even that turned her on. She had it bad. Big time.

"Always been a dreamer I guess. Reach for the stars, my mom always said. I guess it's sentimental in a lot of ways."

"And this?" Nate asked, trailing his finger under the star necklace she always wore.

"A gift from my dad, a few months before he died." She snuggled closer to Nate.

"How did he die?" Rye asked.

"He and his partner were investigating a homicide when a call of a robbery in progress came over the radio. They responded because it was a block away, and as they got out of their car and other police arrived, the bad guys opened fire and shot and killed him and Shane."

"He was in law enforcement, too?" Nate asked.

"So was my brother."

"Brother?" Nate asked.

"Mickey. He died in the line of duty as well. Bad family tradition I guess," she said as tears filled her eyes.

"Shit, sorry, Frankie," Rye said and kissed her shoulder.

"It's okay. It's the whole law enforcement thing that got me caught up in Kevin."

"Your ex?" Nate asked, not looking too happy.

"He was a good friend of Mickey's. He said the right things. He manipulated my weaknesses, and I was stupid and weak and…"

"Hey, hey, slow down," Rye told her as he leaned up and pressed her to her back. She reached for the sheet to cover her breasts, but Nate was there to stop her.

"We all make mistakes. It's whether you learn from them or not." Nate trailed his fingernail along her nipple, making her gasp and hold his gaze.

Rye pressed one leg over hers, sliding her thighs apart.

"The dick's name is Kevin. Where was he a cop?" Nate asked.

Rye leaned down and licked her other nipple then suckled her breast.

She couldn't focus on their words, their question, only their touch.

"Chicago PD," she whispered.

"Patrol officer?"

She shook her head at Nate. "Detective."

Rye released her breast.

"He was abusive?" Rye asked her.

She looked at him, could feel his hard cock against her inner thigh.

"Among other things."

"Like?" Nate pushed.

"Being dirty," she said.

Both of them stopped.

"He was a crooked cop?" Nate asked.

She nodded. "I didn't know at first, but the last several months, I started noticing things and meeting people he said were friends. They weren't good people."

"Who were they?"

She shook her head. "It doesn't matter."

Rye touched her chin and cheek. "Sure it does. You ran from this dirty cop."

"He got busted, and I figured a few months was enough time to disappear," Frankie told them.

"He went to jail for a few months," Rye asked.

"He screwed up some big deal. Had some rough guys after him. The day I tried breaking things off with him, some gangster guys showed up. They were crazy and ruthless. I got stabbed."

Nate rubbed a finger along the scar on her hip and groin. "Here?" he asked.

She nodded. "Their boss showed up, too. Stopped them from killing both of us. I was so scared, and then the gangster guy had his men take me out of there and made me swear to keep my mouth shut. They brought me to some special hidden place. Fixed up my hip and made sure it wouldn't scar badly then brought me home to my place. They left."

"So you took off?" Rye asked.

She shook her head and was silent. She didn't know how to tell them this part.

"The truth, Francesca."

"The gangster guy wanted me. He got Kevin jammed up on some drug possession charge to get him out of the picture. He expressed an interest and had been watching me for quite some time.

"Are you fucking kidding me?" Rye asked.

"Who?" Nate asked.

"It doesn't matter. I got out of there. I ran from them both."

"They're the ones you're afraid might come looking for you?" Rye asked.

She looked at him and held his gaze. She ran her fingers along his soft, bare, muscular chest. He was exquisite. "They will come looking. When they do, I'm out of here, or I'm going to die. That's why I didn't want to get involved with you guys."

"For fear that we would be like them?" Rye asked.

"For fear that these men who want her will take us out to get to her," Nate said.

She felt her eyes fill with tears. "I don't want that to happen. I'll have to leave if they come."

"No you won't. You've got us. You're ours now. No other men will try to take you away. That's not going to happen," Nate told her.

She looked at Nate, could see the anger, the superiority in his eyes and his expression. He was being honest. He would risk his life, their lives for her. She swallowed the lump of emotion in her throat.

"I don't know why this happened to me. I had a decent life. I had a career. I was professional, working my way up in the company. It all turned on me. I was supposed to be strong the way my father and brother taught me to be. But I guess losing them, missing that tough, disciplinary quality that cops just seem to have made me accept Kevin's advances. I hadn't realized how alone, how lonely I was until he showed up after Mickey died. He was there for me during and after the funeral. He pledged a promise to Mickey that he would watch over me."

"He manipulated you. Used you when you were in mourning," Rye told her as he caressed the tears from her cheeks.

"I didn't sleep with him right away."

"I don't want to hear about that," Nate said in a strong tone.

"But you need to know that I waited a long time to let him have me. I never had sex before. He was my first and only boyfriend. I think that's why I tried to make it work even when I knew he was not being honest. But when I overheard things, when I was sent pictures of him with another woman, I had to end it."

"He cheated on you?" Rye asked her.

She felt the tears roll down her cheeks. She wondered why she still got emotional from that.

"He did, and that's another fear I have with you guys."

"We would never cheat on you. A ménage relationship is sacred and a total commitment from all of us," Nate said to her in such a tone that it made her feel as though she'd committed a crime for even suggesting they would cheat.

"I mean if I wasn't good enough for Kevin, for one man, how can I be good enough for four perfect men like you and your brothers?"

"Oh hell, Frankie." Rye gripped her chin as Nate clenched his teeth.

"That son of bitch fucked with your head good. It wasn't you. It was him. He used you. He wanted you for his own selfish reasons, and when it came to protecting you, to putting you first, he failed. We're not him. It's time to move on and put him behind you. We're not using you for anything. We want to be with you. Last night was beautiful. It was perfect, just like you, baby. God, you need looking after. You need to be shown what love is. What honesty and commitment is. Let us show you, Frankie. Let us become one family."

She got choked up from his words and his honesty.

"You still want me?"

Nate cupped her breast, and Rye smirked.

"Fuck yeah, we want you. We're going to protect you. We're going to resolve all this shit, and you, Francesca, are going to let us because you're our woman now. You got that?" Nate asked her.

She pulled her bottom lip between her teeth and nodded.

"Now, a hot, relaxing bath will help ease those sore muscles. Then it's back to bed. Rye and I are going to be learning every inch of this sexy body. We're going to figure out what turns you on and what makes you scream for mercy."

He pinched her nipple then massaged the ache he caused. She felt it straight to her pussy as she parted her lips and held his gaze.

"I don't know if I'm ready for that."

"Oh, we're going to get you nice and ready. Then, by the time Turbo and Mike get home, you'll be ripe for the taking. Now I'm going to get that bath started. You be ready to get your ass in there."

Rye leaned forward and kissed her then slid off the bed. She watched his ass, his thigh muscles, and flanks like a stallion. It made her nipples hard and her pussy swell with desire. She felt Nate's fingers against her chin, turning her face toward him.

"I think I want you begging for us after that bath."

She felt his fingers stroke apart her pussy lips, and she held his gaze.

"Open for me."

She hesitated, and he raised one of his eyebrows.

"Don't make me ask twice," he said, and she felt her body hum with desire.

His firm tone was such a turn-on, never mind his large muscles, the tattoos along his shoulder and chest, and, of course, his extra large size.

She slowly opened her thighs and felt his fingers explore her cunt. As one digit pressed up into her, she gasped and closed her eyes.

"Open your eyes. Don't look away from me," he whispered.

She couldn't believe how deeply his words, his commands affected her. This was intimate, personal, erotic. His dark-brown eyes bore into hers as he stroked faster and added a second digit, which had her panting.

"Look at me," he ordered again when she closed her eyes, the sensations nearly overwhelming.

He pumped and stroked, hitting some special spot that nearly had her shooting off the bed.

His eyes roamed over her breasts then her belly then to her eyes again.

He lifted up, and she reached for his wrist.

"Arms up."

"Oh God, Nate, please," she begged as she counterthrust against his fingers.

He knelt up, fingers deep in her pussy, fingering her, drawing out more juices, more moans of pleasure. He gripped both of her wrists in one hand and raised them above her head.

"Spread your thighs wider. Offer me this pussy, this body, now."

She moaned louder, spreading her thighs wider like he asked as her body tightened like a bow about to break.

"Who do you belong to?" he asked her, shocking her.

She locked gazes with him. The intensity, the control, and the power he had over her were overwhelming.

"You." She moaned.

"That's right. Now come for me. Let go and give me all of you."

She rocked her hips, and he thrust faster then used his thumb to circle her clit and apply just the right amount of pressure.

"Nate!" She screamed his name and came so damn hard she shook and shivered in the aftereffects.

He leaned over her, pulled his fingers from her pussy, and kissed her deeply. He explored her mouth and then moved between her thighs, aligned his hard cock with her cunt, and thrust into her.

"Oh!" She moaned, her hands still up above her head, his grip firm with one hand as he used his other hand to massage and tease her breast, thrusting into her like some athletic fantasy lover. His thigh muscles were flexing and banging against her inner thighs, and she felt herself coming again. How the hell did he do that?

"Francesca, I don't want to hurt you. Is your shoulder okay like this?" he asked, and she was shocked he could even think about her shoulder when his extremely hard, thick cock was ramming into her sensitive pussy.

"Harder, Nate. I need it harder. I don't feel anything but pleasure, but you inside of me."

She noticed the small vein by his eye pulse. His face turned red, his grip on her wrists tightened, and he began a series of hard, fast thrusts into her. She raised her thighs higher, and he thrust down and in, rubbing against her inner muscles as her moans grew louder, deeper.

She lost her breath as he thrust his hips.

"Oh!" She moaned and came just as Nate roared out and shoved even deeper, coming inside of her, marking her as his woman once again.

He pulled her into his arms, rolled to his back so as not to crush her, and cuddled her. He kissed her skin and rubbed everywhere until she closed her eyes and wondered if life could always be like this. Perfect, content, and in the arms of her four amazing lovers.

* * * *

The sirens were blaring, the horns honking as Engine 19 made its way through the intersection on Luana Highway. They were headed to Beach Road after receiving a call about a house fire.

As they pulled up on the scene, Mike noticed a couple of police officers bent over coughing. It appeared they might have entered the house to save some of the occupants.

"Anyone else inside?" Chief Martelli asked the officers.

"Yes. Two adults, a grandmother, and maybe one more kid," one of the officers told them.

Mike felt his adrenaline pumping as Chief Martelli pointed to him, Lance Martelli, Ace Towers and Marcus Towers. "You guys do the sweep of the house. Hal, Billy, Bull, get that water on the fire to the right. It appears like the problem started in the kitchen."

Everyone moved in quickly. Like a team of experts, they checked their gear, put on their masks, and entered the home. As the guys worked the water hose and began to wet down the fire shooting from the kitchen windows, Mike and the others entered the front door.

He pulled down his mask and adjusted his eyes the best he could due to the smoke. He felt around for the stairs, and the smoke seemed to clear as he climbed several steps upward.

Lance called out, "Got one here on the stairs."

Mike looked ahead of him and saw the two adults. No child, and no elderly person.

"Let's get them out of here," Lance ordered, and Ace and Marcus lifted the two unconscious victims over their shoulders and carried them down the stairs and out of the house.

"Side by side. You and I are going to do a sweep. Not sure of the number of residents in this home. Let's make it quick," Lance told him.

"I'm right here with you," Mike said, and then they heard their radios go off.

"Got the grandmother and a small child, four years old, still missing. The other children say grandmother lives in an apartment downstairs," Chief Martelli radioed to them.

"Got it."

"Let's head down the stairs. Maybe they're in there."

In the next instant, they heard the explosion. The entire house shook, and they both knelt down and covered their heads. Pieces of wood and railing hit them, covering them.

"Shit. You okay, Mike?" Lance asked.

"Yeah. You?"

He nodded, and Mike felt the ach in his arm and leg. One look at Lance and he saw the expression of pain. They were both hurt, but there were two people trapped inside this house. They needed to get to them.

Painstakingly, they made their way down the staircase leading to the lower level. Their chief radioed in to make sure they were okay.

As they descended the stairs, more smoke began to encase the lower level and the side walls by what appeared to be a bedroom covered with flames. The heat was unbelievable.

Mike scanned the room. They had to move in closer. They checked the bed. Lance checked the closet mere feet from the fire. Mike moved around the bed to the floor. There were no windows. The basement was a death trap.

He saw the ponytail.

"Lance," he called out and knelt onto the floor. The little girl was crying and shaking her grandmother, who lay unconscious on the floor.

"We got her. Come on now, honey," he said to the child, who was coughing. Her face was blackened from the smoke.

"I got the woman. You take the child," Lance said.

The little girl was hesitant, but he lifted her up and into his arms. Lance bent down for the woman. As they headed out of the bedroom, another explosion rumbled the house. The stairs they'd come from erupted in fire and smoke. They covered the woman and child as best they could.

"We need help in here. The staircase by the front door is engulfed in flames. There no other way out," he called into the radio.

"Coming in now," Chief Martelli said over the radio.

A few seconds passed, and then the sounds of creaking made Mike wonder if he was going to get out of here alive. But then water began shooting from the staircase. The fire sizzled to smoke, and there were Bear, Hal, and Marcus, shoving wood out of the way and making a pathway to escape.

"We need to move. This house isn't going to be standing much longer," Marcus said as Mike and Lance carried the victims from the home with their fellow firefighters right behind them.

The paramedics were there, including Johnny Landers, who took the little girl from Mike. "Great job, Hawk," he told Mike, and Mike watched the little girl reunite with her family.

Two other paramedics were working on the grandmother. She wasn't breathing.

Breathe, damn it. Come on now. Breathe.

He felt Lance right beside him.

"She'll make it. We got to her in time. She'll make it," Mike told him, hoping that the woman lived.

"We got a pulse. It's weak, but we have one. Let's get her to the ER," Johnny said, and Lance and Mike looked at one another.

"That was close."

"Tell me about it," Mike said and then undid his turnout coat.

He could instantly feel the pain, the bruising against his arm and ribs. He flinched, and Lance squinted at him.

"You okay?"

"I'll be fine." He started to head toward the truck and to begin cleaning up. Lance grabbed his arm, and Mike cursed.

"If you're hurt, you have to get checked out. It's protocol," Lance told him, saying it loudly so the others would hear.

"Hawk, get your ass over there now. That's an order," Chief Martelli yelled at Mike. Mike shook his head at Lance. He didn't need to be pampered or fussed over. He would check himself over at the Station. But there was Ace, giving his back a shove.

"Come on, tough guy. I'll hold your hand."

Mike shook his head as the teasing began, and he chuckled. When he took off his turnout coat by the ambulance, Mercury St. James was the paramedic checking out his injuries.

"Damn. This is going to be nasty for a while. What the fuck happened?" Mercury asked, and Mike explained about the railing and walls exploding over him and Lance but how he'd been closer.

He pressed along his ribs, which were sore, too.

"Could be broken. You may need X-rays."

"Fuck that. I'll be fine," Mike said and pushed his shirt down.

Mercury crossed his arms.

"Come on now. Don't be bullheaded. You're the most sensible of all of them," Mercury teased.

"Hey, what the hell?" Lance said as he joined Mercury and Mike.

Ace chuckled then headed back to help the others. One glance up toward the house and Mike could see that the fire was out and now stood an unrecognizable house of smoldering smoke, broken windows, charred nearly to a crisp siding and what could have been all of their graves. The house would be demolished. It was located on such a beautiful spot right across the street from beach. One of the older dwellings in Treasure Town.

Mercury chuckled. "Tell your boy he needs to go for X-rays. Now."

"What's this about X-rays?" Chief Martelli asked as he approached. Mercury lifted up Mike's shirt.

"Shit. Go. Now. That's an order." Martelli pointed at Mike, and Mike blew out his breath.

"This is stupid. I don't need to go by ambulance."

"Then you can go in my car." Mike looked up to see his brother Turbo standing there in uniform, all official.

"That works for me. We'll work out the report together later, Turbo. Just get him checked out," Martelli said.

"You got it, Chief."

"Come on," Turbo said, and Mike tensed up as he walked.

His buddies wished him well and teased him a bit, but it was all good. No one had died today. They could have lost the family of six in that house, but they didn't. So what if he was a little banged up. He would live to serve another day. That was life as a firefighter.

* * * *

Rye couldn't take his eyes off of Frankie. She wore one of his shirts, which hung to right above her knees. Her breasts filled out the top of the shirt, and since they'd hidden her bra and panties, she was naked underneath. He pulled her close as she tried to clean up the dishes from breakfast.

Wrapping his arms around her waist, he stared up into her eyes as she stood in front of him placing her hands on his shoulders.

He was sitting in the chair, legs spread, wearing sweatpants and no shirt.

He ran his hands under her shirt and massaged her ass. "I think I can get used to seeing you in just my shirt all the time."

She smiled down at him as she ran her hands over his shoulders and then gently massaged his neck.

"I don't think that would work," she whispered, and he squeezed her closer then pressed a finger down the crack of her ass to her pussy. Her lips parted.

"Why not?"

"I would never be able to leave the house."

He pressed one digit up into her cunt.

"That's the whole idea."

She stepped closer and lifted one leg up and against his thigh, giving him better access to her pussy.

"You feel awfully wet, Frankie."

She held his face between her hands and moved her lips closer. "I guess you turn me on."

He thrust a little harder. "You guess, or you're sure?"

"Oh. Oh God, sure. Definitely, positively sure that you turn me on."

"Good.

He pulled his fingers from her cunt, lifted her shirt up and over her head, and then lifted her by her hips, placing her ass on the table.

He shoved his sweats down, his cock hard and tapping against his belly, and stepped out of them.

"Lie back. Hold your thighs open. I want dessert."

"Oh jeez, you're so wild." She panted as she lay back.

He grabbed her hands, placed them on her inner thighs, and began to direct her in spreading them wider.

He released them and watched her.

"All the way back. I'm exploring this pussy and ass then fucking them. Got it?"

She nodded and pulled her thighs back.

"What do we have here?" Nate asked, and she began to close her thighs when Rye stopped her.

"Don't you dare. This body belongs to Nate, too. Open for both of us."

She bit her lip and spread her thighs as wide as she could.

Rye rubbed his hands together and stared at her glistening cunt.

"Now this is a feast made for kings." He licked her from anus to pussy. Back and forth he wet each hole then pressed a finger to her cunt, pulling more and more juices from her body.

Nate leaned over by her side and held her hands up and above her head then licked across a nipple.

"Delicious," he whispered.

"She sure the fuck is. Ass or pussy, bro?" Rye asked him.

"I think I'll watch." He pulled on her nipple, and Frankie moaned louder.

"Fuck, watch and learn, bro. This is how you satisfy our woman."

Rye pulled fingers from her pussy and stood up. He aligned his cock with her pussy and stared at her as he stroked the muscle back and forth against her pussy lips.

"You like that?"

She shook her head.

"You don't like that?" he asked.

"Why not?" Nate asked her.

"You're teasing me."

Rye felt his chest tighten and his cock harden even more.

"What is it you want, baby? Tell me?"

"You."

He shook his head.

"Say it. Tell me what you need right now. Don't be shy."

"Rye please."

Nate pinched her nipple. "Tell him you want his cock. Tell him you need him to fuck your pussy and then your ass right now."

She swallowed hard. "Jesus, you guys are crazy."

"Say it," Nate and Rye told her at the same time.

"I want you. I want you to fuck me right now, Rye. Right now." Her face turned red before she shyly looked toward Nate.

"That's my girl. Now you get rewarded."

Rye aligned his cock with her pussy and slowly pushed into her wet cunt. Frankie moaned and thrust downward, and Rye couldn't go slow. He grabbed her hips and began to thrust in and out of her pussy. He loved the soft moans she made, the scent of soap, their soap, and the feel of her soft, toned skin. Her breasts bobbed and swayed with every stroke of his cock into her pussy. Nate suckled and pulled on her nipple, arousing her, making her counter Rye's thrusts.

"Oh God yes, yes." She screamed her first release.

Rye thrust over and over again, but he didn't want to come in her cunt. He felt so primal and in need to possess her.

He ran his finger down underneath her to her ass. He felt her cream. She was sopping wet. He found her anus and rubbed her honey back and forth over the spot.

"Oh, Rye. Please, Rye, stop teasing me. I can't take it."

"Then tell me what you want."

She moaned and thrust. She spread her thighs wider and pressed her ass down against his finger.

He breached her ass with his digit and she cried out.

"More. More."

He thrust his cock into her pussy then pulled his finger from her ass and massaged her ass cheeks.

"Rye," she reprimanded.

"What, baby? What is it?" he asked her, teasing her.

"I think she wants to get fucked in the ass," Nate said as he tortured her breasts.

"Yes. Yes," she said.

"You need to ask for a cock in your ass, baby."

"I want you to," she said softly, making him nearly lose his mind with desire for her.

He rubbed her clit as he moved his cock slowly in and out of her cunt.

"Your pussy feels so good though."

"I want your cock in my ass, Rye. I want you everywhere."

He slowly pulled out and then thrust back in. Frankie moaned another release as cream dripped from her pussy. He pulled his cock out of her cunt and used it to coat her anus with her own juices.

She lifted her thighs.

"No, no, no. You keep them spread. I've got plans for this pretty pink pussy of yours, baby," Nate told her as he played with her pussy and stroked a finger into her. He eased his finger out and drew circles on her pussy lips.

"Oh God, I can't take that."

"You will take that," Rye said then aligned his cock with her anus and slowly pushed into her ass.

"Oh, Rye!" She moaned.

Nate leaned down and licked across her breasts as he played with her pussy. Rye began to stroke into her ass then rubbed her thighs while spreading them wider.

She was completely open to them, and Rye felt as though he was on fire. He watched every stroke as his cock appeared then disappeared into her ass. Her pussy lips swelled, and Nate would lean over and lick, tug, then nibble her clit, making Frankie moan and scream their names.

She started to lift her hips. "More, Nate. More. I feel something. Oh God, I feel something."

She carried on, and Nate rubbed her clit as Rye fucked her in the ass. She shocked them when she pushed Nate aside and pressed her own fingers to her cunt. She countered Rye's thrusts then pushed her fingers in and out of her pussy.

"Holy fucking shit," Nate said aloud, watching her. He latched onto her breast and sucked and pulled her breast. Nate shoved his pants down, and Rye lost his focus and control. He rocked into her three more times and came.

Frankie moaned. "Oh God, I'm right there. Right there."

"Move, Rye. I'll finish her off. She's so fucking hot. Goddamn, she's made for all of us," Nate said.

Rye pulled out of her ass and moved to the side. Nate pulled her lower, lifted her up, and kissed her deeply. When he released her lips, she moaned.

"I need, Nate."

"I know what you need." He put her down, turned her around, and bent her over the table.

He thrust a finger into her pussy, and she moaned and rocked her hips.

"You need that tight, aroused pussy fucked, don't you?"

"Yes. Yes, Nate."

Smack.

"Oh!" she cried out as he spanked her ass.

"You're a naughty little thing. Being so dirty with Rye and telling him you need more."

Smack.

"Yes. Yes." She shook, and Nate pulled his fingers from her pussy, aligned his cock with it, and thrust into her cunt.

Frankie screamed out and gripped the table.

"Yes, Nate."

"Mine. You're all mine now." He thrust faster and faster.

Rye watched as Frankie moaned louder. Her eyes closed, and she screamed out an incredible orgasm. Nate followed, grunting and thrusting into her pussy then shaking as he froze and released his seed up into her cunt.

Nate wrapped his arms around her and hugged her tight as he cupped both breasts.

"Fuck, you're so beautiful and perfect. All ours, Francesca. All ours."

He kissed her neck and then slowly pulled from her pussy.

Rye lifted her up and sat down in the chair with her on his lap. She hugged his neck and laid her head on his shoulder. She looked so sexy. Her large breasts pressed against his chest and forearm as he kissed her temple, her forehead, and then her nose.

"I'll never get enough of you. Never."

Nate squeezed her ass and thigh, making her gasp.

"Me either, gorgeous." Nate leaned down and kissed her.

Then Nate's phone started ringing.

* * * *

Buddy and Jake had just finished up at the state police forensics facility when Nate phoned that Engine 19 had been involved in a serious fire on Beach Road. Mike had sustained possible broken ribs and had been taken to the hospital. They would head there next.

"Well, that wasn't exactly the forensics information and helpful evidence I was hoping for, Buddy," Jake said as he sat back in the unmarked police car as Buddy drove out of the parking lot.

"Yeah, well, we should have figured Sal Baletti wouldn't leave a fucking fingerprint or even a hair follicle behind. These men are good at what they do."

"Could we at least bring Sal in on the simple fact he was the last person seen with Gloria? Perhaps we can shake him up a little. You know, let him know that we're not buying his bullshit."

"I think that would be fine, Jake, but we need to be careful. When we do prove that he had something to do with Gloria's death, even if not solely himself, then we don't want anything stopping us in court from succeeding in locking him up."

"What about that other thing we discussed? Detective Bryce Moore?" Jake asked.

Buddy exhaled. "I've been thinking a lot about the guy and how he wasn't up front with Turbo and myself."

"He's never given any problems. He has a clean file from what I recall," Jake said.

"Do you recall where he moved from?" Buddy asked.

Jake squinted at him. "No."

"Chicago."

Jake looked just as shocked as Buddy felt when he'd looked that up this morning.

"Coincidence?" Jake asked, sounding totally unsure about even saying that out loud.

"I'm not big on coincidences, but we have to assume it isn't coincidence. It wouldn't hurt to look a little deeper."

"No, it wouldn't." Jake looked out the window.

"Maybe look back at some phone records?" Buddy added.

Jake turned back to look at him.

"You think that's necessary? You really want to open this can of worms and risk hearing from union officials about protocol and right to privacy?"

"If this son of bitch is involved, the last thing he'll try to pull would be going to the union. These Balettis are bad news. If he has ties to them, or anyone else affiliated with their criminal activities, then he's going down, too."

"I agree. Let's do this."

* * * *

Frankie's heart was pounding. She was surprised by her reaction to learning that Mike had been hurt in a fire. The tears emerged immediately, and then Nate explained that Turbo said no burns or anything major, just maybe broken ribs.

She tried to calm her breathing as she quickly got dressed in her skirt from the other night and one of Rye's T-shirts, which would have to do. She tied the long shirt to the side on her hip in a knot. Not exactly fashionable but it did the job.

During the entire ride over to the ER with Nate and Rye, her mind began to jump from one thought to the next. She was shocked as she gripped Rye's hand and held on to Nate's thigh as he drove. She needed the comfort of their bodies because the shock had made her think of her brother, her father, and Oscar. She didn't want to go through another one of those funerals. She didn't want to hear the bagpipes, hear the gun salute, look on to a sea of blue uniforms and know that she'd lost a part of her and wonder if the pain would ever ease.

Mike was a firefighter and Turbo a police officer. Their jobs were dangerous, and she would worry all the time and be fearful each time they left her. Then she worried about Rye and Nate. People were injured and got killed doing construction every day. Not to mention, all four men could be in danger because of her now. It didn't seem fair to them. They hardly knew her, yet she was giving them the responsibility of committing to her when she really should keep a distance and let them be safe.

Her heart ached terrible. *But I love them. God, I totally, absolutely am in love with them. Why can't I have a normal life? Why does my life have to be filled with fear, with pain and trepidation of what's to come next and destroy any happiness I feel?*

"Hey, baby, you're squeezing my hand pretty tight. It's okay, Mike's a tough guy. Some bruised or broken ribs aren't going to keep him down," Rye told her.

She couldn't look at him. She would cry. She would break down and tell him she loved them but that she couldn't stay with them. This couldn't work out. Not unless Kevin, and Carlotto, too, gave up on her.

Rye brushed her hair from her cheek and kissed her softly. Nate rubbed her hand against his thigh and gave it a squeeze. They were so big and masculine. She felt feminine, cared for and protected with them. But then came the guilty feeling.

I know if I stay and the danger comes then I'll lose them. How will I live with myself if they're killed because of me?

* * * *

Rye waited with Frankie as Nate went to check if Mike was okay and if they could see him. Rye's phone went off. He saw it was Pete, one of Cassidy's boyfriends.

"Hey, Pete, what's up?" Rye asked as he wrapped his arm around Frankie. She sat in a chair in the waiting room, legs crossed and foot shaking, appearing nervous. He wasn't liking the feeling he had. She'd seemed to change the moment Nate had gotten the call from Turbo.

"How is Mike? We heard at the department about the fire. Cassidy was concerned, too."

"We're at the hospital now, waiting to see him. Turbo said just maybe some broken ribs and bruising. He needs X-rays."

"Damn. Well give him our best. Is Frankie there? Can she talk to Cassidy?"

"Sure thing. I'll put her on."

Rye looked at Frankie. "It's Cassidy. She wants to talk to you."

"Oh, okay."

He handed the phone to Frankie then watched her walk away toward the window.

Rye kept an eye on her. She was so gorgeous and had an amazing body. Even now in his shirt tied to her side and the short black skirt, she looked hot. But he felt that bit of anxiety, an almost strange sensation as though something had changed. He didn't know why or what it was, but he would find out.

* * * *

"I'm so glad that you're okay and that you have your men with you. It was a pretty frightening experience."

"It sure was, Frankie. Thank God Nate is so hung up on you. Things could have turned out differently," Cassidy told her.

"I know."

"Hey, you sound funny. Is everything all right? They weren't rough with you were they?" Cassidy asked.

"No, of course not."

"Yes! So you slept with them. I'm so happy for you. They adore you, Frankie."

Frankie turned to look at Rye watching her. She bit her lower lip and turned.

"Cassidy, I'm kind of freaking out right now."

"About the whole ménage thing? It's too late for that. Besides, you belong with them. They care so much for you."

"My brother and father were police officers. They both died in the line of duty."

"Oh God, Frankie, I'm so sorry. You're worried because Mike got hurt on the job?"

"Yes." She held back the tears that wanted to fall.

"Honey, that's completely understandable, but you can't worry about them getting hurt or killed. You should focus on your time together and about the positives. Any of us can die at any moment and without warning. Isn't it better to have loved them, experienced life with them, than to deny your feelings?"

Frankie thought about that a moment.

"That's a lot easier said than done. I'm in a panic right now. Things moved fast."

"Hey, slow it down then. They'll understand. You have to work tomorrow night, right?"

"Yes, even though Lure and Charlie tried to make me take the night off."

Cassidy chuckled.

"I'm off for another week. Can't be sporting this nasty black eye and cheek at the club. Besides, my men want me with them and to clear up a few things."

"Clear up a few things? Is everything okay?" Frankie asked.

Cassidy chuckled.

"Oh, they're great. It's just that the guys feel I need a little discipline and to learn to trust them and not keep secrets. I got the third degree from Pete and Jimmy about not telling them about Keith and the order of protection. Never mind not calling one of them when I was scared."

"That's understandable, and I think I get the discipline part."

"They spanked your ass, too, huh? Go figure," Cassidy said, and Frankie gasped.

"We'll talk details in a few days. Go take care of your sexy firefighter."

Frankie said goodbye then hung up the phone.

"Baby, everything okay?" Rye asked her.

She turned around to look at him, her handsome boyfriend, the one she'd just made love with on the kitchen table at his place.

She handed him his phone. He put it away, and she placed her hands on his chest.

"I'm being a hundred percent honest with you when I say I got a little freaked out earlier."

He wrapped his arms around her waist and pulled her close. He smiled down at her.

"Kind of figured that. Want to talk about why?"

She shook her head. "Not now. I wonder when we can see Mike."

"Guys, come on," Nate called to them. He was standing there with Catalina.

"Long time no see, girl," Catalina teased, and Frankie smiled as Rye held her hand and they followed Catalina. "How's the shoulder?"

"Good. Just bruised a little."

"Bruised a lot," Nate added firmly as he placed a hand on her waist and guided her along with Rye. She loved the feel of both of them touching her at once.

As they rounded the corner, there was Turbo in uniform, talking to a nurse. Frankie felt an instant jealous sensation for the first time. She paused, and Catalina spoke up.

"Hey, Gracy, he's off limits. Got his and his brothers' woman right here," Catalina said, and Gracy looked Frankie over and smiled.

"Nice one, Catalina. But you do know I have three boyfriends. In fact one of them works with Turbo."

Catalina smiled.

"You got those wild Murphy boys to stay committed? Good for you, girl. Is Mike still in X-ray?" Catalina asked as Turbo approached.

Frankie didn't hear the rest of the conversation, since Turbo pulled her into his arms then kissed her.

She felt his gun belt wedge against her belly, but she didn't care. The scent of his cologne, the feel of his strong arms, and the significance of him in uniform aroused her and made her hug him tight.

He released her lips.

"Hey, it's okay. He's fine. The chief wanted him to come in for X-rays because he was in pain," Turbo told her.

He cupped her cheeks and held her gaze. Nate placed his hands on her shoulders from behind.

"Do you know what happened? How he got hurt?"

Turbo glanced to right. "Why don't I let Mike explain?"

She looked in the same direction and saw him slowly walking toward them with Catalina.

"The stubborn man nearly threw the wheelchair at Gracy," Catalina said, and Rye chuckled.

"Mike, you're hurt. If they think you need a wheelchair, you don't mess around," she scolded him. Mike raised one eyebrow at her as Catalina opened the door. They walked into the room, and Mike sat down on the bed.

"Now wait here and I'll get your discharge papers," Catalina told Mike.

Before she walked out, she placed her hand on Frankie's arm.

"He's okay. Just badly bruised ribs, not broken." She winked before she exited the room.

Rye and Nate walked closer. Nate placed his hand on Mike's shoulder. "Bad fire, huh?"

Mike looked at Frankie then back at Nate.

"We got everyone out," Mike said.

"What exactly happened?" Rye asked after he squeezed his brother's shoulder.

It was all quite overwhelming to watch. The love between them. The camaraderie shared by first responders. Her eyes welled up as she twisted her fingers together.

As Mike explained what happened, she began having that anxious, worried sensation again. He sat on the side of the bed, his legs apart as he told the story about the fire, about the family of six and rescuing the child and grandmother. It was commendable but also frightening.

"Did they wrap your ribs then?" Nate asked, and Mike lifted his shirt.

She saw the bandages. "They're sure they're not broken?" she asked, moving closer but not getting too close.

He looked at her. He had soot on his cheeks and neck, and the smell of smoke lingered in the room and especially on him.

He reached out, grabbed the knot of her shirt, and pulled her between his legs. His hands squeezed her ass.

"Not broken. Only bruised. Everything is fine, Frankie."

She pulled her bottom lip between her teeth and held his gaze. He used the grip on her ass to pull her closer. She placed her hands on his shoulders to be sure she wouldn't press against his ribs.

"Mike, your ribs," she scolded.

"Kiss me, Francesca. Now," he ordered.

Frankie held his gaze. She saw the desire, the need in his gorgeous brown eyes, and she kissed his lips softly. He plunged his tongue between her lips and pulled her tight against him. His hands explored her body over her skirt and T-shirt. He finally released her lips, and they were both panting.

"I missed you. I didn't want to leave you this morning."

"I missed you, too. I especially wish you hadn't left me either. But then that grandmother and her grandchild might not have made it. I'm glad that you're safe."

He hugged her to him as Catalina came back into the room with discharge papers.

* * * *

Turbo headed back to work, Nate and Rye had to answer some phone calls, and Frankie helped Mike get undressed so he could shower.

Mike watched her and could feel her hands shaking. She was very upset about him getting hurt. He felt a mix of emotions. For one, he never really worried about getting injured on the job or off because he knew it was part of being a fireman. There had been plenty of times there was concern or each of them had gotten hurt. But having Frankie in their lives made things feel different. He was more worried about her, and today's events had made him realize how much he already cared for her.

"I can do that," he whispered as she undid the bandages and began to unwrap his ribs. She gently held his upper arm, and her dainty fingers against his muscles aroused him. He licked his lower lips and watched her.

"Let me, Mike. You need a shower. Then Nate can re-wrap these and you can get some rest."

She finished removing the bandages, and as his purple and reddened skin appeared, she bit her lower lip and looked so sad.

He caressed under her hair and against her neck and head, making her look at him.

"I'm okay, baby. Please stop worrying so much."

She turned her head slightly, with tears in her eyes, and kissed the inside of his wrist. His cock hardened.

"I don't like seeing you injured. I don't like bruises."

He stroked her lower lip with his thumb. "I don't either," he said and glanced toward her shoulder that the T-shirt covered.

"I'm fine. This is more serious."

"Not from my perspective. You deserve pampering and gentleness, not to be shoved against a mirror and wall."

She held his gaze in silence then lowered, keeping her eyes glued to his as she bent down on one knee. She kissed his belly then along his ribs. His cock hardened, his body ached, and he hissed when she undid his pants and pushed them down. He stepped from his jeans and briefs as he ran his fingers through her hair.

She licked the tip of his cock, and he pulled back.

"Fuck, baby. I want to be so deep inside of you right now."

"You can't be. You're hurt."

"Fuck, I ain't that hurt."

He pulled her up, his hand under her hair gripping a handful, and he kissed her deeply. She kissed him back, and he felt hotter than the damn fire he'd been in today.

Their lips parted, and he reached for her top.

"Get undressed and come in the shower with me."

"I want to, but..."

"I'm telling you to."

He pushed her shirt up and over her head. Her large breasts overflowed from her bra. She was a damn pin-up model, and she belonged to him and his brothers.

She reached back to undo her skirt, and he unclipped her bra and cupped her breasts. He felt frantic. He flinched and gulped as he leaned forward to suckle her breast.

"Mike, please. I don't want you feeling any pain."

He pulled on her nipple, speaking to her with it between his teeth. "No pain. Only pleasure."

He swirled his tongue around her areola then suckled more of her breast. She moaned and grabbed a hold of his cock, stroking it with her palm and fingers.

"Shower. Now," he demanded and pulled back.

She looked incredible with her platinum-blonde hair cascading down over her breast. He reached in, turned on the shower, and tested the temperature. He reached for her hand. She looked so sweet, so young and petite. It aroused something carnal, possessive, and needy inside of him.

He pulled her in and under the spray of water from the multiple showerheads. They were surrounded by the vibrating rhythm.

Running his hands along her hips and ass, he pulled her closer and rubbed his cock against her belly and his chest against her ribs. "I love how you feel in my arms when you're naked and pressed against me."

He felt her hands massage his hips then go lower over his ass. He flexed.

"And I love how you feel, too. All muscle, so sexy and hard."

"Hard for you, baby." He cupped her cheeks, leaned down, and kissed her deeply. She covered his hands and pushed them away, and she kissed the inside of them as the water flowed around them. She was such an incredible sight.

Water dripped from her hardened nipples, and her beautiful platinum-blonde hair fell in wet, long streaks over her shoulders. Her mesmerizing blue eyes sparkled with desire as she began lowering to her knees.

When her full lips parted and her tongue peeked out to swipe against the tip of his cock, he moaned.

"God, baby, you're a seductress."

"You bring it out in me." She pulled his cock between her lips and suckled.

He wanted to come right there. To hear her words. For her to tell him he made her feel like a seductress and want to be one fed his ego immensely. He felt harder than a steel rod, and he prayed he could handle making love to her in this shower, but his fucking ribs were sore as hell.

She cupped his balls and massaged them in her palm as she stroked his cock with her mouth and tongue.

"Fuck, Frankie, you're killing me. That feels so damn good. I want inside of you, woman. I want to get lost in that warm, tight pussy."

She released his cock.

"On the bed, not here. You'll hurt yourself worse." She stood up, grabbed the soap, and made quick work with it. They didn't say anything to one another as they shampooed, washed up, rinsed one another, and then turned off the water. She reached for the towel, handing him one first, and then she dried herself.

She shocked him again when she reached for his hand.

"Come on, Mike. I'm going to take care of you."

He gulped down the lump of emotion that consumed him in that instant.

I love her. Holy fuck, I'm in love with Francesca.

He dropped his towel then shoved hers apart and away from her body when they made it to the bed. He kissed her deeply, and she pulled back.

"Let me." She gently pressed her palm against his belly.

He let her run the show. It was out of his control. At least for tonight.

She spread his thighs and ran those sexy, dainty hands of hers up and down the inside of his groin. The tips of her fingers teased his cock and balls. It was torture, but he was enjoying it.

"Frankie, I need you."

She licked his cock and began to suck on him again. His cock grew harder and thicker. He gripped her hair.

He held her gaze. "Get up here," he said, voice shaking because he felt so hungry for her.

She slowly released his cock, and her striking blue eyes locked onto his as she eased her way up his body.

"Any pain?" she whispered.

He didn't respond. She got the hint and slowly took his cock, aligned it with her cunt, and sank down on him.

He closed his eyes as he cupped her breasts and enjoyed the feeling of being so deep inside of Frankie.

"I love being inside of you."

He opened his eyes. Her hair fell over her shoulders, and the wet tips tickled his pectoral muscles.

"I love the scent of you. The smell of your hair, your perfume, your sexy, wet pussy."

"Oh God, Mike." She began to ride him faster. She rocked on top of him, fucking him, milking his cock. He pulled on her nipples, massaged her breasts, and then counterthrust up against her.

"Oh. Be careful," she reprimanded him, and he clenched his teeth and thrust upward hard and fast when she fell forward.

"I'm fine. You do it to me. I fucking love you. Every inch of you, Frankie."

He pulled her down and kissed her. He rolled her to her back and fought the pain he felt in his ribs. They seemed numb against Frankie's body and power over him. He rocked into her as he kissed her and shoved his cock as deep as he could get into her. He released her lips, and she screamed out her release, and he followed, grunting, panting, and then lying over her.

"Oh God, Mike." She cupped his cheeks. She had tears in her eyes. "I love you, too."

He smiled then rolled off of her and to his side. Then the pain kicked in.

* * * *

Frankie kissed along Mike's chest. She used her mouth to explore his tattoos. The floral-like pattern encased in fire, the firefighter's helmet, a date eleven years ago, and an American flag with another date and the word, "brothers." She paused as she realized she had seen the same tattoos on Nate, Rye, and Turbo, too. At first she had seen only the flags. Her focus was on their bodies and, of course, how they made her feel. She lost all focus when they touched her, made love to her, and had her screaming in ecstasy.

Mike reached up and ran his fingers through her hair.

"What are you thinking about?" he asked.

She ran her finger over the flag tattoo and then the word, "brothers."

"All four of you have the same tattoo and the same date."

He glanced down at his arm.

"That was a special day."

She heard Nate's voice and turned to see him standing in the doorway. He looked at her, and she felt all aroused and wet all over again.

"Why don't you tell her about it, Nate? It was a big day for you." Mike used his good arm to pull her against his side. She snuggled up against Mike, despite her attempt at giving him room.

"I'm good, sweets. I want you right by my side," he said, and she smiled at him.

Nate walked over, pulling his shirt up over his head before he sat down on the bed. She reached out and ran her fingers along the flag and the identical date.

"Ten years ago, which seems like a lifetime from now, I prepared to leave for the Marine Corp like I had since joining the service at nineteen."

"Nineteen? You were so young."

He smiled.

"Baby, you have no idea. I had experienced war before. Nearly got killed in a low-profile mission, and when I came back in between tours, my brothers and I talked about our family."

"We discussed the bond we have. We wanted what our mom and fathers have," Mike added.

"Wait, mom and fathers? You mean a ménage?"

Nate smiled. He cupped her chin, and his eyes swept over her bare breasts. "They live a couple of hours south of here. They have a gorgeous place on the beach. They'd love you, Francesca."

She felt her heart race.

"My brothers and I did everything together. And during those first few years apart, things got a little crazy," Nate explained.

"Rye got into some serious trouble. He was fighting, messing around in illegal boxing matches, and then he got in over his head with some mobster types."

"Oh God, how did he get out of trouble?" she asked.

Mike chuckled. "Let's just say Turbo, Nate, and I went into a fistfight packing guns."

"We made it so that Rye would never have to worry about anyone messing with him or trying to drag him back into underground trouble."

She couldn't imagine Rye fighting illegally. He did have big muscles, and he was very physically fit, but still, he was so sweet and didn't seem to fit the personality of a fighter.

"I wasn't that bad off. Don't let them bullshit you," Rye said, joining them in the bedroom.

She looked him over, trying to imagine him in some wild cage fight in an old abandoned warehouse down some dark alley. Why she thought it was sexy she didn't know. But she was glad his brothers had helped him out of trouble and from going down the wrong path.

He climbed right up onto the bed and caressed up her bare calves and thighs to her waist. He kissed her inner thighs. "I was bad-ass, baby. We kicked ass that night." He licked her skin under her knee, and Mike chuckled.

"We were fucking lucky," Mike stated.

"That's why we drank so much afterward. We were on a high," Nate said.

She put it together. "Oh, so you got drunk and celebrated your victory by getting matching tattoos?"

Rye spread her thighs and used his thumbs to manipulate her pussy.

"No, Nate was leaving for a tour of duty in the Middle East on some secret mission. His commanders told him it was dangerous and he might not make it back alive."

The tears instantly filled her eyes, and she saw the seriousness in Rye's eyes and heard it in the tone of his voice. She looked at Nate, who held the same unreadable expression. "Oh God, Nate, you were in Iraq?"

He leaned over and pressed his lips to hers.

"I've been a lot of places, darling. I've done a lot of crazy shit to survive." He held her gaze and looked over her face as if memorizing every detail. "I often wondered why I lived and why I even existed. Now I know."

She didn't know what he meant, and then it hit her.

"To take care of your brothers and watch over them," she whispered.

"For my brothers and me to take care and watch over you." His words hit her straight in the heart, and then he kissed her.

Rye took that moment to stroke a finger into her pussy.

Nate took complete control of the situation and kissed her thoroughly, and then he paused.

"We want you."

"Yes," she whispered.

He got up off the bed and stripped off his pants and briefs.

Rye pulled his fingers from her pussy and jumped up from the bed. He ran to the side dresser, and Nate lifted her up to straddle his body, leaving his legs to hang over the side of the bed. She looked over Nate's head and locked gazes with Mike. He rolled to his side, flinching as he leaned on his arm and elbow, and watched with interest.

"Best fucking seat in the house," he said.

She felt her cheeks warm and then felt Nate align his cock with her pussy and thrust up into her.

She gasped and held on to his shoulders until he worked his thick cock all the way in.

His hands felt so good and powerful as he manipulated her body, cupping her breasts while thrusting up.

She tried to hold on and ride him, but suddenly she felt the cool liquid to her anus and Rye's fingers press into her ass.

"Damn, Frankie, you have got to have the best ass." He leaned down and bit her gently on the ass cheek.

"Rye," she said, but it came out more like a moan than a reprimand.

Mike chuckled. "Her tits look great, too, as they bob and sway each time Nate thrusts into her pussy."

"Mike," she scolded, and Nate held her hips and thrust upward. Sure enough, her breasts moved and bounced.

As they made comments, and she was about to reprimand them some more, she felt Rye pull his finger from her ass and replace it with his cock.

She stiffened a moment and then gasped as she felt Rye's cock sink deeper between her anal muscles.

Both Nate and Rye began to move into her, thrusting, rocking, and grabbing her everywhere. Rye cupped her breasts from behind as he thrust into her ass. She felt her belly tighten and her heart soar with love and adoration for these men. They were such a deep part of her, and the realization brought tears to her eyes. She suddenly wanted to give them everything she could. She thought she heard the bed dip but could hardly focus as her body erupted and she screamed her first release.

She was trying to recover, her body building up again already as Nate and Rye continued to make love to her. They slowed their pace. Nate cupped her breasts, and Rye grabbed her hips and massaged her ass cheeks. Then she sensed Mike moving closer. His eyes scrunched together, but he held his cock in his hand and looked determined.

"I want in, too."

She licked her lips. She wanted to ask if he was okay, but that fierce, determined look in his eyes warned her not to. She moved her head closer and immediately pulled his cock between her lips. From there on out, she was in some kind of erotic fog.

* * * *

Nate locked gazes with Rye, and then they looked at Mike. Mike was staring down at Frankie, caressing the hair from her face as he thrust slowly into her mouth.

"That's my girl. It feels so good," Mike told her as he caressed her cheeks and held her hair and head while she sucked him down.

Nate felt his brother's love for Francesca. Hell, if he could let himself go and believe she was as amazing as she seemed, he would admit to loving her, too.

"I'm coming, Frankie." Rye moaned and thrust faster.

"Me, too, baby," Mike said.

Nate heard both of his brothers moan then Mike's face tightened and he closed his eyes as he grunted and came in Frankie's mouth. Mike fell back to the bed, exhausted and more than likely in pain. Frankie lowered her head and moaned as Rye kissed along her shoulder then pulled out of her ass slowly and with care.

Nate was overwhelmed with emotion. He rolled her to her back, lifted her hands above her head, and entwined their fingers. He held her gaze as he rocked his hips, thrusting his pelvis and cock as deeply into her as he could get. She was a fantasy. Her large breasts rocked and bounced with his every thrust. Her head tilted back, her pelvis lifted, and the sight of her throat, her breasts, and rapid panting sent him closer to his climax.

"I love your body. I love being inside of you, Francesca."

"I love it, too. You feel so good. I'm coming, Nate. I'm coming."

She moaned again, and he picked up speed. He rocked his hips and thrust his cock into her tight, wet cunt until he could hardly focus. He heard her cry out. He felt her hot cream drench his cock and her vaginal muscles grip the thick muscle, and he lost it.

"Francesca. Oh God." He came. He jerked and spasmed, letting all his seed fill her to her womb, and the thought brought on a surge of possessiveness and deep emotions. He wanted everything with her. He wanted to always feel like this and be this close to her and to his brothers.

He leaned forward and kissed her. He let his weight press her to the bed a moment as he relished the feeling of knowing she was their woman and no one else's.

He released her hands and cupped her cheeks then kissed her again. When he pulled from her body, she moaned softly, and he cradled her in his arms.

"This is where you belong. Where I need you to be. Right here in my arms with my brothers and me. Always."

Chapter 10

Turbo's head was pounding. It had been a long day and a long night. After having to go to the hospital with Mike and then heading back to work to assist Buddy and Jake in the investigation, he was exhausted. He tried to be as quiet as possible as he put his service revolver into the locked box, then hung up his belt and placed his badge on the dresser along with handcuffs and other items. They were all right across the hallway in Mike's bedroom. He'd missed making love to Frankie but was thrilled that his brothers were getting closer to her. Especially Nate and Rye, who held back the most.

Turbo reached into his pockets, finding spare change from lunch, which had been a chicken wrap from one of the local mom and pop shops near work. He'd just placed the change on the dresser, instead of dropping it into the glass jar, so it wouldn't make noise. Easing his shoes off, he walked toward the bedroom to check on his family. The thought had him pausing in the doorway.

My family? When had he considered Frankie as part of the family? As part of him and his brothers?

Tightness formed in his chest.

He looked at them. Mike was lying flat on his back, an expression of discomfort on his face, even in sleep. He'd saved lives yesterday. He'd risked his own, and things could have turned out worse. Mike and Lance could have gotten caught in that house fire and died. They were heroes for saving the grandmother and child. He shook his head.

Then he looked at Nate and Rye. Frankie was sandwiched between them, her face against Nate's neck, Rye's body pressed tightly against her back and his arm around her waist. She was completely naked, her sexy, curvy body encased by his brothers, as though they were some kind of protective shields. He was concerned about her past and about the men she'd run from. If they were still after her, still wanting her, it wasn't a matter of if they would find her but when.

He eased his way out of the room and headed down the hallway to the other bathroom. His need to feel Frankie in his arms, to make love to her, to get lost inside of her would have to wait.

He undressed the rest of the way and turned on the shower. His muscles ached from leaning over the computer at work for hours and holding the phone to his shoulder and ear as he made phone call after phone call. This case seemed more complicated and risky than any of them had expected.

He got in under the multiple sprays of hot water and nearly moaned. He placed his hand on the wall in front of him, hung his head, and just let the hot, steaming water loosen those aching muscles.

His thoughts still on the case, he wondered if they would find anything concrete to charge Sal Baletti with Gloria's murder that could hold up in court. Looking into the guy, and his family, more deeply, Turbo, Buddy, and Jake had found out what a scumbag he actually was. Plus, he had ties to other big-shot gangsters. Turbo shook his head. He'd thought mafia types were long gone, something from the past that had died out. This seemed to be a newer, more violent type of gangster mentality and activity. Buddy had some connections across the United States. He found out about other cases, cases that appeared to be connected to the Baletti family as well as to another crime family out of Chicago by the name of Carlotto. Buddy knew the name and knew some background.

Carlotto was one bad-ass gangster that kept his hands clean of blood by having his employees do his dirty work. None of these men rolled over during interrogation. Instead, they took the fall. They did the time. It seemed this Carlotto guy was very feared and respected.

Buddy told Jake and Turbo that his connections said a debt with Carlotto is never paid. You always owe him, and he owns you for life.

Turbo heard the door creak open and turned to see Frankie. Her cheeks were a nice shade of pink, her lips full like a woman well loved. He just watched her approach.

"Did I wake you?" he asked.

She shook her head. "I missed you."

He looked her over. She wore a T-shirt, something belonging to one of his brothers. "Come in here then."

She didn't hesitate. She lifted the shirt from the hem up and over her head, her glorious, sexy body instantly right in front of him like a feast to enjoy after hours of hard mental labor.

He saw the love bites on her breasts and her collarbone. He pulled her under the spray of water, and then he pressed his palms against the wall behind her. She stared up at him then pressed her palms against his chest. He moved one hand to her collarbone and trailed a finger along her skin, down her breast where one love bite stood out.

"Had some fun with my brothers I see."

She glanced down, the water cascading over her breasts, her nipples making his mouth water.

He lowered, cupped a breast, and licked the tip. Frankie leaned back, giving him full access to her breasts. He continued to suckle the pretty pink bud then traced a pathway down from under her breast below her belly button and to her pussy.

She opened for him immediately. He released her breast with a *pop*. "That's my girl. You know how to please my brothers and me, don't you?"

She ran her hands up his chest to his cheeks and then his head. He leaned forward and kissed her on the mouth as he pressed his fingers into her pussy.

She moaned into his mouth and lifted one thigh up against his thigh as he pressed forward and thrust fingers fast up into her cunt. He plunged his tongue deeply and explored her mouth with his tongue and teeth as he explored her pussy with his digits.

The feel of her thigh rubbing up and down against his aroused his cock. He was hard and needy for her cunt. He wanted to possess every inch of her, leave his mark on her body and her soul as his brothers seemed to have done earlier.

He released her lips and continued to kiss her jaw, her neck, and then he suckled, leaving his own love bite against her skin for all to see. She moaned, counterthrusting against his fingers.

"I need you."

"Yes. I need you, too." She squeezed his arms and then wrapped her body tight against him, squeezing his ass cheeks.

He pulled his fingers from her cunt, lifted her up, and pressed her back and ass against the tile wall.

"I ache, baby, and only you can ease that ache." He held her gaze, and those gorgeous blue eyes of hers bore into his and went straight to his heart.

He gripped his cock with one hand as he used his hips to hold Frankie up against the wall. She squeezed her thighs against his sides and rubbed her breasts up and down against his pectoral muscles.

"Fuck, I love this body." He aligned his cock with her pussy and shoved right up and in.

Frankie tilted her head back and moaned. He nipped her neck and licked along her throat to her collarbone as he thrust up into her.

He felt so needy, so out of control.

"Hold on," he ordered in a deep, hard tone even he didn't recognize. He gripped her ass cheeks and began to thrust faster, harder into her tight cunt. The water splashed, and her moans echoed in the natural acoustics of the shower and bathroom. It was all so erotic and wild. She ran her fingers through his hair, gripped his head, and pressed her breasts against his mouth as he fucked her so hard, so fast his legs began to ache and almost cramp. He grunted and moaned, pulled a nipple between his teeth, and yanked hard.

"Oh!" she screamed out and pressed harder against his mouth. She counterthrust against his cock, and he lost it.

"Frankie. Come with me. Come now!" he roared, and he rammed his cock into her pussy over and over again.

He felt his climax coming, and then Frankie's vaginal muscles clamped down on his cock as she screamed out her release, and he followed, calling her name and thrusting until he couldn't take the feel of her cunt anymore. His cock was so damn sensitive and spent he pulled from her body, hugged her against the wall, and remained like that until they both calmed their breathing.

* * * *

Frankie hugged Turbo and kissed along his neck and shoulder. She felt so protected and loved in his arms. He turned off the water and then set her feet down.

"Let me grab the towel for you." He stepped out and took the towel he had for himself and wrapped her in it.

"Get your towel so you don't get cold, Turbo," she whispered.

He licked his lower lip then reached out and caressed down her cheek and jaw with his pointer. "After that? Hell, baby, you set my body on fire."

You set my heart on fire, Turbo.

She smiled then watched him walk to the linen closet, grab a red towel, and dry off. She stared, in awe of his body, lean, muscular, the dips and angles like a fine work of art. He must work out really hard to have such an amazing body.

He turned to look at her, the room quiet.

"What?" he asked, and she didn't want to come across as some lust-stricken woman, so she quickly glanced at the tattoo he and his brothers shared.

"Nate, Mike, and Rye told me about the tattoo you guys share. I like it. That's very special." She lowered her eyes to dry off. She released the towel, dried her wet hair as best she could, and then reached for the T-shirt she'd thrown on earlier.

Turbo gently took her wrist into his hand and stepped in front of her. He lowered to his one knee and leaned forward to kiss her star and moon tattoo.

"Have I told you how much I like this tattoo of yours?" he asked then licked the tattoo and nibbled on her hipbone, making her giggle and pull back.

"No, you haven't," she teased. He pulled her back by her hips then leaned forward and kissed her belly.

"Well I do. I love this sexy body. I love your scent, the feel of you in my arms, and mostly I love getting lost inside of you." He kissed the top of her pussy, and she ran her fingers through his damp hair.

"I love your body, too, and all these muscles and the tattoo you and your brothers share and getting lost with you inside of me, making me feel safe and loved."

He wrapped his arms around her and hugged her, his cheek pressed against her breasts. They stayed like that a moment until she felt his tongue lick the underside of her bosom then along the tip. He pulled her nipple between his teeth and tugged.

"Turbo." She gasped.

She felt his hands move along her ass then spread her cheeks. He ran a finger down the crack.

"I nearly forgot," he said, pulling back and stroking his finger back and forth over her anus. "I love this ass, too."

He stood up, picking her up into his arms in one smooth motion as if she weighed nothing at all. She straddled his waist, and he turned and headed out the door, flicking off the light switch. As they walked down the hallway, they met Nate.

"How's our girl?" he asked.

She felt every body part react. Nate stood there in only his briefs, looking like some sexy male underwear model.

"Fine. Why wouldn't she be?" Turbo asked, now sounding concerned, as if she hadn't told him something was bothering her.

She was confused, and then Nate approached and now they stood in front of another bedroom doorway. Nate reached out and stroked a finger along her back and ass.

"Because I heard a whole lot of gasping and moaning. Sounded like she's really in need of more loving from her men. What do you think, Turbo?"

She pulled her bottom lip between her teeth as she watched Turbo lock gazes with Nate.

"Her ass is calling to me."

That was it. He carried her into the bedroom, and in a flash, both men had her spread on the bed and were licking, nipping, and arousing every part of her body. She moaned and squirmed as Nate feasted on her breasts while Turbo grabbed things out of the dresser drawer.

They both lay on either side of her, a hand to her inner thigh spreading her wider.

"Open all the way and let us get this body ready for both of us," Nate told her. His voice firm, his tone commanding.

She panted, and her breathing grew rapid.

"Arms up behind your head. Don't let them down, and we'll reward you," Nate told her as he traced a nipple with his fingernail.

She slowly raised them upward above her head, and Nate and Turbo pulled her body lower to the edge of the bed.

Nate held her gaze as he traced her pussy lips with his finger.

"How does that feel, baby?" he whispered, stroking her pussy and then pressing his finger deeper. He dipped it in then pulled it out teasing her.

"Good. So good." She moaned.

Her legs tightened, but they remained open as Turbo slid to the floor. He pressed one hand against her inner thigh and stared at her pussy.

"That's fucking hot. Watching my big brother finger your cunt and get it ready for his cock."

"Oh God, Turbo." She moaned and felt her cream drip from her cunt.

Turbo smirked.

"That's right. Get those juices flowing, Frankie. You're about to get fucked in your ass and your pussy by Nate and me."

He leaned down and licked her anus. She nearly shot up off the bed.

"Hands up. Lie still," Nate ordered, and she widened her eyes at him.

He was so forceful and demanding. It turned her on beyond belief as her pussy leaked more cream. She felt the cool liquid and moist finger press against her anus.

"Look down there. Watch us feast on you," Nate said.

She tilted her chin to her chest and saw Nate fingering her pussy. The lips were moist and wet, and then he stuck his tongue out and licked all around it, making her belly tighten and her pussy swell with need. Nate was between her legs. He nipped the sensitive part of her ass cheeks that bordered her anus. She tightened and lifted and then felt the tip of his finger press through the tight rings of her ass.

"Oh God, I can't take it. I can't take it." She moaned and rolled her head side to side. Both men began to finger her ass and pussy faster. They stroked and thrust, and when she went to close her legs because they were shaking, both men's large, firm hands held her wider. She screamed her release, thrust, and rocked on the bed until she felt them remove their fingers.

Frankie had nearly cried out, demanding they give her more, when suddenly Nate lifted her up so she straddled his waist, and he aligned his cock with her pussy and pulled her down as he thrust upward. She gasped, losing her breath as the thick, hard muscle filled her to her womb. Behind her, Turbo spread her ass cheeks, pressed the mushroom top of his cock to her anus, and began to slowly push in. She wanted, she needed, so badly, she pressed her ass back.

"Easy, baby. I don't want to hurt you," Turbo said, sounding as though he was being tortured. He put her needs first, and she loved him for it, but her hunger, the overwhelming need to feel both men inside her was greater.

"Get in, Turbo. Get in now." She moaned as she lowered and lifted on Nate's cock.

Nate gripped her hips and squeezed. "Watch it. We're in charge in the bedroom." Nate was firm.

She parted her lips when she felt Turbo push his cock deeper.

"I don't know, Nate. I kind of like the fact we make her so fucking horny she demands a cock in her ass." He shoved all the way in, and she couldn't respond to his comment. Instead, she held on for the ride as both men fucked her together until she felt like a rag doll and came two more times.

Nate grabbed her, bringing her down lower as he covered her mouth and kissed her deeply.

Turbo moaned then held himself in her ass as he came, smacking her ass cheeks then massaging them as she moaned.

He pulled from her ass slowly, and as soon as he was out of the way, Nate rolled her to her back and pounded into her, entwining their fingers above her head. She held his gaze and watched his teeth clench and his face turn red, and they both moaned together as they came.

Turbo appeared with a washcloth and cleaned her up then kissed her tattoo, her belly, her breasts, and then her lips.

Nate pulled her into his arms and brought her up higher on the bed and under the covers.

Turbo turned off the light and got into bed behind her, and both men adjusted their bodies around her like a shield of armor. She couldn't help but smile.

"I love you guys. Goodnight." She fell into a deep sleep, feeling content and sedated.

* * * *

Rye watched Frankie get dressed.

"Call in sick. Charlie and Lure won't care."

He didn't want her to leave, even though he and Nate had work to do and Turbo, too. Mike was going into the firehouse to do paperwork but had to see the doctor before he could get back onto active duty.

"Rye, I can't. I'm scheduled for multiple parties the next few nights. It's good money."

He grabbed her hips and pulled her closer. He was sitting on the edge of the bed. They'd all showered and kissed her and expressed how much they didn't want her out of their sight or their arms.

"We can take care of you."

Her eyes widened. She looked hurt or maybe shocked. He wasn't sure. Sometimes Frankie was hard to read.

"Rye, this is my job for now. Please don't make this complicated. We had an amazing two days and nights together. I'll see you in a few days." She pressed her palm against his cheek.

"A few days, my ass. We'll go by Prestige tonight and see you."

"No, Rye. You can't. I'll be in the private back room. It will be an interruption. Let me do my job like you guys do your jobs." She cupped his cheeks between her hands, and he held her ass and hips.

"I'll miss you." She leaned down and kissed his lips. He pulled her closer and fell backward then rolled her to her back on the bed.

"You watch your ass, you hear me. Any fucking guys flirt with you, tell them you're taken," he demanded and was surprised at his own firm tone. He didn't want to come across as some possessive asshole. It might scare her.

"I love you. Remember that."

"I love you, too." He kissed her then hugged her, hoping he could survive the next twenty-two hours without her.

Chapter 11

"So that's who Gloria was so jealous of. Very fucking interesting," Sal said as he licked his lips and watched the waitress taking orders from the other men at the private party.

"She has a fucking hot body. She could be a centerfold model. Look at those tits and that ass," Chino said, watching her with lust in his eyes.

Sal glanced at Ralphy. He was straight-faced as usual.

"Ralphy, what do you think?"

"About the blonde or about this place Prestige and the opportunity to gain back some business Gloria cost us?"

Sal smirked. "First things first. The blonde."

Ralphy glanced back toward her. She was headed their way to take their order.

"I'd fuck her, but I would break her."

"Break her heart. She looks too fucking sweet to have that siren body," Chino added.

Sal held her gaze. His brother had to see her. He nodded as he took a picture.

"Good evening, gentleman. May I take your drink orders?" she asked.

"Sure thing, baby. What's your name?" he asked.

She looked a bit timid. His cock hardened. He kind of liked that.

"Frankie."

He squinted at her.

Ralphy spoke first. "That's a guy's name."

She gave him a dirty look. "Well, obviously I'm not a guy," she retorted, and Sal watched Ralphy's body language. He was a fucking animal and had a mean streak in him for disobedient women, as he referred to most of the opposite sex.

Ralphy eyed her body over.

"Further examination may be needed to clarify that, darling."

"You wish. Can I get you guys drinks or not?" she asked firmly with attitude, and Chino chuckled.

"Martini, dry, no olives, Kettle One."

"Same here, Frankie," Sal said. She looked at Ralphy.

"Scotch. Straight up. You might as well bring over the bottle."

"I'll be back shortly." She then walked away. They all watched her.

"Cocky bitch," Ralphy stated.

"She didn't like your insulting comment," Chino replied.

"She has a fucking guy's name. What the fuck?" Ralphy said.

"Gino has to see what she looks like. Let's get a picture."

Ralphy rolled his eyes but stood up and made his way to the bar area and Frankie. Sal watched as he very inconspicuously took several pictures of Frankie, including her ass in the short, tight black skirt.

"Oh yeah. Gino is going to love her," Sal said.

Ralphy returned.

"This place is fucking crowded. The bartender said every fucking night they're open. We can easily squeeze some more people in here to sell."

"I agree. The only thing that concerns me are the owners. From my understanding, they're very alert and have a good hold on their employees," Sal said.

"Gloria got in here no problem. She was a fuck-up, too, but still brought in a shitload of money each week. We need to rectify that fuck-up and make nice with Carlotto," Chino stated.

"Carlotto is sending some of his own men here. We'll figure this out. We may need to meet with these owners and apply the pressure like you guys did today at Riley's and the Beach House," Sal said.

"They have a few more hours to call us. If they don't, they just might be putting out a fire and damage to their businesses where they'll need a loan," Ralphy stated.

"You all set with the plan for arson? We don't need any more fuck-ups," Sal said.

"Chino and I have it covered. Like I said, if we don't hear from these owners, and they're not on board with paying a little security each month, then this first and only warning should make them very cooperative," Ralphy told Sal.

Sal nodded. His guys knew what to do and how to apply the pressure. He pulled out his cell and looked at the pictures Ralphy had taken. The woman Frankie was fucking hot. He sent his brother the pictures and a text.

This is the broad Gloria was jealous of. What do you think?

* * * *

"They're there now, Louie. Ralphy and Chino said a few of the other places would bring in some nice funds, too. They applied the pressure, spoke to the owners, and gave our terms of agreement," Gino told Louie Carlotto over the phone.

Gino's cell phone went off, and he read his brother's text message.

"So if your brother believes these to be lucrative businesses, then I expect results fast, or you're going to have to find another way to pay off the debt."

Gino felt his chest tighten. They were all going to get knocked off if he didn't make nice with Carlotto and get him more money.

"We'll do it. Just give us this week, and we'll have everything in order."

"You'd better. I have men in town now. So watch that you don't fuck up. My informants tell me your brother is being watched and investigated by the police. I don't need pigs on my ass. I've had to buy enough cops, and I'm not buying local beach bum ones."

"I understand. By the way, my brother just sent me a picture of the woman Gloria attacked at Prestige. Pretty fucking hot stuff. Big tits. A real sweet beauty."

"Send me them. We'll be in touch."

Carlotto disconnected the call, and Gino sat up straight in his chair.

The blonde was pretty fucking hot. He sent the photos to Carlotto and then read his brothers message again.

"What man wouldn't fuck a piece of ass like that?"

He texted back.

Maybe she'll be a perk to our new business in Treasure Town? Find out what you can, but lay low. Give me an update as soon as Ralphy completes phase one.

* * * *

Carlotto disconnected the call from Gino Baletti and sat back in his chair.

"How did that go?" Pasqual asked him.

"I'm not sure if he'll pull through. We may need to cut our losses and move on. It's not like we need the extra business."

"But those clubs on the beaches with all the damn college kids are gold mines.

"Ruffio and Santana did their own research. They think the businesses are very lucrative."

Carlotto heard his phone go off. He glanced at the text message.

"Fucking Geno. He's sending me a picture of the waitress Gloria assaulted when she got caught dealing. He says she's a knockout."

Pasqual smirked.

Carlotto opened up the text and had to do a double take. He leaned forward and grabbed onto the desk.

"What is it? What's wrong?" Pasqual asked, standing up and coming closer.

"He fucking found her. Gino found Francesca."

"What?" Pasqual asked as he came around his boss's desk and looked over his shoulder.

Carlotto took in the sight of her in the tight, barely there waitressing outfit.

"She looks so different," Pasqual said.

"She's hiding out in the same fucking town, working at the same fucking club we're about to take over. We've searched everywhere for her. Tell me this isn't fucking fate and that she doesn't belong with me?" Carlotto said as he stared at her pictures. She looked incredible. He'd spent nights dreaming of that body, of fucking her. He'd even tried fucking blonde whores just to get her out of his head.

"What do you want me to do first, boss?"

Carlotto looked at Pasqual.

"First things first. Kevin is going to be a problem to deal with."

"We can take him out. Problem solved."

"I still need him and his connections in the police department. Plus, he owes me his life. His debt will never be paid unless I tell him he's free if he gives me Francesca."

"I say fuck that bastard. He doesn't own her. She took off to get away from him. He cheated on her, abused her, and put her in direct line of fire. She took off and has been on her own. She's working at a fucking bar and nightclub instead of the professional career she loved. Fuck that prick."

Carlotto chuckled.

"You really hate Kevin, don't you?"

"Like I said, give the okay, and he's gone. Forever."

"I want to be careful here. If the feds and the local police have their eyes on Gino and Sal Baletti, then we don't want to be seen with them. We don't need to go take Francesca and cause more trouble."

"Then what do you suggest?"

"Call Kevin. Tell him I found something he lost."

"You're going to give him Francesca?" Pasqual asked.

Carlotto looked down at the picture on his phone and leaned back in his chair.

"I'm going to let him do the dirty work. Let him go out to New Jersey and grab her. He'll bring her back here, and then we'll get rid of him."

Pasqual smirked.

"That's one hell of a plan. But aren't you worried he might hurt her or maybe fuck her another time?"

"He fucked her for over a year. What the hell is one last time? It's the least I can allow him before I put him in his grave."

Pasqual chuckled.

"Call Rufio and Santana. Give them the heads-up that Kevin is coming and have them find out all they can on Francesca. That way we make it easy for Kevin to grab her. In forty-eight hours, she'll be back in Chicago and in my bed. Where she belongs."

* * * *

Jake McCurran tried to remain controlled and not blow his stack. The owners of both Riley's and the Beach House had asked for a private, secure meeting out on the docks in Bayline. He was shocked as they told him about the men approaching them from out of town and threatening them. They asked for money each month and also the ability to freely sell drugs at their clubs. They told the owners, Brian from Riley's and Chester from the Beach House, that if they didn't comply, then they would apply a bit of pressure and force them, too. They threatened their business, their families, and their patrons.

As he gathered all the information he needed that evening, a call came over the radio as Chester's cell phone rang.

The Beach House was on fire. Engine 20 was currently putting it out.

As they rushed to the scene, Jake called Buddy and Turbo and had them meet him there. This was all too much of a coincidence not to investigate full force and immediately. No gangster thugs were going to come into Treasure Town and try to force the hands of hard-working citizens in the community. Organized crime was a serious matter and now he wondered who else in town might have been confronted and who was giving in out of fear?

Jake stood by Chester and Chief Raul Sanchez of Engine 20. One of his main firefighter, Collin Caldwell, was giving them the details.

"Looks like the fire started out back by a Dumpster," Collin told them.

"The Dumpster? That's right by the back door to the kitchen. How is the kitchen? Please tell me the kitchen is okay," Chester said, sounding frantic.

Collin touched his arm. "Chester, the Dumpster was moved to the other side of the building and nowhere near the kitchen. It was against the other side. You have some damage to one of the back rooms, but really, it's minor. Nothing that would close you down for more than a day of cleanup and freshening up," Collin told him.

"My God, Jake. What am I going to do?" Chester said and covered his mouth then ran his hand along his chin as he exhaled.

Jake cleared his throat.

"We're going to take care of this together. I've got men patrolling the streets near Riley's, too. I hope if anyone else was threatened they will come forward now like you and Brian," Jake said.

"What's going on, Jake? I got your text message," Buddy said as he joined them, along with his brother, arson investigator Trent Landers.

"Glad to see you guys. Trent, I need a thorough evaluation here. We may have ourselves some trouble in Treasure Town."

* * * *

Turbo couldn't believe the call he got from Jake. He was looking over the information he'd uncovered on Sal and his brother, Gino Baletti. As he searched for a location of their primary residence, the phone rang. He answered it.

"Hey, Turbo, it's Charlie."

He heard Charlie's voice and was immediately concerned.

"Is everything okay? Is Frankie all right?"

"Yes. I didn't mean to freak you out. Listen, I know you, Buddy, and Jake are working Gloria's murder case. I remember us talking about some of the players around town and possible suspects who were selling drugs in my club. Anyway, Shark is working the bar tonight for a private party. There's nearly a hundred people in there, but Shark recognized someone you might find important."

"Who is that?"

"Sal Baletti."

"Are you kidding me?"

"No I'm not."

"I'd better call Buddy and Jake. Keep an eye on Francesca."

"Hell, buddy, you don't need to ask me that. I always have my eye on her," he joked.

"Watch it, Charlie. I'll forget your close friends with my brother.

Charlie chuckled, and Turbo disconnected the call. He immediately called Jake.

* * * *

Francesca didn't like the three guys at the table that reminded her of gangsters. She especially didn't like the attitude of the one guy who she swore had stood by the bar and taken pictures of her with his cell phone. It was creepy and made her feel like some object on display for anyone to look at, bother, or even touch. She hoped they didn't try something.

She was relieved when the party finally came to an end. It was after four in the morning, and the cleanup over.

"Frankie, your ride is here," Charlie told her, and she wondered who he meant.

She had told the guys she was going to be really late and that she needed to catch up on sleep. She felt antsy, uptight, and in a bad mood, despite the great tips she got. The three guys at the table had given her three hundred dollars, a hundred each in tips, and the one with the attitude had asked for her phone number.

She was getting sick and tired of this shit. She wanted her old career back. She wanted to be respected and not treated like some piece of ass.

She walked toward Charlie, wondering whom he meant and saw Rye and Nate. Both men smiled.

"There you are. All set?" Rye asked her as Nate looked her over.

She bit her lower lip. Nate hated the uniform she had to wear. She knew that. His disapproval had her mind spinning. She was getting tired of this type of work, but she needed money to survive. She wouldn't let these men take care of her. It wouldn't be right, and she would feel wrong about it.

"What are you two doing here? It's so late. I thought you would be in bed sleeping."

"Without you? Not a chance in hell," Rye said and pulled her closer for a kiss. She saw Charlie give Nate a wink.

"So it's official. You belong to the Hawkins brothers?" Charlie asked as Lure joined them. She looked at Rye and Nate, who apparently were leaving the answer up to her.

"It's true, and the Hawkins brothers belong to me," she said, and Charlie chuckled.

"We're happy for you guys. Have a good night and see you tomorrow, Frankie. You have two smaller parties. One at five and another at nine," Lure told her.

"I'll be here."

"Hey, let the woman get some rest, will ya," Lure teased before walking away.

Nate took Frankie's hand.

"Rest is overrated." He rubbed her arm then leaned down to kiss her. "How is your shoulder?"

"Feels fine. I totally forgot about it, actually."

"Good. Then let's get you back to our place," Nate said.

"I didn't have extra clothes here, and like I said, I really need my sleep."

Nate frowned.

"We'll bring you to your place to pick up some things. We can stay there with you, or you can come home with us, your choice, but we're not leaving you so soon," Rye said.

"Okay, but I really do need extra sleep. I've had it tonight."

They followed her down the hallway to the employee room where she stored her stuff.

"Hey, you seem upset. Did something happen tonight?" Rye asked.

"I just get tired of this job and some of the people who come here. That's all. Sometimes I miss my old job." She pulled on her light hoodie sweatshirt. It was gray and had the word *Pink* stretched across the back. She grabbed her bag and locked up her stuff.

Nate took her hand and stopped her before she headed toward the door to leave with them. He brought her fingers to his lips. "Rough night?"

He kissed her knuckles. She was overwhelmed with emotion, with the fact that he understood her upset and felt concerned. She appreciated that so much.

She glanced at Rye then back at Nate.

"Thank you for coming here and giving me a ride home."

Rye placed his hand on her shoulder and squeezed.

"We'll be making this a habit. Don't you worry."

She felt her cheeks warm as they headed out the door and into the early morning hour. She was starving but didn't say a thing until they got into the truck and her stomach rumbled.

"Hey, are you hungry or something?" Nate asked as he started the truck, and Rye chuckled.

"Starving."

"We can stop and get you something," Nate said.

"You don't have to."

"Baby, if you're hungry, then we'll stop. Sullivan's opens at five a.m. They have an awesome egg sandwich combo," Rye told her.

"Sounds great, then it's shower and bed for me."

"Shower and bed for us," Rye said and winked.

She felt her body come alive and get a boost of energy. Having four lovers was definitely going to take a lot of energy out of her. But, oh, what a way to get drained of it.

Chapter 12

Turbo stopped by Frankie's apartment during the day. Nate had called him and told him about getting her from work, going for an early breakfast at Sullivan's, then coming back to her place. He hadn't told his brothers about the investigation or about the things that concerned him about Frankie's safety. After meeting with Charlie and Lure, along with Buddy, they went over surveillance camera footage from Prestige and identified that Sal Baletti and two of his associates had been at Prestige and talked to Frankie a lot.

He would need to ask Frankie some questions to cover all their bases in the investigation.

Currently, Buddy and Jake were visiting other clubs along the strip on the boardwalk in Treasure Town and trying to find out if Sal and his men had threatened them like they'd threatened Brian and Chester. Trent, the arson investigator, along with his team, gathered evidence and found accelerants all over the Dumpster and the side of the Beach House. They were canvassing the neighborhood, trying to see if any witnesses saw anything suspicious or out of the ordinary. Without more specific evidence than one person's word over the other, they wouldn't have enough to bring Sal and his buddies in for questioning.

As Turbo parked the patrol car, locked it, and made his way toward Frankie's apartment building, he felt annoyed, angry, and concerned. Although he understood her thinking for picking such a place to hide out in, it didn't seem necessary for her to live in this crappy complex anymore. Not when they had plenty of room at their place and wanted to be with her all the time. But he struggled with making that serious commitment. It was obvious he was still fearful of admitting his love for her and taking the huge step of living together. But considering how strongly he and his brothers felt about her already, it seemed the most logical thing to do was to ask her to move in with them right away.

As he walked down the hallway to her place, he noted a guy leaning against the wall, who always seemed to be there.

"What's blondie doing running a brothel?" he said then took a slug from his brown bag that appeared to be a bottle.

"What did you say?" Turbo asked.

"You arresting her for prostitution or you fucking her, too?" he slurred.

Turbo had to bite his tongue.

"What the hell are you mumbling about? Go inside your place, or I'll arrest you for drunk and disorderly conduct."

"Men coming and going, knocking on her door, asking if she's home and where she works. Ain't no one come around for months. Now you and these other cops, the two big guys and guys in suits, too."

"What guys in suits?" he asked the drunk.

The guy waved his hand at him.

"You gonna arrest me?"

"Not if you're straight with me."

"I see a lot of things sitting here. A lot of things, copper." He drank from his bottle again, and Turbo ran his fingers through his hair. He wasn't going to get anything true or concrete out of this guy. Why was he asking him anyway? He was most likely delusional and drunk all the time.

"Whatever. Just get inside."

The drunk mumbled something, and Turbo walked back to Frankie's door, deciding it was better to get her out of this shithole than take a chance of someone trying to hurt her. Gun or no gun, she deserved better than this.

The door opened immediately.

"Hey, bro, what's up?" Rye asked, giving him a chest bump and a handshake.

Turbo entered the apartment, and then Rye locked the door and all the bolts Frankie had on it. Her apartment smelled great, was decorated nicely, and was a huge contrast to what was right outside.

"Frankie just finished showering."

"Hey, Turbo, what's going on? You sounded funny earlier when you called." Nate shook Turbo's hand hello and gave a chest bump.

"Just working all night. I got a few hours this morning but not much. This case we're all working on is getting complicated."

"How so?" Rye asked.

"Some guys are coming into Treasure Town and pushing to force owners of the local clubs to give money for protection and also allow drugs inside."

"What? Who are they? Do you have any leads?" Nate asked.

"Well, don't repeat this, but we had the owners from the Beach House and Riley's confide in Jake and ask for help when someone sent a message to Chester about accepting their offer. Jake was gathering information but I guess Riley and Chester didn't respond fast enough to the thugs. They set the Beach House on fire."

"No fucking way," Rye said and shook his head.

"Was everybody okay?" Nate asked.

"The fire was just a message. Some accelerant, enough to need Engine 20 to put it out. We believe the guys who did this are also connected to Gloria's murder."

"What?" Frankie asked, holding her arms around her waist as she entered the room. Her hair was blown dry and done up, but she wore only a baby blue silk robe that matched her eyes perfectly.

He stared at her, wishing he could make love to her right now.

He rested his hand on his holster and took in the sight of her.

"Good afternoon, Frankie." He then licked his lower lip.

She hesitated coming to him, but then he raised one eyebrow, and she got the message. She walked right up to him, leaned up on tiptoes, and kissed him hello. He couldn't resist touching her, holding her in his arms. He wrapped her up close and felt how feminine and petite she was, which made him feel more concerned and protective of her.

"I missed you, baby. My brothers taking good care of you?"

"Yes, Deputy," she said, and Nate and Rye chuckled.

Turbo gave her a wink and tapped her ass. He could tell she was naked under the robe. The lapels parted, and he saw her full breasts and no bra.

"Hungry?" she asked him.

His cock hardened, and he cleared his throat. She quickly stepped back and headed toward the kitchen.

"I was going to make something to eat before work."

He instantly remembered why he was here. Police business.

"Actually, talking about work, I need to ask you a few questions about last night."

"Questions?" she asked, turning toward him.

He walked closer and ran his finger down her jaw. He gave her a soft smile.

"Some guys may have been at Prestige last night. I spoke with Lure and Charlie about it this morning. They believe you may have served them drinks at their table."

"Who are they? What did they do?" she asked.

Nate approached and placed his hands on Frankie's shoulders.

"These guys the ones who threatened the store owners and set the fire?" he asked.

"What?" She covered Nate's hand with her own.

"Not sure really. But if they are, we're trying to build a timeline of events and figure out who they are and why they're here. Maybe who else they're working for and connections to some other things. They may have looked like gangster types. Anyone stand out as different than the normal crew of patrons?"

"Oh, you don't mean three guys with city accents, do you? They stood out in that big party I worked."

"These aren't the ones you told us about, are they? The ones you think took your picture and flirted with you?" Nate asked.

"The ones that got you all fired up last night about working at a professional job again instead of at Prestige?" Rye added, sounding pissed.

"Wait, back up. They took pictures of you?" Turbo asked.

"It seemed that way. The one creepy guy who had an attitude came up to the bar and looked like he was doing a selfie, but then I saw the flash. He was pointing it at me. It pissed me off, but unfortunately, other asshole guys think they can do that, too."

She exhaled in annoyance.

"Guys take pictures of you?" Turbo asked, feeling his blood boil.

"My ass, my breasts when I deliver drinks, sometimes they ask me to stand in the pictures. It's annoying. It's not like it happens a lot but enough to piss me off."

"I don't like this one bit. You didn't recognize them? You never saw them before?"

"No. They weren't from around Treasure Town. Why? You think they're the ones who started the fire and threatened the store owners?"

He ran his fingers through his hair. "Not sure but it's a good possibility. I want to make sure you're safe there. One of us will drop you off and pick you up from here on out. In fact, you should pack some things. I think it's better you stay with us for a while, maybe longer."

"Why? Do you think I'm in danger?"

His gut twisted. He didn't know what he was doing. He was being jealous and protective.

"I would just feel better if you weren't coming and going from here late at night all alone. That drunk guy in the hallway is always watching you."

"He's harmless. Give him a bottle of cheap scotch and he's your best friend."

She stood up and walked further into the kitchen.

He glanced at Nate and Rye, who looked concerned. He gave them a nod, asking for their help with this.

"Frankie, I'm serious. Things are going great between all of us. It would be nice to have you at our place. You're safer there."

"Listen, Turbo, I know you've hated my place form the start, but I'm taking care of myself. This is my place. We'll work out staying over. Nate and Rye stayed here with me last night. I could bring an extra change of clothes in my bag for work if you want me to stay at your place now and then."

"How about all the time?" He wrapped his arms around her waist.

He thought about what the drunk guy in the hallway had said about men knocking on her door. Were other guys bothering her, trying to get what was theirs? He couldn't clear his head.

"Turbo, I need some space here. I don't want to mess this up. It took a lot to trust the four of you and let you into my heart. Please give me a little more time."

He exhaled.

He released her.

"Fine, but one of us will drop you off and pick you up from work tonight. End of story. I have to head back. I'll be home late. Pack something so you can stay tonight at our place."

"I'm meeting Cassidy for lunch tomorrow."

"We'll drop you off wherever you're meeting her. I'll talk to you guys later." He left the apartment and felt his head spinning. Something was bothering him. He just couldn't put his finger on it. Was it the case? Was it this new relationship with Frankie? Whatever it was, he couldn't figure it out. There was too much going on. He would think about it later. Right now he needed to meet Buddy and Jake. Maybe they had more info on the Baletti brothers.

* * * *

Kevin couldn't believe his eyes. She was alive, she was well, and she looked so fucking beautiful even in the skimpy uniform. What really pissed him off was that, the past two nights, guys had dropped her off and picked her up. They kissed her and had their hands on her, and there seemed to be four of them. Seeing her get picked up this morning at four in the morning by a deputy really did a number on his nerves. Was she seriously fucking four guys? Was she fucking some local beach bum cop?

He gripped the steering wheel and tried to control his breathing. He couldn't believe how difficult this was. The last six months he'd sat in a cell thinking terrible things, wondering if Carlotto had his hands on Frankie and if he was fucking her. But his woman had been smart. She still loved him, still wanted him, so she'd taken off and hid. A cop's daughter, a cop's woman, she knew what had to be done. But obviously these four men had manipulated her mind. She was young and naïve, an inexperienced woman. Fuck, it had taken him half a year to get her to spread her thighs for him so he could take her virginity. He owned her. She was his, and it wouldn't matter how many guys she fucked while he was locked up. She still belonged to him.

He took a deep breath and exhaled as he watched her apartment complex. She lived in a fucking shithole. Why? If these men cared for her at all they would get her out of there. Why was she living here?

He couldn't wrap his brain around it. He thought about Carlotto. Carlotto had found out about Frankie by accident. His connections wanted in on this tourist area and the strip of clubs in several consecutive towns. There were a lot of cops. He thought about the deputy that had his hands on Frankie's ass as they walked to his patrol car. He'd personally put a bullet in the fuck's head just like he'd done to Oscar, that fucking piece-of-shit friend of hers and her brother. Oscar Finery had wanted what Kevin owned. Frankie. Oscar had the fucking nerve to threaten him, to order him away from Frankie, or he would lock him up for the crimes he was committing. See how far that threat had gone. He was as good as dead even before he walked in on that drug deal in the warehouse.

Kevin needed to be patient. He needed a plan. Carlotto had sent him here to bring back Frankie and make things right. He wanted Frankie, too. She was that fucking special. But she was his and no one else's. He couldn't give her up to Carlotto. He saw the way Carlotto looked at her and wanted her. There had to be a way that he could get Frankie, take her out of here, and disappear together. He had funds. He had a bag of money with him now. He just needed to be careful and get it done in the next twelve hours. If he didn't, then he would send in Pasqual. Carlotto wouldn't keep Kevin alive this time. They'd get rid of him just like he'd gotten rid of all the others who'd betrayed him.

Kevin rubbed his hands together. When would she come out of there? It was nearly lunchtime. The minutes were passing by so quickly. He had to grab her and disappear. *Come out, Frankie. Come on now. It's time to be together again. I missed you so fucking much. I need you. Without you, none of it matters.*

The minutes passed by, and soon another thirty passed. Finally a truck pulled up in front of the building. He clenched his teeth and growled low. One guy got out. He looked as though he was favoring his side as he stepped out of the truck. He was one of the guys she was fucking. Kevin looked at his watch then waited as the time passed by. Ten minutes, twenty minutes, thirty minutes. His blood was boiling. The guy was probably fucking her right now. Thirty minutes in an apartment with Frankie and that's what he would be doing. Fucking her so hard, making her scream his name until her voice was hoarse and her body limp and spent. He was so fucking hard just thinking about having her. Those breasts, that ass, her sweet innocent glow. Twenty-three and perfect. She was his, not theirs.

"I'll fucking kill you. I'll kill you right now." He gripped the revolver and reached for the door handle. He imagined his next move. Get into the apartment building, shove through the door, put a bullet in the fucker's head, and snag Frankie.

He'd begun to click open the door handle when he saw the door to the apartment open up. He watched them closely. She was hugging the guy's arm, smiling, face glowing, and the pompous bastard looked so fucking satisfied as he held her around the waist with his hand on her ass. Kevin's heart pounded.

He watched the guy press her against the truck and kiss her deeply, plunging his tongue down her throat as he pressed her hard, tight against the truck.

He pulled back and smiled then helped her up into the truck. Kevin watched with daggers in his eyes, hatred in his gut, as the guy walked around the truck to the driver's side, still favoring his side. Either he had an injury there or he was a lot older than he looked and something was wrong with him. Kevin didn't care. He was as good as dead. Today that guy would meet his maker.

* * * *

Frankie smiled at Mike as he drove her into town.

"I told you I could have taken the bus. You should be resting still."

He ran his hand under her skirt along her thigh.

"Resting? I'm fine. Didn't I just prove that to you when I made love to you on your kitchen table?" he asked, all cocky with one of his eyebrows raised up.

She felt her cheeks warm. He drove her insane. One minute he was greeting her and telling her how beautiful she looked in the skirt and blouse, and the next thing she knew, she was on the table, thighs spread, and he was feasting on her cunt.

"I suppose so."

"You suppose so? Honey, you were moaning, scratching at my chest, and calling out my name. I think I succeeded in showing you I'm fine."

She slapped his shoulder. "Mike," she reprimanded, and he pulled her by her inner thigh closer to him.

"Get over here. I want to feel you right next to me at all times."

"You're dropping me off so that I can have lunch with Cassidy. Don't tell me that you're going to be sitting somewhere nearby stalking me."

"Stalking you?" he asked, sounding shocked but laughing.

"Well, you know what I mean. You all have so much stuff to do. I don't need a babysitter."

"Hey, we watch over you because we love you and you're ours. We want to be with you as much as possible."

She hugged his side.

"I know that, and I love you guys, too."

"Good. End of discussion. While you're having lunch with Cassidy, I need to grab some stuff at the hardware store and will probably stop by Sullivan's to have lunch with a couple of the guys from Engine 19."

"Really? That's great. When do you think you'll get the okay to start up work again?"

"Probably today. At least I'm hoping today, even though I love spending the days with you in bed."

"I love them, too, but I guess we need to get back to a routine. You know, I work late hours and need sleep. I've been dragging these last two weeks."

"You'll get used to it. Besides, it would make things easier if you would just move in with us. We told you we have that spare bedroom if it makes you feel better. Even though you'll hardly use it, and when you do, one of us will be in it with you."

She chuckled.

"I told you that it was a big decision. I don't want to screw this up. I want this relationship to work and to last."

"As do we. Take your time. I expect an answer by the end of the week."

"What? The end of the week is two days away?"

"That's right, baby. You seem to be a person who needs specific deadlines, or you just keep saying you're thinking about it. Now you have a date to make a decision."

"And if I'm still not ready?" she asked, feeling the instant anxiety.

"Then you're not ready. But I think you know you are and you're just letting the past get in the way of making this decision. We understand your fears now. We're not going anywhere, Frankie. Just remember that."

He pulled the truck along the sidewalk in front of the small café on the edge of town.

She leaned up and kissed him deeply.

"What was that for?"

"For being amazing." She kissed him again. Their lips parted.

"And that?" he teased.

"For being patient." She held his cheeks between her hands and kissed him thoroughly, plunging her tongue into his mouth and moaning against his lips.

"And that?" he asked, sounding out of breath.

"That's for fucking me on my kitchen table this morning."

She scooted across the seat and waved goodbye as Mike stared at her in shock.

"We'll catch up later, Frankie."

"I'll be back in an hour."

She waved and started laughing as she walked away from his truck. She felt so happy and giddy. She never would have said anything like that to a man, but her four boyfriends, the men she loved, made her feel so alive and special. She knew she could drive Mike as wild and crazy as he drove her.

She was headed toward the café when she saw Cassidy at the table. She waved and gave her a kiss hello and a hug.

"I missed you. How are you feeling?" she asked Cassidy as she took the seat at the table.

"Great. And how about you?" She winked.

"Pretty good."

"Pretty good, huh? You look…satisfied." Cassidy wiggled her eyebrows up and down.

Frankie chuckled.

"Well, you know I don't kiss and tell."

"Well, that's going to change. You and I have a lot to catch up on."

"We do? We've spoken every day for the last week."

"But not about the juicy stuff. Do you find it hard to recover from having sex with four guys one after the next and together? Because, damn, I know fucking five of them is like a full-time job. I've never been so exhausted."

Frankie started laughing. She felt so happy, content, and loved right now. She just couldn't imagine anything bad or negative.

"Well then, I guess we better order some drinks and some food. Sounds like we're going to be here awhile," Frankie teased, and Cassidy chuckled as the waitress came over to take their orders.

They talked about their men, their protectiveness, and about moving in with them.

"They asked you to move in with them?" Frankie asked Cassidy.

"I've pretty much been at their house more than mine anyway. I'm just not sure it's the right thing to do. I mean it's been like a month of dating, well, mostly having sex and spending every waking hour with them. I don't even want to go back to Prestige. I don't think the guys want me to either."

"I don't blame you or them, Cassidy. I've been having the same thoughts. Back in Chicago, I worked at an advertising agency. I had a professional career and was moving up the corporate ladder fast. I'm getting sick of guys looking at my body, flirting, taking pictures, and all the bullshit lately. I worry about Turbo and the guys. And the other night these weird men in suits came in and gave me the creeps."

"That's terrible. Hey, I heard that there were some threats to some of the businesses and that the Beach Club had a fire set on purpose."

"Where did you hear that from?"

"Peter told me about it. He and his brothers were worried about me working at Prestige, too."

"I think it's all connected to a case Turbo is working on with Jake and Buddy. They had gotten the heads up about threats to business owners for payoffs and protection. Pretty scary stuff," Frankie told Cassidy.

"Shit, I heard about this from Peter. These thugs didn't try anything at Prestige with Lure and Charlie, did they?"

"Are you kidding me? Those two psychos would shoot someone and probably get rid of the body before anyone knew anything. Lure and Charlie are resourceful. I can tell you that much," Frankie said, and Cassidy chuckled.

"They are very mysterious men. So do you really think you'll quit and look for something like you had in Chicago? I'm so glad you trust me enough to tell me more about your past. It makes me feel good," Cassidy said.

Frankie smiled as she reached over and patted her hand.

"I do trust you. You're my best friend."

Frankie felt teary-eyed, and with one look at Cassidy, she could tell her friend was tearing up, too.

"I'm you're only female friend," she said, trying to act tough and not sound mushy.

Frankie laughed. "True. I don't waste time with the fake friends. So sounds like we both have some decisions to make. Move in with our men or hold off awhile longer."

"Mine gave me until tomorrow," Cassidy said.

"I've got two days," Frankie said then sipped her margarita.

Cassidy chuckled then sipped her drink. "It's not like it's going to be hell. I can basically have cock any time I want."

Frankie nearly choked on her drink as she laughed, shocked at Cassidy's statement.

"But that also means they can have pussy as much as they want, too. I don't know if mine can handle so much," Cassidy added.

"I didn't really think of it like that. I'm focusing on how much more independence I'm giving up by moving in with them and letting them take care of me. There's this fear that they could lose interest or get pissed at me and some of my bad habits."

"That's part of living together. I fear the same thing. They continue to live in their place and do their thing, and my life is turned upside down, and it's like starting over. The only familiar thing to focus on is their bed."

"I'm in love with them," Frankie admitted as the waitress delivered their salads.

Cassidy reached over and covered her hand with hers. "I figured as much. I think I'm in love with my men, but then I get this ache, this fearful sensation in my gut, and imagine one of them striking me, beating me like Keith did."

Cassidy leaned back.

"Oh, Cassidy, they would never do that."

"I know. It just pops into my head. Sometimes, when one of them goes to reach for me or approaches from behind, I flinch or tighten up. Peter and Jimmy get pissed. Toby, Sam, and Reggie try to console me and tell me they understand and to not be fearful. It makes the atmosphere change."

"Well, it's understandable that you have those fears. Perhaps living with them and having them always around will help you realize they wouldn't hurt you and that they love you, too."

"That's the big decision," Cassidy said then forked a piece of grilled chicken and lettuce and popped it into her mouth.

Frankie took a bite of hers, and then they both smiled.

"You know we're probably going to give in to their demands. They're all just too damn sexy," Cassidy stated.

Frankie nodded. "They sure are, and they make me feel things I've never felt before or thought I could."

"I hear you."

Cassidy's phone buzzed, and she looked down at it.

"It's Reggie. He was working late. I didn't see him this morning."

"Answer it," Frankie told her.

She listened to them talking and then caught Cassidy's eye. Frankie whispered to her, "I'm going to go use the ladies' room. I'll be back." She winked and smiled, wanting to give Cassidy some privacy.

She headed toward the hallway that led to the bathrooms and back door. Just as she began to push open the door, she felt the tight grip on her arm and was shoved hard against the doorframe.

She gasped then tightened up as she heard his voice.

"Hello, Frankie. Did you miss me?" Kevin asked.

The tears emerged, and she lost her ability to react in any way other than in shock. He turned her around and pressed her against the wall.

She was speechless and totally shocked. Then she remembered Cassidy and worried about her friend. She turned that way then back toward Kevin. The men popped into her head. What if he'd seen her with them? What if Kevin had been watching her this entire time and he knew about Turbo, Mike, Nate, and Rye?

His one hand held her hip as his other lay against her throat. He used his thumb to gently caress her skin. But she knew he was pissed. She saw the anger, the rage in his gray eyes, despite his calm tone. How had he found her? How long had he been watching her? Were Turbo, Nate, Mike, and Rye okay, or had Kevin done something to them already?

"Kevin."

He gripped her throat tighter. "No talking here. You're coming with me. Don't make any attempts to run, or your new girlfriend Cassidy won't live to finish her salad."

He knew her name. He must have been watching her for a while.

She nodded, and he turned her toward the back exit. He shoved it open and led her to an SUV with black tinted windows.

As they got into the back seat, she saw two guys. One was driving, and the other she recognized from Prestige. He'd been with the three men she'd gotten annoyed with that night. Who were they?

"I'll call Carlotto and tell him we're on our way to the airport," the guy said and turned around in the passenger seat.

"Carlotto?" she whispered.

Kevin held her gaze.

"He's waiting on us in Chicago," Kevin told her then pulled her hands together and wrapped them with duct tape.

"You're hurting me," she cried out as he placed her hands over the back seat headrest of the passenger side of the car then taped them to the headrest so she wouldn't be able to move or get free.

Her ass lay halfway off the edge of the back seat in the large SUV because she was so petite.

He sat down on the left side behind the driver's side of the car.

"That's nothing compared to what Carlotto is going to do to you for taking off," the guy in the passenger seat stated.

"You work for Carlotto?" she asked.

"He works for Gino Baletti. The driver you probably remember from Chicago. Santana."

She did remember him. He was one of Carlotto's right-hand men. They were going to take her back to Chicago and back to Carlotto. Did Kevin realize that Carlotto wanted her for himself?

"Why are you letting them do this? Why are you helping them?"

He ran his hand up and down her back then under her blouse. She tightened up and scooted closer to the passenger seat to evade his touch, but he wouldn't have that. He used his other hand to move up her thigh and under her skirt.

She closed her thighs as best she could, and he gripped tighter.

"Come on now. You know you missed me. I missed you. Can't wait to get you back home to the penthouse after I do business with Carlotto."

"Missed you? I hate you. I hate you even more for being under Carlotto's thumb and now handing me over to him."

"I'm not handing anything over to him."

"Sure you are. Why do you think he sent you to come get me? He wants me for himself. He's going to kill you. That's why I ran. He wanted me in his bed. He's using you."

Kevin just smiled softly at her. The SUV came to a stop at a red light.

"Don't you think I know what I'm doing? Haven't I always done right by you?" He slowly pulled the revolver from his waist, and in a flash, the situation took a turn for the worse.

She screamed as he shot the driver in the back of the head and then the guy Santana, Carlotto's man. She screamed and cried out, trying to pull her hands and arms from the headrest as Kevin hopped over the front seat. He shoved one body out onto the street and closed the door then shoved the other body out on the street and closed the door. The light turned green, and he sped off with horns honking and chaos all around them. She was crying hysterically, not knowing where he was taking her or what he had planned.

Kevin was alive and here in Treasure Town. She'd just witnessed him killing two men, one being Carlotto, and now he was taking her somewhere with him. She was going to die. She was never going to see her men again, and she cursed herself for wasting time. She should have said yes immediately to moving in with her men. She should have enjoyed that time with them because, now, she would never see them again. Kevin would make certain of that.

* * * *

"Baletti is working for Carlotto, and they both have men here in Treasure Town. I just spoke with a detective there working with the feds in an anti-crime unit," Buddy told Turbo. Jake stood next to him, eyes wide, face bright red, appearing pretty upset.

"Okay, so how do we connect Gloria's murder to them and the threats to the club owners?" Turbo asked.

"Turbo, there's more. The feds and this detective unit have been trying to track down a woman of interest. It's Francesca," Buddy told Turbo.

"Francesca?" Turbo asked and stood up from the desk.

Buddy lowered his voice.

"There is a major fucking investigation going on. Francesca was involved with a cop." Buddy paused.

Turbo nodded. "He was dirty, involved with some illegal stuff. She said she was running from him after he wound up in jail."

"Yeah, well, he's out, and the investigators say he's in the vicinity."

"Oh God, we have to find Frankie. We have to get to her."

"Make the call, but there's more. We have investigators and some federal agents on their way here," Buddy told him.

He dialed Mike's number, knowing that Frankie was with him. She was going to have lunch with Cassidy first, and Mike was right down the block at Sullivan's. They planned on all meeting at the house for dinner.

The cell phone kept ringing, and Mike didn't pick up.

"Turbo, the feds have wire taps. Phone conversations with Carlotto and Baletti's plans. Carlotto wants Francesca. She was running away from him, too."

Turbo felt his chest tighten and his stomach ache. Mike answered his phone call and sounded frantic.

"Holy shit, Turbo. There's been some kind of shooting. People are screaming. Two guys are on the ground in the middle of Luana Highway."

"What the hell do you mean two bodies?" Turbo asked as Jake's phone and Buddy's phone both rang.

"We have to go. Ask him where Francesca is," Jake said.

"Mike, where is Francesca? Tell me she's with you."

"I'm headed to the café she and Cassidy were at. I'm just trying to get through the crowd."

"Mike, her ex is in town. He works for the Carlotto and Baletti, the men we think murdered Gloria, threatened Chester and Brian, and set fire to the Beach House. Carlotto is after Frankie," Turbo explained as he ran alongside Buddy and Jake. Other officers were on route to the location.

"Oh shit. Oh God. I see Cassidy but not Frankie."

"Find her, Mike. I'm on my way."

Turbo called his brothers and told them to meet him.

"Maybe she's fine. Maybe she went to the ladies room at the café or something," Jake said to Turbo.

"I don't believe this. She told us about her ex and mentioned some other guy threatening her and wanting her and that was why she took off. She never gave us any names. She didn't recognize Baletti or the other guys at the club the other night. She just said some guys creeped her out and she thought one of them took her picture."

"It was probably to send to Carlotto to confirm her identity," Buddy said from the back seat.

"The ex was in jail. If he, at one time, worked for Carlotto and knew Carlotto was interested in Frankie, then why would he grab her and bring her back to Chicago?" Turbo asked.

"We're assuming that's what's going on, but we don't have any facts," Buddy said as Jake pulled up on the scene.

Jake's men already had the area taped off and people away from the crime scene. Sure enough, there were two dead bodies, gunshot wounds to the backs of their heads, lying in the middle of the right-hand lane in front of a major intersection.

Turbo spotted Mike and Cassidy. Cassidy was crying, and Pete was running toward her with his partner, Todd.

"Where is she? Where the fuck is Frankie?" Turbo yelled.

Mike cursed and ran his hand through his hair.

"We can't find her," Mike said.

"We were having lunch and talking. Reggie called, and Frankie got up to use the ladies' room to give me some privacy. Then a few minutes later I heard screaming then sirens. Someone said a black SUV with tinted windows was stopped at the light. Two men were shot and shoved out of the SUV, and then the driver took off."

"You checked the ladies' room, the entire restaurant?" Turbo asked Mike, and Mike nodded.

"She's not in the restaurant. She's in the SUV. There were witnesses sitting on the benches by the corner. Two of them said they heard the gunshot and watched some guy shove a body out of the passenger seat. They saw a woman with her hands tied to the back headrest of the seat. She was screaming and crying." Buddy then walked back over to the policeman that had detained witnesses.

Sirens continued to blare in the distance. Crowds of people were gathering around the crime scene and the restaurant to get a closer look. It was total chaos.

Turbo ran his fingers through his hair. "He has her. Her fucking ex has her, and he's going to hand her over to Carlotto."

"Her ex? You mean the guy she ran from?" Mike asked in a panic.

"Yes. What are we going to do?" Turbo asked Jake.

Jake looked around at the chaos. "We have a description of the vehicle. We have all these witnesses and the feds on their way here. We have to find that SUV." Jake ran over to the car and to Buddy as Mike spoke to Jake.

"I shouldn't have left her. If I hadn't left her, he couldn't have grabbed her."

"He probably would have killed you, Mike, just like he killed those other two guys like it was nothing. She's probably so scared right now."

"Turbo, we got a sighting on the SUV. It's heading out of Treasure Town. That's all we have. That investigator and some federal agents are ten minutes from here. We need to head back to the Station and set up a command center. Buddy has them issuing roadblocks with the state police in every direction. They won't be able to get off the island or out of the four surrounding towns. Let's move."

Chapter 13

He knew the whole area. He seemed to have a plan as he maneuvered through side streets she would never be able to get through without getting lost. He was a street cop from Chicago. Resourceful, tough, a planner. His strategic abilities had kept him out of jail for years, working under the radar, playing both a cop and criminal.

She was shaking and cold now that they were in some sort of warehouse with old boats and smelly garbage.

How long had he been watching her? Were Mike, Turbo, Nate, and Rye okay, or had he done something to hurt them, too? She couldn't stop the shaking.

He was talking on his cell phone. Yelling then speaking calmly, demanding a time. A time for what? There seemed to be police everywhere, and was that a helicopter she heard in the distance?

She wished she had her gun, but her purse was in the SUV. It didn't look as though Kevin was planning on going anywhere else in the vehicle.

He disconnected the call and looked down at her. His hand on his hip, he paced a moment then turned.

"Did you sleep with Carlotto before you took off?"

She gulped and shook her head. He stomped toward her and grabbed her by her blouse, ripping the material. "Don't fucking lie to me. I know you're fucking five guys, so don't for one minute think you can lie to me about fucking Carlotto, too."

"No. I didn't. I took off so he couldn't touch me. I had to leave my job, my home, and disappear because of him and because of you."

The strike across her mouth was so sudden she wasn't sure what stunned her more. The fact that he'd hit her or the pain that radiated along her jaw and split her lip.

He got down low, stared at her face, and shook her.

"They're dead. All five of them are dead. It's just you and me. Do you understand?"

She wondered if he was lying. How could he have killed her men, her lovers? Then again, she wouldn't know because she'd been at the café enjoying lunch with Cassidy instead of with them in their bed.

She shook her head as the tears rolled down her cheek.

"You didn't. You didn't kill them."

He smirked then grabbed her throat and held her snugly. "Oh yes I did. They're gone forever. You'll pay for fucking them. You'll pay for the rest of your life. I'm taking us away from here. No one will ever find us, not even Carlotto."

He shoved her back, and her head hit the concrete wall she leaned against.

She was going to die. There was no way she would let him take her away and have his way with her. She would rather die. There wasn't anything to live for anyway, not with her men dead. She sobbed uncontrollably. She loved them so much.

"Shut up. We leave in ten minutes."

* * * *

"It's been two hours since she was taken. The SUV hasn't been seen anywhere, and every street with access in and out of the surrounding towns is covered by State Police. Where the hell could he have taken her?" Turbo asked as they all gathered around the main meeting room at the sheriff's department.

Three federal agents were there, two detectives from Chicago, Detective Rick Smothers and Detective Roger Prentice, along with

Jake, Buddy, Nate, Rye, and Mike. Turbo was pissed off and losing his patience.

"Deputy Hawkins, we understand the distress you're under, and we're doing our best here. Carlotto is already under arrest in Chicago. We have the surveillance tapes, recorded evidence, and ultimately your girlfriend's statement as a witness to Kevin Lang and Carlotto's involvement in the murder of Officer Oscar Finery."

"Whoa, slow down there. When did this happen?" Nate asked, interrupting.

The federal agent gave Nate the once-over, and Nate held his ground. Nate was definitely in his zone here dealing with government officials. The moment the federal agents saw him and got his name, they stayed clear.

"Back in Chicago, about two weeks before Francesca took off, she was involved in a confrontation between Carlotto's men and her boyfriend at the time, Kevin Lang. We listened to recordings of the interrogation of three of Carlotto's men we arrested, and from the gist of them, it seems Kevin screwed over Carlotto and he wanted some kind of payback. Men came in and confronted Kevin, and Francesca was stabbed."

"What?" Rye asked.

Turbo immediately thought about the scar on her hip and groin. It was very light but still noticeable.

"Carlotto's men took her to some private facility, and within a week, Kevin was behind bars for a slap-on-the-wrist crime. He was caught with some drugs, but with his lawyer, he got six months with early parole. He was fired from the police department, stripped of his badge and gun, and got out early, as I mentioned. We believe that Francesca found out that Kevin and Carlotto killed Police Officer Finery. He was a friend of her family. She attended the wake then disappeared. Even we lost sight of her and had no idea where she went to," the federal agent told them.

"These men you interrogated, they didn't provide enough evidence to put Carlotto behind bars and to keep Kevin there?" Nate asked them.

The agent looked at the other agents then at the detectives.

"We were waiting on this big deal, a shipment coming in from the Atlantic. We only have drips and drabs of details."

"So you were holding out, and now this fucking psycho who just shot two guys in the head and tossed them on the street in the center of town has our girlfriend, a witness and woman you all should have been protecting." Nate pointed at the federal agents.

"She wasn't a witness for our case yet. Just a person of interest to question," the agent told Nate.

"Are you fucking kidding me?" Rye raised his voice. "And you think we're going to trust you with saving our girlfriend from getting killed by these people?"

* * * *

Nate placed his hand in front of Rye as Rye stepped toward the agents. Even Nate was losing his patience. He understood how these men worked. They were out for one thing—the big bust.

"I think we need to step back here and look at the big picture. We have Carlotto in custody. We have the wiretaps and recordings and the three guys who ratted him out on enough crimes to put him away for quite some time. Kevin is a cop killer. But he also may be a main connection to international drug cartels shipping drugs here to the U.S. In fact, we believe these connections Carlotto had selling drugs in clubs is just touching the surface of a major operation across New Jersey. This is huge."

"So looking at the big picture, you couldn't give a shit whether our girlfriend lives or not. This was an opportunity to snag Kevin and try to intercept the import of drugs to the state?" Turbo asked.

"Fucking great. We see where your focus is. Well, we have ours. What's your plan to save Francesca from this guy?" Nate asked.

The agents were silent.

"You're not privy to our plans. We're just providing professional courtesy to the local law enforcements. We'll need everyone's assistance because you all know this area better than we do. As far as the ultimate plan, you're all on a need-to-know basis."

"Is that really how you want to play this?" Buddy asked the agent.

"We're in charge. You all take orders from us. Now we need to get back to work. All non-law enforcement personnel directly associated with this case can leave," the agent said, dismissing them, basically telling them they were not going to be kept abreast of the situation and they were being shut out.

"You can't do this. She's our girlfriend. It's not right," Rye yelled.

Mike grabbed his arm. "Screw these guys. Turbo can stay. Let's go."

"Are you sure that's how you want to play this? Are you certain you don't want us involved in helping to locate them?" Nate asked as he started thinking of what he needed to do next to save Francesca. He was the oldest. He was the one responsible for them, and apparently he and his brothers were all Francesca had as hope to survive.

"As I said, all non-law enforcement can leave. Now please do," the agent said with attitude and then he began speaking to some of the other officers and giving orders.

Turbo followed his brothers out of the room. Jake and Buddy stayed in there as they all discussed their next move.

"What a bunch of control-freak dicks. They're going to get her killed," Rye stated then paced in front of the desks.

"We see what their agenda is. It's about the big bust. She'll fall under collateral damage," Nate told them.

"Fuck, I'm not standing here and doing nothing. There has to be a way to help find her. She has to be so fucking scared," Rye said, and

Nate could tell his brother was freaking out. Rye always paced when he felt out of control about something.

"I wonder why she lied about the scar and didn't tell us about hearing the confession of murder?" Mike asked.

"Because she was protecting us from him and Carlotto. Just like she probably went willingly with Kevin today so he wouldn't hurt Cassidy. The man's a monster. He killed two men in front of her and shoved them out of a car. He'd think nothing of hurting her," Nate told them.

"Then we need to do something. God knows what he's done to her already," Rye said with his fists by his sides.

"Well, those assholes in there have their own agenda. They're looking for the big bust and couldn't care less if Frankie lives or dies. We can't stand here with our thumbs up our asses and let them decide her fate," Turbo told his brothers.

Mike ran his hands over his mouth and locked gazes with Nate. "Nate, we need you. You've got the connections. You did shit for the government. She'll die if we leave her rescue up to those agents."

Nate held his brother's gaze. The tightness in his chest was overwhelming. His brothers were strong men. Never had any of them asked for help. They were always there for one another. A family, a team, brothers in every aspect. They shared Francesca. They'd fallen in love with her together, made love to her together, and bound their hearts with hers together. It was up to them to save her life.

He stepped closer to them, and his brothers gathered around.

"We can't talk here, but we need to keep abreast of what's going on. Turbo, we need ears here. We'll need to know what the feds' plans are and when they'll make a move so we can be steps ahead of them," Nate told Turbo.

"So you want me to stay here while you guys make a plan and go rescue her?"

"No, you need someone you can trust," Nate told Turbo.

Nate looked around the room, his eyes landing on plenty of people before he saw Detective Bryce Moore on his cell phone and heading toward the back hallway.

"Hold that thought. I think I have something even better." Nate watched Turbo walk away.

"I don't know what he's up to, but we catch up with him elsewhere. Mike, Rye, we need eyes and ears out there. Anyone within the vicinity that may have seen that SUV or perhaps something suspicious going on. As the federal agents mentioned, they believed Kevin was involved with importing and exporting drugs, possibly supplying the local dealers with product across New Jersey. The only way in and out internationally would be by boat. I'm going to call Jinx and Raphael. They run the crews for the patrols on water and are connected with the Coast Guard for any potential foreign boats and barges coming into the ports to the south. If something is up, if they get the heads-up on a possible situation for backup, they would be the ones these federal agents would contact."

"That's great. You really think this guy would still let a shipment come through here with the feds and local police hunting him down?" Rye asked.

"It's all about the money. He couldn't care less about who he kills in the process. Look at what Kevin has done so far," Mike said.

Just then Buddy walked out of the office, looking really pissed off. Jake was with him and barking out orders for deputies to gather in the main part of the office.

"Hey, Buddy, what's going on?" Rye asked him.

Buddy shook his head. "It's fucking crazy. They got insight on a location for Kevin and Frankie. They also have a boat five miles from here that came in from out of the country. They think it contains the product that's being smuggled in. They're going to raid the boat and the warehouse they think Kevin and Frankie are in. I'm sorry. It's a fucking mess."

"They can't just go in there guns shooting. She's a civilian, a hostage. There are rules, aren't there?" Rye asked Buddy.

"Somehow I don't think these guys give a shit. They seem to feel risking one life to save the thousands that would be affected by drugs is more important. They don't play by our types of rules. They have their goal to capture Kevin and confiscate the drugs and the people who are on that boat. Nothing else matters," Buddy told them.

Nate looked at Rye and Mike. They were running out of time. This situation truly was out of control, and now despite all he knew, all the connections he had, it might not be enough to save the only woman he and his brothers had ever loved.

* * * *

"They're onto the bait. They'll be miles away from the real location, and you and your woman can disappear. Yes, they're organizing the raid and getting set to go. Of course I will keep you posted. Move in ten minutes to the second location. When I get the text, I'll call you immediately," Bryce said. He stood by the back door of the police precinct.

The second Bryce put his phone away, Turbo shoved him out the back door then pressed him up against the wall.

"You double-crossing piece of fucking shit. That's my woman he has."

"What the hell are you doing? What are you talking about?" Bryce tried to act dumb, but Turbo was so onto him.

He was helping Kevin. He didn't know how they were connected, but he would find it. This was his and his brothers' chance at saving Frankie.

"You didn't want me to see the names in that file the feds sent. You thought Francesca had told us about Carlotto and Kevin and that I might recognize their names. You've been working for them for how long? How fucking long?" Turbo demanded to know.

"I'm not talking," Bryce said, and Turbo pulled back then slugged him in the stomach.

Bryce started coughing and bent over. Turbo pulled him back up and shoved him against the wall.

"Oh, you're going to talk, even if my brothers and I have to beat it out of you."

"Fuck you," Bryce said and reached for his gun.

Turbo immediately stopped him, pulled it from Bryce's holster, and placed it under Bryce's chin.

"No, fuck you, asshole. You're mine, and if you double-cross me and my brothers, you'll regret it. In fact, you'll pay with your life."

* * * *

"What are you doing? Where are you taking me?" Frankie asked as Kevin lifted her up and practically dragged her toward the back of the warehouse and outside.

The early evening air was warm, and the sun was setting. There was probably less than an hour until dark. Why hadn't anyone come to help her? Kevin had shot two people in broad daylight and dropped their bodies in the center of an intersection. How the hell could no one find her? She was shaking with fear.

Kevin stopped and then looked to the right. There was a small dock with three medium-sized boats. Was he taking her on a boat? What was his plan? To take her out to sea, kill her, and then dump her body? *Oh God please. Please don't let this happen.*

"What are you doing? Where are we going?"

He gripped her upper arm and squeezed tight. "Shut up and do what I tell you, Frankie. You're in enough trouble as is."

"I didn't kill a cop and two gangster thugs from Chicago and dump them on a main street. You did."

The backhand came out of nowhere. He pulled her close as she cried, her face throbbing from the strike to her cheek. She felt the instant swelling. The pain radiated down her neck to her shoulder, and her lip was split and aching. He thought nothing of striking her. He would kill her if necessary.

"I killed them to save you from Carlotto. You think I didn't know he wanted you? He fucking drooled every time he saw you. He asked me all these personal questions. You're mine, and he wasn't going to stand between us."

She yanked her arm free from his hold as he undid the rope from the buoy.

"You were doing a great job of that all by yourself. You cheated on me. I got the pictures and the weekly schedule of your screw sessions," she yelled at him.

She was shocked when he grabbed her, lifted her in the air, and threw her into the boat. Her head hit the wooden seat. Her back hit the floor, and she thought she lost focus a moment.

She moaned from the pain and felt the blood ooze from her head. It seemed like only seconds passed.

The small hum of an engine, the rocking up and down, the nauseous feeling, and the weakness.

The sound of a phone ringing. Kevin's voice echoed in her head. What was he saying?

What's wrong with me?

"We're on our way. I see the yacht. We'll be boarding momentarily. Make sure that plane is ready to take off."

A plane? A yacht? Boarding? She tried opening her eyes and moaned aloud. He grabbed her by her shirt, and she still had difficulty focusing. Her head throbbed something terrible.

"You stupid bitch. You had to piss me off with that damn tough-girl mouth of yours. You're fucking bleeding all over me." Her shirt ripped, and he gripped her face between his hands.

"Look at me. Focus, Frankie," he yelled, and she moaned louder. She couldn't focus.

"Fuck," he yelled out.

She felt the boat stop. She heard voices then he lifted her up and over his shoulder. All the blood rushed to her head, and she felt her stomach react, and she vomited all over the place.

"What happened?"

"Concussion. She'll be fine. It won't matter where we're going. This is only the beginning of her punishment anyway. Is everything in place?" Kevin was talking to someone, and she was trying not to throw up more. She felt horrible.

Someone else took her from him. He set her down on a seat. He checked her head and face.

"This is her? I see why you risked so much," the man said as he eyed over her exposed breasts and licked his lips.

"Get this fucking thing moving. We don't have much time."

He was going to win. He was taking her somewhere by boat and had a plan. She saw the gun on the guy's waist. She saw the one on Kevin's hip in the holster. If she could get her hands on one of them, she could perhaps save herself. As she moved, she felt the pounding pain, and then her gaze roamed slowly over her hands. Her wrists were taped together. How could she grip the gun and shoot?

She practiced the motion, pretending to grab a gun and grip it then shoot. It would be difficult but not impossible. She was probably going to die anyway. She wouldn't let him win.

He would own her forever. He would have his way with her body. He wouldn't be staying in the country. How could he as a wanted killer?

"What the fuck is that? Get us out of here now," Kevin yelled at the man.

Kevin grabbed her as the engine started and the boat jerked forward. She couldn't even stay upright. Something was happening. She heard the sound of rotors and saw flashing lights in the distance. They were headed in the opposite direction, toward the ocean and complete darkness. Was help coming? The engine roared louder. She held on to the railing on the side of the boat, and Kevin pulled her up and against his chest.

"Get downstairs." He shoved her to the floor. She crawled forward, sickness consuming her stomach again.

"I'm going to be sick," she said.

The boat rocked and bounced on top of the water. She heard the engine roar as it leaped through the air then slammed down on the wakes and swells of the ocean. She was so scared.

"Get us the fuck out of here. Their boats are far enough behind us for us to lose them. Turn off the lights and let's do this."

The boat went dark. No cabin lights, no side lights on the bow. Nothing but darkness and the sound of the engine.

"Over there. Head that way toward the shoreline and that cove before the open ocean." Kevin gave orders, and the boat headed that way.

Frankie looked behind them. The lights, red and blue, turned to the left. They were going the wrong way. They couldn't see the boat. She cried out. "Oh God no. Come back please."

Kevin lifted her up by her hair. He dragged her to the hatchway leading below deck.

"Keep us on course. Don't let them catch us, or you'll never get your money," he threatened the guy driving the boat.

She smelled the aroma of suede and leather as they entered the cabin below. It was fancy and large, filled with a small wet bar, a couch, another set of doors, and brass fixtures everywhere.

"Sit down." He shoved her onto the small couch then went around to the bar. He pulled out a snifter, filled it with liquor then drank down the contents. He filled it again then walked closer with the bottle in one hand and the glass in the other.

He smirked at her.

"Our new lives have begun, sweetheart. We'll be sitting on our own private beach living the lives we've dreamed about for far too long."

He sat down and brought the glass to her lips. Her head throbbed, and her heart ached. It was over. Kevin had won.

He looked at her head then placed the glass back down on the table with the bottle. He pulled a handkerchief from his pocket and reached up to wipe away some blood from the cut on her head. She flinched, feeling the rawness and sting.

"You'll need stitches. I can't promise where we'll going that you'll have the best doctors, but a little scar by your temple I can live with." He eyed her breasts and then ran a hand along her thigh and under her skirt. She scooted back and pressed his hand away.

"Don't," she said.

His eyes turned darker. He clenched his teeth and forced her thighs open as he fell to the floor between them. His grip was painful on her groin, and he pulled her closer and forced her onto her back.

"You seem to forget who you belong to. I think you need a reminder, Frankie." He ripped her blouse wide open then grabbed her taped hands and placed them above her head with one hand. His eyes were wide and bore into her skin as he stared at her breasts and pushed her thighs open wider with his own.

"Don't, Kevin. Don't do this."

"You need to be reminded about who you belong to. Don't fight me, Frankie. This can be pleasurable for both of us or just plain painful for you." He leaned forward and licked along her skin, pressing his tongue into the cleavage of her breasts.

She was so angry and disgusted she didn't think twice as she shoved her head forward and head-butted him.

The blood splattered from his nose as he pulled back and held it. She slammed her hands against his face and screamed at the top of her lungs.

He was disoriented as she pushed herself up and off the couch. As she turned to head toward the stairs, she heard his roar, turned, and side-stepped just as he swung at her. He caught her shoulder, and she slammed against the railing, cried out in pain, and fell to the step. He was struggling to get up when she screamed and panicked, crawling up the stairs and back into the open. Lights were flashing in the distance, and the boat was moving fast through the darkness.

She'd run toward the side when she felt the hands on her skirt, pulling her back. Kevin tackled her against the side of the boat, and she struggled against him. When she felt the gun on his waist, she pulled it from his waist. But then he punched her in the jaw.

The sky illuminated with colored lights. A chopper in the distance moved closer, the white spotlight zigzagging until it landed on the bow of the boat. There were other boats moving in closer, surrounded this boat.

With her hands taped, she could hardly grip the gun.

"You stupid bitch!" Kevin roared.

He pulled back, and she pulled the trigger, hitting him somewhere, but she didn't know where. His eyes widened in shock, and she climbed higher, waiting to see if he were badly injured and unsure what to do. He reached for the gun when she dropped it, and she knew that look. He was going to kill her.

She ran up the side of the boat toward the front just as a deep voice echoed over some sort of intercom.

"This is the United States Coast Guard. Put down your weapons."

The shot rang out as she turned back toward Kevin. The impact of the bullet hitting her arm sent her over the railing, and she plummeted into the darkness and the cold ocean water.

* * * *

"Jinx, he's going to kill her. Hurry," Nate yelled to Jinx as the Coast Guard boat sped in front of the boat with Kevin and Frankie on board.

They could see the struggle. Nate and his brothers saw her ripped clothing then her scrambling for the railing of the boat as Kevin pointed a gun at her.

The shot rang out. He saw her body swing backward, and then she fell into the darkness.

"Woman overboard. Woman overboard," Raphael called out to the other crewmen.

In record speed, they approached the boat. The marine police were pulling up fast in the distance, but all Nate and his brothers cared about was getting to Frankie.

There were sirens blaring and lights flashing, and a spotlight landed on the water, trying to locate where Frankie fell in. It looked like a pool of black. There was chaos around them as men jumped into the water, and then Nate did, too. He couldn't see a damn thing. He nearly hit his head on the boat as he surfaced, looked around, and saw others doing the same thing.

"Over there. Look over there, Nate," Rye called from the boat.

They were all holding lights onto the water. He'd almost missed it. Her platinum-blonde hair then the piece of her blouse.

"There," he yelled and pointed then swam to her, diving under water and grabbing a hold of her.

It felt as though it took forever to get her onto the boat, and then Turbo was helping him up. Mike was lying on the floor of the boat next to her doing CPR.

"Breathe, baby. Breathe," Rye ordered as they stood over her. "God, she's all beaten up. Look at her head."

Nate looked toward the boat where Kevin was. They'd kill the fucker.

"Kevin is dead. Bullet wound to the stomach. No pulse," Raphael told him as he spoke into a walkie-talkie.

Nate looked back at Frankie as Mike did the compressions on her chest then blew air into her mouth. He held his breath and then he heard the gurgling and Frankie choking. Mike pressed her onto her side.

"That's it, baby. Good girl. Get it all out," Mike said as he rubbed her back.

The medics came over with blankets and special covers that would heat her body. Someone placed one over Nate's shoulders as he shivered, standing there watching her, relieved that she lived.

Mike looked at Rye then Turbo and Nate.

"You did it. You saved her."

"We all did it together. Like always," Nate said as the medics began to evaluate her injuries and call in for an ambulance to meet them by the closest point of the shoreline.

"Hey, are you okay?" Rye asked Nate as he stood next to him, placing his arm over his shoulder, hugging him, looking as though he had tears in his eyes.

Nate ran his fingers through his hair as he looked around at the chaos and at the federal agents who had now joined the other boats on another U.S. Coast Guard boat, carrying on and demanding to know what happened.

"We committed several felonies to get to her. You know that?"

Rye smirked.

"I don't know what you're talking about, Nate. We were just out with our friends, who just happen to work marine patrol when we noticed that yacht moving at an excessive speed. Marine patrol called into the Coast Guard, and as we got closer to assist with the evaluation of the potential situation we caught glimpse of our woman and the marine patrol called in for backup. We were along for the ride and had to jump in to help once we noticed it was our woman on board being held against her will."

"You seriously think that will work?"

Rye smirked.

"That's the way it went down."

"That's what happened exactly," Jinx added, and then the other crewmembers said the same thing.

Nate smiled at his brothers and the rest of them.

"Well, thank God we were all hanging out tonight then, huh?" Turbo added, and they chuckled.

Treasure Town was a close-knit community. Friends made were friends made for life. The bonds they shared with each other were unbreakable, and it was times like these, in the midst of serious danger, that those friendship bonds were tested.

He looked at Frankie, bent down, and caressed her lower lip, avoiding the cut.

She moaned softly.

"We're going home, baby, and whether you like it or not, you're moving in with us."

Chapter 14

Frankie's arm was wrapped and in a sling. The bullet wound to her arm was only a flesh wound but enough to give her twenty-four stitches. Her head was still pounding, especially right now with the federal agents and detectives from Chicago questioning her.

She saw the anger on her men's faces, especially as the federal agents tried to order them from the room.

"There's no reason for you to be present. Your John-Wayne ways could have cost us an entire operation. So don't push me, Hawkins," the one federal agent said to Nate.

Nate kept a straight face and remained by her bedside, along with Rye, Mike, and Turbo.

"If it weren't for them, I would probably be dead right now, and you wouldn't have the opportunity to use my testimony against Carlotto. So I suggest you start showing some respect to these four men because, as I see it, they're the real heroes."

"I understand you're upset. You've been shot, sustained a concussion—"

"Was beaten and practically raped by Kevin and left to be collateral damage as part of your operation, so don't try to sugar the bullshit," she said, finishing his sentence and shutting him up.

She held her hands to her head and closed her eyes.

"You don't need to do this now. They can wait," Jake said from behind the agents.

She opened her eyes and held the one federal agent's gaze. He was the one who'd threatened Nate with jail time, for interfering with a federal case and a list of other charges. She didn't like him, nor did anyone else seem to.

"I'm fine. This is the deal. I want all charges, by you and the government, dropped against Nate Hawkins and his brothers. I want them commended, government-style, for their quick thinking and use of obvious military skills to save me as they stumbled upon the scene. In return, I will cooperate and testify against Carlotto and be a witness to his admission of being part of killing Officer Oscar Finerty. Oscar's family should receive his medal, the one acknowledging his sacrifice to help bring down such a large and wanted gangster as Louie Carlotto and a cop killer like Kevin Lang."

"That's a lot to ask for. I'll have to speak with my superiors and determine if that's enough to accept and give into your demands," the federal agent said.

She looked him over.

"You do that, and perhaps mention that I may, or I may not, have other information that could prove to be vital in putting Carlotto away for life."

"What kind of information?"

She took a deep breath and slowly released it. She thought about the meetings she'd sat in on and how, at first, she hadn't understood what Kevin and his buddies were talking about, and then how it all made sense. She'd written down names and phone numbers, locations, and keywords she thought might be code for something when she'd found out Kevin had been cheating on her. Could they mean nothing? She wasn't sure, but her gut told her there was information there. Other men were involved in the drug operation and distribution. Other cops, too. It was why she had feared going to anyone for help in the Chicago PD.

"Maybe names, locations that could help a task force bring down more individuals connected to Carlotto's operation. Maybe Carlotto isn't even the largest fish for you to catch, Agent. But I guess whether you get that information or not depends on how you treat my heroes.

Now if you'll excuse me, recovering from a concussion, a bullet wound, an assault, and nearly drowning is taking its toll on me. I need to rest now."

He nodded and glanced at the men and the other detectives.

"You take care of yourself, Francesca. I'll be in touch."

"I look forward to it," she said, and then they all walked out of the room except for her men, Jake, and Buddy.

"She's a keeper. Don't fuck this up with her," Jake said, and Buddy chuckled.

Jake and Buddy walked closer.

"You rest and don't worry about those agents. They're more scared of you right now than you realize." Jake winked, and then he and Buddy exited the room.

Frankie closed her eyes, took a deep breath, and released it. She felt her eyes well up with tears, and then she felt Nate's hand against her cheek.

She opened her eyes, and he stared at her with such an expression of love that she felt the tear roll down her cheek.

"Are you a spy?" he asked her very seriously.

"What?" she replied in shock and confusion. She heard the others chuckle as they moved closer.

"You just manipulated three federal agents, ate them up, and spit them out like a pro."

"I was scared out of my mind," she admitted.

Rye clasped her hand and squeezed it. "You were incredible."

"Definitely made for us Hawkins men," Mike added.

"I don't know. I think she needs a little discipline," Turbo added, and when she locked gazes with him, he winked as he gave her a smile.

"I think I need aspirin."

"We've got plenty of that at our place," Nate added.

"Your place? But I—"

He covered her lips with his finger gently so as not to hurt her bruises.

"Baby, we love you, want to marry you, raise a family with you, and live in Treasure Town with you for the rest of our lives. Now how the hell are we going to do that if you're not living with us and making love to us in our bed every night?"

The tears rolled down her cheeks, and she sniffled.

"You love me and want all those things with me?"

"Sure do, sweetness. You need looking after, by all of us," Mike added.

She knew he felt responsible for her abduction, despite how it all happened.

"I'm going to go see about getting you released. We can take a hell of a lot better care of you at home," Turbo told her.

"I love you guys, too. I want all those things. A family, your love, and to wake up with you every morning and to go to bed with you every night."

"Then you'll move in right away?" Rye asked her.

She looked at Turbo.

"Deputy, use some of that sexy charm and powerful authority to get me out of here. I have the feeling that the four of you can definitely make me feel a lot better in your bed at home."

"Damn, you'll be out within the hour. I guarantee it, honey. You just get yourself ready for loving." Turbo headed out the door, and the others smiled.

"You know you have to rest. They'll be no making love for at least a few days," Nate told her and ran his thumb along her lower lip.

"Oh, I think it will be a lot sooner. I trust you guys will take really good care of me."

"Baby, you have no idea," Rye said as he rubbed his hands together.

"Just you wait," Mike said and slowly leaned forward and gently kissed her lip.

She closed her eyes and smiled, the pain in her head a light buzz as the love of her men destroyed any feelings of pain and replaced them with happiness.

She'd never thought for a moment when she came to the area that she would ever fit in or be able to become part of a place like Treasure Town. Rye, Nate, Turbo, and Mike had set her heart on fire and made her see that true love did exist and that happiness could be found with the right people at the right time. She was starting over again, not alone, not in fear, and not on the run, but in a place filled with first responders, just like her father and brother had been. She'd found her future, in the arms of four men she would love and cherish for the rest of their lives.

THE END

WWW.DIXIELYNNDWYER.COM

ABOUT THE AUTHOR

People seem to be more interested in my name than where I get my ideas for my stories from. So I might as well share the story behind my name with all my readers.

My momma was born and raised in New Orleans. At the age of twenty, she met and fell in love with an Irishman named Patrick Riley Dwyer. Needless to say, the family was a bit taken aback by this as they hoped she would marry a family friend. It was a modern day arranged marriage kind of thing and my momma downright refused.

Being that my momma's families were descendants of the original English speaking Southerners, they wanted the family blood line to stay pure. They were wealthy and my father's family was poor.

Despite attempts by my grandpapa to make Patrick leave and destroy the love between them, my parents married. They recently celebrated their sixtieth wedding anniversary.

I am one of six children born to Patrick and Lynn Dwyer. I am a combination of both Irish and a true Southern belle. With a name like Dixie Lynn Dwyer it's no wonder why people are curious about my name.

Just as my parents had a love story of their own, I grew up intrigued by the lifestyles of others. My imagination as well as my need to stray from the straight and narrow made me into the woman I am today.

Enjoy *Hearts on Fire 5: Loving Frankie* and allow your imagination to soar freely.

For all titles by Dixie Lynn Dwyer, please visit
www.bookstrand.com/dixie-lynn-dwyer

Siren Publishing, Inc.
www.SirenPublishing.com

Lightning Source UK Ltd.
Milton Keynes UK
UKOW06f1932070915

258236UK00020B/482/P